Grandma's Teacup

Mary Elizabeth Becker

PublishAmerica
Baltimore

ISBN: 1-4137-5769-3
PUBLISHED BY PUBLISHAMERICA, LLLP
www.publishamerica.com
Baltimore

Printed in the United States of America

Dedicated to my children, Shannon, Stacy, Patrick and Katie, who bring so much joy into my life. Although there wasn't an actual legend about grandma's teacup, you did have your grandparents' love and commitment to each other and to their families as an example to help you become the exceptional individuals you are. I am very proud of you.

Special Thanks:

To the wonderful people of Akumal, Mexico. Your friendly and caring attitude makes visitors feel like family.

To Jenni Murrill for once again putting this book into proper form.

To Bill and Karen Sager for continuing to come at my beck and call when my computer decides it is smarter than me.

Prologue

The rocking chair squeaked as it was pushed back and forth.

Her feet couldn't reach the floor, but she maintained the rocking motion by shoving her hand against the magazine table that sat beside it. The noise of the rocker was obscured by the voices in the room. There were people standing everywhere. She only heard fragments of conversation, "I didn't know she had a bad heart."

"It's such a shame, she wasn't that old."

"I wonder if she just lost the desire to live after Joe died."

She could see her big brothers outside the living room window. They had come home from college for the funeral. Her father was outside talking with them. They were twenty and twenty-two. She was only eight. A late surprise, her parents always said.

Bringing her gaze back to the living room, she spied the little china cup sitting on the mantel. She loved the story Grandma had told her about the cup. Grandpa had given it to Grandma when they were young, before they were married. He was going away to war and gave it to Grandma the night before he left. He had called it his Promise Cup. He had said it was filled with all their hopes and dreams and love and that he would return one day to make it all come true, and he did.

Grandma was gone now and Jessica wondered who would take care of the cup. It almost looked like it had tears overflowing it instead of promises.

I hope whoever gets you next, fills you with good things again, she thought.

Jessica spotted her cousin Katie sitting on the stairs. Jessica scooted out of the rocking chair and walked to where she sat. She plopped down beside her. Resting her elbows on her up-drawn knees and holding her face in her hands, she said, "I sure am going to miss Grandma."

"Me, too; I love coming here. I just don't know why people have to die," Katie replied.

Jessica just shrugged her shoulders as if to say she didn't understand either. Looking over at Katie, Jessica asked in a shaky voice, "You won't die, will you?"

Katie was a year older than Jessica and had always tried to look out for her when they were together, especially when her older brothers or some of the older cousins would tease her or leave her out because she was so little.

"I plan to live until I'm really old. We will always be best friends and we'll be there for each other. I have an idea. Why don't we become blood sisters?"

"How can we do that?" Jessica asked.

"We need to find a needle and stick our fingers so they bleed. Then we mix the blood together and promise to be each other's sister forever. We won't tell anybody else. It'll be our secret."

Jessica's eyes lit up as they stood and made their way to their grandmother's sewing room. Soon they were putting their fingers together and promising to be there for each other no matter what the future held.

Chapter 1

Akumal, Mexico, eighteen years later

It was high season. The weather was perfect. Tourists wandered through the specialty shops, drinking up the sun on the beaches, slipping on their wetsuits and collecting their diving equipment. Children's laughter could be heard as they built castles in the sand and chased each other into the still water of the lagoon. All seemed perfect and normal in this paradise by the sea. For Katie, all this beauty and activity was seductive and exciting.

She had lived here going on seven years, working first as the director of the kid's program at the hotel down the street and now as the manager of a villa rental agency. She had made real friends among the local people and was a hit with the visitors with her easy smile and helpful attitude. She wasn't rich, but made enough money to live comfortably and to be extravagant on occasion.

Standing at the window of her office, the sights, smells and sounds of this tropical paradise filled her. She loved it here and loved the life she had created for herself. So why, over the last few months, had she had this sense of nervous energy and longing inside for something…just something?

She gave a soft sigh as she stretched her slim five-feet, four-inch body, turning away from the window and back to the computer on her desk. Her cousin, Jessica, had sent an email and she needed to write her back. Jessica was doing so well now. She would be graduating from college in a few months and Katie couldn't be more pleased. She would write Jessica first and then she had just a few other e-mails to answer and she could close up the office. Before she went home she would go meet the two new families who arrived today, making certain they had everything they needed for their dream vacation. One family had small children, so she would take them information about the kid's club and local babysitters.

An hour later she shut down the computer and stacked the information on the new arrivals for tomorrow in a neat pile. She skimmed over the papers quickly to make certain everything was ready for them. A smile crossed her face as she reread the request from the group of retired friends. They wanted a villa that, as they put it, was a "real party house." The second request brought a slight feeling of curiosity. It was for a three-bedroom villa for a K. J. Dalton, a daughter, and an assistant. It asked for something quiet and away from the main tourist area, with a fully stocked kitchen but no cook service, and a driver and car to pick them up at the airport and to be available to them upon request from ten in the morning until ten at night throughout their stay. The most unusual part of the request was that they wanted the villa for four weeks. It was probably a newly divorced woman who wanted to get away for a while but wanted to bring her daughter with her. An assistant could either be there to take care of the child or, more likely, it was the woman's new love interest dressed up in a nicer name. Katie had met a few others like this, newly divorced women who wanted to spend some of their hard-won alimony money on a luxury vacation. They usually didn't bring their kids though. She just frowned and shook her head, hoping the child wasn't being used as a pawn between mother and father.

Getting up, she shoved her long blond hair back behind her ears, grabbed her purse and the brochure for the Lol Ha Kid's Club and headed out the door. Most of the villas were close so she decided to walk to greet her new clients.

Having made sure everyone was settled and happy with their accommodations and answering some of their specific questions, she returned to her car and headed home. She decided the restaurants and night spots would be crowded with tourists tonight, so a long soak in the tub, a salad for dinner and a long walk on the beach with her dog, Mimoso, would be the extent of her evening plans.

She made it a point to stay away from the nightlife spots during high season. She had learned a few years ago that being in her mid-twenties, reasonably pretty and American definitely had their drawbacks. Most of her clients were Americans and had come to

Mexico to have a good time. A lot of the single men, and even some of the married men, after having a few drinks, had thought her wish to please her customers and provide whatever they needed extended to a little more than usual services. She had to evade more than a few physical advances. In the light of day, these same people were polite and even a little embarrassed by their activities of the night before. She learned it was easier to be absent once the sunset.

Most of her friends were busy this time of the season, as their jobs centered around the tourists, too. So for a few months out of the year she spent her evenings alone. Maybe that was what was bothering her; she was just lonely.

K. J. Dalton, businessman, entrepreneur, father and widower, leaned back in his first-class seat, closing his eyes, hoping to catch a few minutes of sleep. His seven-year-old daughter had curled up in a little ball with a blanket tucked around her and was fast asleep. He hoped she would stay that way. He knew if she had one of her nightmares and started screaming she would probably cause complete panic and pandemonium on the airplane.

He had wanted to fly during the day to avoid just that possibility but, as luck would have it, their plane got delayed twice; once in Boston and then missing their connecting flight out of Atlanta. He probably should have stayed overnight in Atlanta, but he just wanted to get away so badly.

He hoped the booking agent in Akumal had gotten his e-mail that they would be late and to keep the driver and car at the airport for them. He hated to drive. In fact he hadn't driven for over two years. Roger, his assistant, could drive but his skills weren't very good, as he had never owned his own car, being from New York City, and now he just had Dalton Industries' chauffeur drive him about.

He planned this vacation to get his daughter away from their home, where too many memories lingered. Would it help? He didn't know. She had become withdrawn, hardly speaking, and those terrible nightmares weren't getting any better.

The psychiatrist had said she was suffering from severe post-traumatic stress syndrome. He said it would take time and that she needed to talk about that awful night of the accident. But she wouldn't talk to anyone about the wreck. If you asked her about it, she just stopped talking altogether.

He knew it was probably his fault since right after it happened he was so despondent that he threw himself into his work and hired a woman to take care of her. He went for days without even seeing her. He had spent weeks at a time away on business trips and stayed late into the night in his office when he was home. It had taken him a full year to realize he had basically deserted his own daughter. When he had finally come out of his own cocoon it was to find that his sweet, happy and lively daughter no longer existed.

The first night he had heard her terrible screams, he had rushed to her bedroom only to find the woman he thought would be a kind, grandmotherly type yelling at the girl to stop that bellowing immediately or she would be punished. He fired her on the spot. Then he tried to comfort and quiet his daughter. When she finally awakened, she looked at him as though he were a stranger, curled up in a ball, pulled the covers over her head and didn't say a word. He sat there so dazed that it took him a full hour to realize his little princess, Megan, had fallen back to sleep.

That was over a year ago, but things hadn't improved much. He could get her to smile on occasion and even hold her now after her nightmares, but she wouldn't tell him what she dreamt and she was still sad and quiet.

Roger had been hired a year before the accident happened as a lower executive in Kaleb's company. He was intelligent, warm and capable, and a real "nerd" in the eyes of the world. He moved up to be Kaleb's assistant because he was the one who brought Kaleb back to reality.

Roger had been working on a construction project that Kaleb became engrossed in after his wife was killed. He kept encouraging Kaleb to get more rest, to eat, not push so hard and to spend time with Megan.

For his efforts, he usually got a "Go to hell!" or "Stay out of my business" reply. One thing about Roger, he was persistent, but not overly pushy, and Kaleb liked him.

One day as Roger quietly pushed Kaleb to go easy on himself, Kaleb snapped, "How would you know about losing the woman you love?"

"I don't, but have you ever thought about asking God for a little help with all this pain and anger?"

Kaleb just stared at Roger. He had gone to church as a young boy, but men in multi-million dollar businesses didn't talk to each other about God. Then he became angry.

"If God is who and what people say He is, why did He take my Lucy from me? Answer me that."

"I don't pretend to know why God took Lucy when He did, but God has always wanted Lucy with Him, just like he wants you and me to be with Him some day. He did give you six wonderful years together and blessed you with Megan. Maybe you should thank Him for your gifts and seek his help."

Kaleb had no more energy left to fight and just walked away. But it made him think and gradually the anger started to die. The pain and loneliness remained.

A few weeks later, Roger again started pushing Kaleb about spending time with his daughter, telling him that she needed him.

When Kaleb turned to snap something back, Roger just held up his hands saying, "No, I've never been a father, but I have been a kid."

And so the relationship grew, and now Roger was a strength that Kaleb relied on.

Chapter 2

Katie couldn't believe it. This K. J. Dalton expected someone to sit at the airport at her beck and call. The driver she hired had refused. Being conscientious and knowing she only had to work a half-day tomorrow, since it was Saturday, she gathered her energy and set out for Cancun Airport about seven o'clock. She hoped Mimoso wouldn't tear her house apart, since he was used to her walking him on the beach this time of night. She had checked the flights coming in from Atlanta and knew one got in at nine this evening, but the other didn't get in until one in the morning.

Nine o'clock came and went without Dalton emerging through customs. Now she had several hours to kill. She decided a few cups of coffee and a book might keep her going until one o'clock. All she knew was this lady better be real appreciative. Most likely she was really rich and used to having her own way. She probably didn't know anything about Akumal. She no doubt thought the name sounded exotic and thought she was headed toward a swanky, high flyer's paradise. Most likely she would hate it and leave in a few days.

Renting a villa for a week, taking in the sights and lying in the sun were great, but for four weeks? The woman had rented a villa for four weeks, for God's sake. If she was accustomed to a glitzy nightlife and high society, she was definitely coming to the wrong place.

Katie wandered about the airport, trying to keep awake and alert for the drive back. She thought about the little girl coming with her mother and hoped she wasn't getting worn out. Stopping dead in her tracks, she shook her head.

Now why did she assume the daughter was a little girl? Nothing had been said about how old she was. She could be fifteen and as demanding as her mother.

Could she be wrong about that, too? Could K. J. Dalton be a man? Oh great, just what she needed, an overbearing man who demanded everything, and a rotten teenager. And the assistant was probably a high-heeled, short-skirted sexpot. Just thinking about it made her angry.

About that time she glanced at her watch and saw that it was one-thirty. If they were on this flight, they should be clearing customs soon. Watching the gate, she tried to guess who her companions were going to be. She held a cardboard sign with Dalton written on it.

First class would deplane before the other passengers. She watched avidly as each passenger walked by. The first woman coming out was about fifty, dressed casual but rich. She walked by Katie straight into the arms of a well-dressed man about her own age.

The next people out were two scantily dressed young women laughing together. They headed straight for the car rental booth.

Then she saw a man about thirty, wearing slacks and a polo shirt, holding the hand of a little girl about seven or eight. The little girl looked like she was half asleep and not really interested in all the activity around her. This could be her client, but where was the sexy assistant? The person behind them was dressed in a suit and carried a briefcase.

Dismissing them, she was stretching her head to one side to try to see past them when the man holding the little girl's hand stepped in front of her and asked, "Are you to direct us to our car and driver?"

Startled both by the sound of his voice and by the fact that she had already dismissed him, Katie took a step back and jerked her head up to look at the face of this rugged but not quite classically handsome man. His voice was soft, with a thread of authority running through it. His eyes appeared speculative, with just a hint of sadness.

Katie pulled herself together, forced a polite smile on her face and extended her hand, saying, "I'm Katie from the rental agency. Welcome to Mexico, Mr. Dalton."

He nodded his head in acknowledgment of her greeting, not taking her hand, as one was holding his daughter's hand and the other held a carry-on bag. If he thought it unusual that the booking agent would personally welcome him to Mexico, he didn't comment on it.

Dropping her hand to her side, she continued, "If you'll follow me, we can go to the car."

Looking at Roger, Kaleb said, "I'll get Megan settled in the car, and maybe Miss...I'm sorry, I don't know your last name."

"It's McKay, but you can just call me Katie."

"No, Miss McKay will do. Could you have your driver come help Mr. Collins with our bags?"

Tension tightened Katie's face at the implied lack of professionalism. She nodded to the man called Mr. Collins. He returned her nod with a smile and said, "Katie, I'm Roger."

Some of the tension left her face. Turning to Mr. Dalton she stated, "I will show you and your daughter to the car, Mr. Dalton, and send a porter to help with the luggage." Then she smiled at the little girl and said, "Hi." She got no response.

Katie's mind was racing as she led the way out of the airport entrance. Who was this man? He acted as though he was on company business instead of on a vacation. She dealt with the rich and famous as much as she did with common people who had saved their money for years to take a special vacation. It was part of their success that they treated everyone in a casual, relaxed manner, causing the common people to feel welcome and at ease and the rich and famous to feel like common people who no longer had to maintain an air of perfection. Was he really here on vacation or was he here on a business venture?

As she passed a porter on the sidewalk, she spoke to him in rapid Spanish, instructing him to help with the luggage. That taken care of, she directed Mr. Dalton to the car she had rented for the trip. Her personal car was too small for four people and luggage, so she had rented a Ford Expedition.

Mr. Dalton helped his daughter into the back seat of the car, fastened her seat belt and took a small blanket from his carry-on bag and placed it over her legs. The night air had cooled enough to warrant the blanket. He then turned to Katie, asking where their driver was.

She held the keys out in front of her and said, "You're looking at her."

His faced tensed and with more volume in his voice he spoke only five words, "I prefer a male driver."

After his initial put-down in the airport, Katie had suspected that he wouldn't be pleased with her being the driver, so this time she was prepared for his curt manner.

She smiled and said, "Your original driver refused to wait on your arrival, so you have me. If you prefer, you can drive."

If possible, his face tensed even more and his skin appeared to turn pale. Before he could comment further she assured him that she was a good driver and that she would drive with great care to protect the welfare of his daughter and Roger.

He caught the fact that he had been excluded when she promised to protect her passengers. A bit of admiration sparked in his eyes for her audacity, but it was quickly replaced by his own fears.

Kaleb's thoughts were in a tangle. He knew he couldn't drive. Maybe Roger could. But no, Roger had little experience, and to drive in a foreign country, where he wasn't sure if the road signs were in Spanish only, would be asking too much.

The young lady seemed capable enough. He had dealt with her over the computer to make the arrangements. She had been here to meet them when, if she hadn't come, they would have been left on their own, and he had heard her speak to the porter in Spanish, so she had shown good business sense in learning the local language. He knew his daughter was exhausted and needed to get to bed. What choice did he have?

He looked again into the expectant face of Katie, not sure of what he saw. He was tired, too. She was pretty, he decided, and warranted at least civility from him. He would let her drive and hope they would all survive. Maybe, after he got some rest, he would stop by her office tomorrow and thank her for picking them up. After all, it wasn't her fault they were so late. He might even see her smile again.

He had noticed how her eyes sparkled when she smiled, but tonight he was just too tired to put forth any effort. He knew he would be white-knuckled all the way to the villa, but he had no other choice.

"All right, you drive," and with that he climbed into the back seat with his daughter.

Roger and the porter arrived with the luggage. Once it was all stored, Roger got in the passenger side, smiled and said, "Well, Miss Katie, let's be off on our great adventure."

Kaleb snorted from the back seat and that was the last either of the two in the front of the car heard from the two sleeping in the back until they pulled up in front of the beautiful Luna Villa.

Kaleb came awake as he felt the car stop and heard the engine die. Opening his eyes, he looked out the window to see the lights on outside the entry to a two-story arched entrance. A smooth, stone walkway, lined with green shrubbery and lit by decorative ground lights, led the way to the door. It crossed his mind that perhaps he would find his daughter again and some rest for himself in this quiet and peaceful-looking place.

Releasing the seat belts and picking Megan up, Kaleb followed Katie into the house. Roger walked behind with some of the luggage. Katie indicated where the two bedrooms were downstairs, opening the door to the first one. It was a cozy-looking room with a double bed. It was decorated in soft shades of blue with splashes of green. The sun would shine through the large window across from the bed when it made its appearance in the morning.

Sitting Megan on the edge of the bed, Kaleb slipped off her shoes. Katie had followed them in and pulled back the comforter so he could place Megan under the quilt. Having tucked her in, Kaleb leaned over and kissed her forehead. For some reason Katie felt as though she was intruding on someone else's private life, so she quickly left the room. She could hear Kaleb whispering something to Megan as she left. For such a stern-appearing man, he did seem to adore his daughter.

As she walked back into the living room she saw Roger gazing at the walls. They had spoken comfortably on the hour drive from Cancun and she had told him about some of the decor of the villa. He stood studying a piece of Mayan stonework that had been inset into the wall. It was a sea scene and one she had always liked.

Turning toward her he commented, "Very nice. Did our little Megan get all tucked in?"

"Yes. Her father is just saying his goodnights and I didn't want to intrude on their privacy."

Roger lifted a speculative brow but made no comment. Instead he complimented the house, or as much of it as he had seen. She showed him about the rest of the villa. In the kitchen she reminded him that they were not to drink the water from the faucet, showing him the bottled water dispenser.

Feeling tired and knowing she would have to be to work in a few short hours, she said goodbye to Roger and reminded him that the driver she had hired for them would be over at ten in the morning, as requested.

As Katie opened the door to her home, she was greeted with a sloppy tongue across her face and enough weight against her chest to send her staggering back a couple of steps. Lowering the paws from her chest and putting Mimoso back on all fours, she gave him several long strokes down his back. She surveyed her living room.

A little shredded paper and some yarn from his cloth dog bone were scattered about, but there was no destruction of any of her personal belongings. She heaved a sigh of relief.

Now that he was older, he seldom chewed up any of her things, but it still happened on occasion. She had lost too many shoes, purses, pillows, and even a couch to his propensity to tear things apart if she left him alone too long to be totally comfortable when something happened that kept her away for a long evening. April, her old roommate, usually watched him if she was gone overnight, but she had hoped to be home a lot earlier than four in the morning.

Slipping the leash onto his collar she took him outside for a quick call of nature. Hurrying him back into the house, she quickly changed into a pair of sweats and collapsed on her bed, setting the alarm for seven. It was going to be a short night, but she had done it before and knew she would muddle through the day somehow. A nap in the afternoon was already being planned, or at least being in bed by seven that night. She closed her eyes and was asleep before the minute hand on the clock had moved.

The sound of buzzing from her alarm awakened her. Katie stretched, feeling Mimoso snuggled against her side. Opening her eyes, she glanced out her bedroom window. Even though her house wasn't right on the beach, she could see the blue water pushing up against the green of the jungle.

A warm feeling spread through her as she thought of her house. It had taken her a few years to save enough money for a down payment, but she had done it. She moved in about six months ago. The place needed work, but nothing major. She had saved enough money to get the backyard fenced so she could leave Mimosa out when she was gone. Now she just had to hire someone to help, get the material and find time to do it.

"Well, Mimoso, let's go for a short run on the beach so I can get my body moving," she said as she grabbed the leash and headed for the door.

It was warm but not hot.

Perfect weather, she thought.

After a brisk jog, she headed back up the path that led from the ocean to her house, passing two other homes on her way. Looking across to her left she saw the upper level of Luna Villa.

She hadn't thought about the three people she had met last night until now. Roger was probably a couple of years older than her and nice-looking with his dark brown hair, brown eyes and average build. Coming to a vacation spot dressed in a suit had made her first impression of him one of being stuffy and a little aloof. But then he had greeted her warmly, despite his boss's presence, putting her at ease. She decided he probably wore the suit because Mr. Dalton demanded it. On the way to the villa he had been easy to talk to. She had asked him if it bothered him that she was driving.

"Not at all," he'd answered. "I can drive, but I'm not very experienced. Growing up in New York City, cars really were not very important and they can be a real hassle."

At her inquiring glance, he'd continued, "New York City has a lot of mass transit and the subway, and if you have a car, parking can be a real problem. In Boston it's much the same. Plus, I can use one of Dalton Industries' cars and a driver any time I need to. I must admit I use cabs a lot more now, but getting my own car has never been a high priority." She had wondered at the time if it was the same with Mr. Dalton.

She also knew that Roger wasn't married, nor did he have a special woman in his life. She had noticed that he didn't wear a ring and the question had just popped out. She didn't usually ask personal questions, but there was just something about him that took you off guard. She felt a little embarrassment thinking back on their conversation.

Katie remembered blurting out, "So Roger, I notice you aren't wearing a wedding ring. Does that mean you're not married?"

"No, I'm not married," he'd replied.

"Anyone special in your life then?" she'd asked.

He'd smiled and said, "Oh, there are lots of special people in my life, but one woman who has captured my heart? No."

She hadn't known what to say, but then he'd asked her the same questions and that had put her at ease.

She never went out with any of her clients, but now she thought maybe going out with Roger might be kind of nice.

Then there was the little girl, Megan. Megan had dark hair with a hint of red through it and the bluest eyes fringed with long lashes. She had been wearing pink shorts, a flowered-print top, white ankle socks and pink tennis shoes.

She must have really been exhausted. Katie had cared for a lot of kids over the years and was able to develop a relationship with them quite easily. Kids just seemed to like her and she liked them. When the children first got there they were usually tired but so excited from flying on a plane and all the fun things their parents had promised them that they couldn't sleep. They would either be cross and demanding or so wound up from excitement that they fidgeted and talked non-stop. She remembered smiling at Megan and saying hello, but Megan had just looked straight ahead and not said a word. She had seemed almost dazed.

Well, a good night of sleep should change all that. She would have to remember to take the brochure for the kid's club and the information on the other activities for children over to Megan's dad.

That brought the image of K. J. Dalton to mind. He had been dressed much more casually than Roger, but he had been the stuffy and aloof one. She had noticed his wedding ring and wondered where his wife was. Most divorced men didn't wear wedding bands. Maybe she just couldn't make this trip. Roger had made her comfortable, but not enough to ask about his boss.

Maybe this was a business trip after all. Was he looking to buy property and set up some kind of venture? If he was here on business, why bring his daughter along?

Then she remembered that flash of sadness she had glimpsed. What was that all about? She had also caught that little look of admiration from him when she had insinuated that she would take good care of Roger and Megan, leaving him out on purpose. She usually went out of her way to get along with the most demanding customers, so she wasn't sure why he had been able to push her buttons so easily.

Walking into her house and glancing at the ornate clock on the wall, she knew she had better hurry if she was going to make it to work by nine. She showered, dressed, grabbed a roll and cup of coffee, gave Mimoso a goodbye hug and rushed off to work.

Chapter 3

Kaleb awoke to sunlight and the sounds of birds. He turned his head toward the window and beheld one of the most beautiful sights he had ever seen. The water was so blue and still, it looked like polished glass, and rocks and the strip of white sandy beach broke the green of the natural flora.

Perhaps this is paradise, he thought.

He wondered what Megan would think of it. Looking at the clock he wondered if she was awake. He wrapped his robe around himself as he left his room. Opening her bedroom door he saw her lying on her side looking out the window, seeing the same sight as he had. He crossed to the bed and sat down on the edge.

Leaning over he kissed her cheek and asked, "Well, what do you think?"

Megan continued to look out the window saying, "I think I might like it here. I didn't have any bad dreams last night." Then looking at him she added, "Did I?"

"No, no bad dreams honey," he re-assured. His heart sped up a little; for this was the first time she had shown any interest in her surroundings for a long time. They both stayed where they were, looking out the window, both lost in their own thoughts. The sounds of activity in the kitchen broke the peaceful spell.

"I better go help Roger get some breakfast put together for us. I put your robe out last night so you can slip it on when you're ready to get up."

She didn't answer but continued to stare out the window. He wondered if she was still seeing the beautiful sight or if she was back in that place in her mind where nothing seemed to touch her.

Roger had the coffee brewing and was looking in the refrigerator when Kaleb walked in.

"What do we have for food? I'd like to make Megan her favorite breakfast of waffles topped with strawberries. Any strawberries in there?"

Roger looked in the bottom drawer of the refrigerator. "You're in luck; right here they are, along with some pineapple and oranges."

"Good. I'll mix up the waffles if you clean the strawberries. Did you sleep well, Roger?"

"Very. This place is really something. You'll have to make a complete tour after breakfast. The cell phone works, too. I called Marge at her home this morning to let her know we made it here, and the connection was perfect."

Kaleb nodded, and then out of habit asked Roger if Marge had received any word on one of the contracts they were working on. Roger shook his head.

"You are not to think about work while you're here. I will let you know if anything comes up that requires your attention. That's why I'm here, remember?"

"Yes, yes," Kaleb replied, a little annoyed with Roger for his admonishment.

Changing the subject, Kaleb asked Roger about his plans for the day. Roger said the only thing he wanted to do was sit on the beach and soak up some sun.

"What about you and Megan?"

"After breakfast I'll take Megan for a walk. I also want to stop by and talk to the booking agent for a moment. Would you mind keeping Megan company for a few minutes while I'm gone?"

"Not at all."

About then the doorbell rang. The driver they had hired was there inquiring if they wished to go anywhere. Kaleb told him to return around twelve-thirty.

The driver nodded his head saying, "I return twelve-thirty."

Well, chalk another one up for Miss McKay, Kaleb thought.

The man seemed to be able to speak fairly good English. He had been afraid he would have trouble communicating with his driver and had attempted to learn a few words in Spanish before he came. He had learned a bit, but listening to Miss McKay talking to the porter last night, the only thing he had understood was *gracias.*

At breakfast, the men chatted quietly while Megan only spoke to ask for more strawberries. After cleaning up the dishes and getting dressed for the day, they all walked through the house, checking it out. It was a pleasant place and would do nicely as their home for a month.

A maid came to make the beds and straighten up. Leaving her to do her work, they walked down to the beach. They had brought some towels to lie on. Slipping off their shoes they waded into the water.

All were surprised by how warm the water was. After walking about exploring the area, they made their way back to the towels. Roger had brought a book and settled back to read. Kaleb glanced at his watch and realized he was going to keep the driver waiting. Pulling his sandals on he explained to Megan that he had to go talk to Miss McKay for a few minutes, but he wouldn't be gone long and Roger would stay with her.

She said, "Okay, but it's Katie."

"What's Katie?"

"Her name."

This time it was Kaleb who said nothing. Maybe his daughter was seeing and hearing more than he thought.

When he reached the villa the driver was already there. He asked the man to give him a few minutes and went to his room and changed from his shorts into slacks. Reaching for his socks and shoes, he shook his head. He was on vacation. So he slipped back on his sandals. Another concession to this relaxing place, he supposed.

As he rode along in the car he was trying to rehearse what he wanted to say. He dealt with all kinds of people in his work and never rehearsed what to say. He had been raised with the knowledge that he would take over his father's business one day and there had always been an air of command about him. He had moved into that position much younger than had been expected when his father had taken ill and eventually died.

That had been hard, but his father had been battling cancer for three years, so it seemed almost a blessing when he died. Kaleb had assumed most of the responsibility for the company during that time and stepped into total control quite naturally. Now here he sat, trying to think of something to say to a slip of a woman he had just met.

By twelve-thirty, Katie had answered the e-mail and handed out the paychecks to the agency's employees, including those who cooked, cleaned, and kept the grounds for the villas they managed. Several of her clients had stopped by to ask questions and one family came in to say goodbye. They thanked her, saying they had such a good time that they planned to come back again. It was those goodbyes and words of thanks that made her job so rewarding.

She decided to go check on the group of retired friends who were staying at the villa just a block away. She had greeted them yesterday upon their arrival. They all had to be in their seventies, but had the spirit of twenty-year-olds. They had said they were ready to have a good time and hoped they wouldn't bother any of the neighbors with their wild parties.

Waiting outside the door, she could hear laughter and music from within. One of the maids at the villa answered. She motioned Katie inside, pointing at one couple dancing on the patio to a Glen Miller song. The other two couples were sitting around a table in the dining area playing cards. The maid spoke to Katie in Spanish, telling her how much fun these people seemed to be having.

One of the ladies noticed her and motioned her forward saying, "Well, if it isn't our Katie here to check up on this rowdy bunch. Everyone be on your best behavior."

Katie chatted with them, learning about their children and grandchildren. They told her stories about how they all had met, and one of the men even told her some jokes. She listened, but mostly she watched. They all seemed so happy. They held hands, touched each other as they passed, and seemed able to communicate with each other without speaking.

Despite being tired, just being around these couples brought a new surge of energy to her step as she walked back to the office to gather some information for Megan's father about children's activities in the area and to lock up. She couldn't help but smile thinking about those three wonderful couples.

Kaleb was just exiting the rental car when he noticed Katie walking back to her office. There was a smile playing across her face as though she was secretly amused about something. She must be weary after he had kept her up most of the night, but her steps appeared quick and her body language didn't denote fatigue.

Very good at her job, he thought once again.

As Katie approached her office she noticed the white Expedition she had rented for Mr. Dalton parked nearby. She had just grabbed the door handle to her office door when she heard Mr. Dalton call out, "Miss McKay, may I have a word with you?"

As he called her name he remembered Megan's assertion that her name was Katie, bringing a smile to his face.

Turning, she saw him walking towards her. He looked rested and less stiff. A small smile actually crossed his face.

Clearing his throat, he said, "I just stopped by to thank you for picking us up last night and..." hesitating for a moment, "...to apologize for my reluctance in allowing you to drive us. You did a good job."

She was surprised by his coming out of his way to thank her, but especially by his apology. Acknowledging both the thank you and the apology with, "You're welcome and apology accepted," she couldn't help her inborn instinct to tease a little. She added, "But as far as the good job driving, I don't think you could know that, as all I heard from you in the back seat was snoring."

He flushed a little and said, "Touché, Miss McKay." Then a look of puzzlement crossed his face and he added more to himself then to her, "I can't believe I actually fell asleep in the car." Turning away he started back to his car. He seemed to remember himself, stopped and called out, "Goodbye."

Katie answered, "Goodbye," and let herself into her office.

Now that was indeed strange, she thought. It was then that she remembered the information she intended to give him. She hurried back to the door but the car was already pulling away. She would just have to stop by on her way home.

Taking the information, she locked up the office and got into her car. Maybe she would go home first and take a nap. She doubted Megan would be ready to get involved in too much activity today, considering how tired she was last night. She would just run the papers over this evening.

Pulling away Kaleb thought, *That went well enough.*

He couldn't help thinking about the way she had teased him about his snoring; gutsy girl. In both of their short encounters she had stood her ground and hadn't let him get away with anything just because he was rich and powerful. But then she didn't know how rich and powerful he really was. Well, maybe that was good.

He hadn't gone out on a date since he and Lucy were courting. Several single women he knew had started making suggestive advances towards him in the last year, but he wasn't interested. Even before he and Lucy had gotten married a lot of women seemed interested, but he had learned early that a lot of them were more interested in his money than in him.

Katie didn't really know anything about him, so maybe he would ask her out to dinner some time. It had been over two years since he lost Lucy and sometimes he just got lonely for female companionship. Well, maybe he wasn't quite ready for an actual date. He could ask her to have dinner at the villa with Roger and Megan and him. Yes, that was a better idea.

Kaleb, Roger and Megan spent the afternoon on the beach. They discovered two hammocks stretched between the trees. Kaleb convinced Megan to lie in one and he used it as a swing, pushing her back and forth. She sat beside him in the sand as he built a sand castle for her.

Kaleb thought she seemed more relaxed and didn't drift off into nothingness as much as usual. He hoped it was true and that he wasn't just seeing something that wasn't there.

They had decided to eat dinner on the patio and had just finished when the doorbell rang. Roger was the first on his feet and said he would get it. Opening the door he found Katie standing outside.

"Good evening. Come on in."

"Oh, no. I just stopped by to bring some information about our kid's club, the Xcarat Park and some other local activities I thought Mr. Dalton might want to look at for Megan."

"He's out on the patio with her, so why don't you go take it to him in case he has any questions." Roger motioned to a patio off of the living room. Katie glanced over her shoulder to where a car sat with the motor running.

"My friend April and I were just coming back from grabbing a bite to eat in town and I hate to leave her sitting by herself."

Roger looked out at the car. "You go on in and talk to Kaleb and I'll go out and meet your friend. If I'm going to be here for a month I should at least meet a few new people," Roger said as he walked past her on the way to the car.

So the "K" in K. J. Dalton stood for Kaleb. She liked the name. She thought it suited him. Shrugging her shoulders, she walked into the house and out to the patio.

Kaleb saw her coming. He set down his drink on the table and stood to greet her.

"I wondered who was at the door."

Megan was sitting across from where her father had been seated, sipping on a straw. The drink was pink, probably some kind of Shirley Temple.

Katie looked up and said, "Good evening, Mr. Dalton." Then turning, she smiled at Megan. "Hello, Megan. You look so pretty tonight. Did you do anything fun today?"

Megan gave her a shy smile and nodded her head. Kaleb had been watching the exchange and was relieved when Megan hadn't just stared past their visitor as though she didn't exist. Katie turned back to Kaleb, holding out some pamphlets and other typed papers.

"I had planned on stopping by earlier to give these to you, but I wound up taking a nap instead. I'm sorry to have interrupted your evening. I thought you might like to look these over before you made plans for tomorrow. We have many interesting places and activities for children here in Akumal and the surrounding area."

Kaleb looked down at the material Katie handed him. He saw Lol Ha Kid's Club written across the top pamphlet. He didn't think Megan would do well in a group, but he said he would look them over. It tore at his heart because he knew that before the accident, Megan would have been begging him to let her go play with the other kids.

Bringing his mind back to the present, Kaleb again thanked Katie for the information.

Katie said, "Well, I have a friend waiting in the car, so I better go."

It immediately crossed his mind that it was probably a man, but he had noticed that she wore no ring, so it wasn't a committed relationship yet.

As he walked her to the door he found himself asking, "I was wondering if you would like to come for dinner some time? I know Roger and Megan could stand some other company besides my own."

Katie hadn't expected the invitation and found she wasn't sure how to answer. She made it a policy to never get involved with her clients, but there was something about this man. She found him disturbing but exciting. She wasn't sure what it was. Maybe it was his air of authority, his attentiveness to his daughter, or maybe she just found him physically attractive. Then she recalled the way he had asked her.

She glanced at his hand, seeing the wedding band on his finger, and thought, *No, he's not asking for himself, but maybe he's trying to play cupid for Roger.*

Trying to be diplomatic she replied, "I'd love to spend time with Megan any time I'm not at work. I have a dog she would love and I only live a few houses over from here, so maybe we could meet on the beach tomorrow. I like to spend my Sundays relaxing and allowing my dog some running time. As far as dinner and Roger, I think if he is interested, we better let him do the asking. Goodnight, Mr. Dalton. I hope I'll see Megan on the beach tomorrow."

With that she turned and walked down the path to the waiting car.

Kaleb was struck speechless by Katie's monologue. Katie and Roger...it hadn't even crossed his mind. He knew they had talked on the way from the airport, because several times today Roger would mention something about the area prefacing it with, "Katie said..."

Was Roger interested? He wondered why she had thought he would ask her to dinner for someone else and not himself. When he had asked, he knew she had been surprised, but he thought she had also been pleased. Something had changed when she looked down.

He looked down himself and noticed his wedding ring. Could that have been it? He had worn it for so many years that he didn't even think about it. It was part of him. Katie wouldn't know that his wife was dead and instead of thinking he, a married man, was coming on to her, she assumed he was playing matchmaker.

Looking out to the driveway he saw Roger walk around the back of the car. He stopped and opened the door for Katie, saying something to her. Then he closed the door, stepped back and waved as the car pulled away.

Chapter 4

Pulling away from the villa, Katie looked over at April's excited face.

"Boy, you look like you just met the god Adonis and he promised to carry you away in his chariot."

"Isn't he just the most gorgeous man you ever saw, and so friendly and nice?"

"I think you've got it bad, and all in about ten minutes. Usually it takes you at least a half hour."

"But this time it's different. I just know it is!"

Katie shook her head. It seemed to her that April fell in and out of love, or at least like, about every month or so.

April was a free spirit, flamboyant and flirtatious. She tended to rush headlong into most situations. She had come to Akumal at the urging of her aunt, who owned the largest hotel resort on that strip of the Mexican Riviera. She had been out beating the pavement looking for a job, having just graduated from a two-year interior design institute, when her Aunt Beth offered her a chance she couldn't refuse, the remodeling of her hotel. April was in her element. She was able to use rich, bright colors, a variety of textures, and was basically able to create what before, only her mind had seen. Once the hotel was completed she worked freelance and never lacked for a job.

Despite, or maybe because of, Katie and April's differences in personality, they were instant friends. Katie's parents had been rather lenient. She was allowed to express her feelings and experiment with new ideas and things, but her basic personality tended more towards the structured, routine and careful lifestyle. Coming to live in Akumal had been her big rebellion, but in her daily life she was still cautious and took few chances. She wore responsibility like a cloak.

April, on the other hand, had been raised in a very strict and prohibitive home. By the time she was ten, she was already chomping at the bit wanting to break free of the bonds of her parents. A visit from her Aunt Beth had set fire to her spirit. She could still recall the visit to this day.

Aunt Beth was her dad's sister. She had left home and gotten married when she was seventeen. Her husband was twelve years older than her and wealthy. Traveling seemed to be their life. They sent April and her brothers and sisters gifts for birthdays and Christmas from all over the world.

Her parents were in an uproar when they received word of the impending visit. Her dad tried to smooth things over with her mom.

She could recall him saying things like, "I know she's the black sheep of the family, but she's my sister and I still love her. Maybe she's changed. It's been years since we last saw her. I'm sure she will be on her best behavior with the children here."

But her mother had not been reassured.

"You know how she is. She dresses so outlandishly, and those stories she tells. Why, I still remember her talking about those natives in Africa and how they spent a week living with them. Imagine what the children would think if she told them about how they were dressed, or rather undressed, and some of those rituals they took part in. I'll just die."

Her parents didn't realize that the more they talked, the more April could hardly wait for her aunt to come. What a wonderful time it had been. She had arrived wearing a flowing gown with red and white flowers and beads and bangles chiming with every step she took. She did tell stories about the places she had been, but April was disappointed that she didn't hear anything about people who didn't wear clothes.

April had fallen in love with her Aunt Beth on that visit and wanted to be just like her.

By the time April was fifteen, she had started to rebel against her parents' rules. She would leave for school dressed in a prim blouse or a sweater with a little Peter Pan collar, but once she got away from the house the top would come off to reveal a low-cut, tight T-shirt or a little sleeveless top that left her midriff bare. She had makeup in her locker at school, and that was her first stop every morning. She did a little baby-sitting, but most of her money for these necessary items came from the lunch money her parents gave her every week. Missing lunch was a small price to pay. Eventually, she got caught and the lunch money was cut off. Her mother started packing one for her. This didn't stop April though. She borrowed clothes and makeup from her friends.

When she finished high school, her parents wanted her to go to college, but she found a job and moved into a little apartment with a friend. When she decided to go to the Interior Design Institute, it was her Aunt Beth who had financed it.

Katie and April seemed to find a missing part of themselves in each other. April could always count on Katie to help her focus and take a little more time to think things through, while April pushed Katie to be more spontaneous and carefree. They were like a rich tapestry; one was the fine stitching and intrinsic pattern, while the other was the vibrant colors and textured material, intertwined to form a strong friendship.

When April dropped Katie off at her house, Katie warned, "Now April, you be careful and don't go too fast with Roger. I don't want to see either of you get hurt. He seems like a really nice guy."

"Yes mother, I'll be good and take things real slow," April drawled.

Katie just laughed. As she closed her car door she added, "The day you take things slow will be the day I fall head over heels in love."

Roger stood watching the car drive away. Wow! He couldn't believe it. He was slow and methodical when it came to his own relationships, but April had bowled him over. He thought she was gorgeous, and when she laughed it was like music to his ears. All he had seen of her was her face, but man, what a face. He was taking her to lunch tomorrow and was already wishing it were time to go. She was going to pick him up at noon.

He turned and strode back to the house. Kaleb was standing in the doorway.

"Well, old man, I have a date tomorrow for lunch. Think you can spare me for the day?"

"Sure," Kaleb answered, a little terseness in his voice. Roger didn't appear to notice.

So there was something between Katie and Roger; so much for meeting Katie on the beach tomorrow. He was glad he hadn't had a chance to tell Megan about the planned outing and Katie's dog. She didn't need any more disappointments.

They all went to bed early. Megan had another nightmare.

Kaleb sat on the bed holding her long after she had fallen back to sleep. As he sat comforting her he wondered what was to become of the two of them. He would give up everything he owned just to have her laughing and playing. He would even love to see her throw one of her temper tantrums. When she was two she would lie down on the floor kicking and crying when she couldn't get her own way. By the time she turned four her temper manifested itself by her stomping around on the hardwood floors of her playroom, where, if she were really upset, she would pick up her toys and throw them across the room. Both he and Lucy had tried to channel her anger into more acceptable forms, but now he wished he could see her stomp around with that frustrated look on her face. Anger was better than terror or nothing.

He knew that Megan had seen her mother die. From what the police had put together from the accident scene and eye witnesses, it appeared that Lucy had been driving down the highway, heading home after picking up Megan from her dance lesson, when a car coming from the other direction had suddenly crossed over the white line. It had smashed into the front driver side of the car. It hit at enough of an angle from the left that her air bag didn't protect her. The driver of the other vehicle had also been killed. Upon autopsy they found that the other driver had suffered a massive heart attack. Megan had been seat-belted into the back seat when the accident occurred and was not injured. He knew she couldn't have seen her mother's broken and bloody face from the back seat, and the people at the scene had assured him that they had gotten her out and away from the immediate area long before they pried his wife's body out of the wreck. What was it that she kept seeing in her dreams?

Lucy had loved cars and loved to drive. She insisted on having her own and driving herself. She had been raised in a small town in upper New York State and thought of a car as a means of freedom. There had been no mass transit or subways there. She had never understood his indifference to cars. He'd had subways, cabs and a chauffeur and car at his disposal all his life. He had learned to drive when he was eighteen, but had driven very little. He thought it was someone else's job to get him where he wanted to go.

Their opinion on cars was one of the few things upon which they disagreed. He had met Lucy in college. They fell in love and married. They had friends in common and loved their little girl. They had hoped for more children but none had come along.

He still loved and missed Lucy but some of the pain had started to fade. He wanted to remember the good times and wished he could talk to Megan about the things they used to do together. But poor, dear Megan just couldn't get past the trauma. Maybe he should let them try hypnosis like the doctor had suggested, but she was so young. He just didn't know what to do. With that thought he fell asleep.

Waking up, he found himself lying in bed next to Megan. She was still asleep, her face relaxed in slumber. The little clock on the bedside stand showed that it was already ten in the morning. He hadn't slept that late in a long time. Climbing quietly from the bed, he made his way to the shower.

Dressed and ready for the day, Kaleb walked out of his room. Megan was just coming out of her room.

He leaned over, gave her a hug and said, "I think a bath is in order for you this morning. Somehow we missed getting you one yesterday."

Megan followed him into the bathroom and waited for him to run the water. He got her a towel and some shampoo. Knowing she didn't always get all the soap out of her hair, he said to holler when she was ready for him to help her rinse.

Leaving her to her bath, he went to the kitchen to start breakfast. Coffee was already made, so he knew Roger was up and about, but he hadn't seen or heard him. The kitchen window looked out on mostly jungle. Perched among the leaves were numerous colorful birds. As he looked out the window he thought that it must be a bird watcher's paradise.

Rolls warmed in the oven and fresh fruit would do for breakfast this morning. Hearing Megan call his name, he returned to the bathroom and helped her finish with her hair.

Megan and Kaleb sat on the patio to eat. He talked to her about the many birds he had seen outside the window and about the butterfly center he had read about in the material Katie had given him. She asked a couple of questions but didn't seem very interested.

Roger came back to the house a little while later. He greeted them with a cheery good morning, said he'd had a nice walk on the beach and then headed upstairs to get ready for his date.

Kaleb decided to take Megan back to the beach. She seemed to like it there yesterday. He packed a picnic lunch and grabbed some towels and sunscreen.

Heading out the door he called to Roger, "Would you let the maid in? I think she should be here soon. Have a good time today."

Roger came to the top of the stairs.

"Okay to the maid and I plan to have a great time today."

Kaleb nodded, said goodbye and left.

Boy, Roger is acting like a teenager, Kaleb thought.

Megan and Kaleb had just laid out their towels and taken off their sandals when they heard a dog barking. Looking down the beach they saw Katie jogging towards them with a big, light-brown-colored dog running beside her. Kaleb glanced at his watch, noting it was a quarter to twelve. Why wasn't she getting ready to pick up Roger?

As she neared, she called out, "I was beginning to wonder if the two of you were coming." Looking at Megan she continued, "I told Mimoso that we were going to meet some new friends today and he was getting sad because you weren't here."

"How do you know he was sad? Dogs can't talk."

Laughing Katie replied, "No, he can't talk, but he puts his head down and walks real slow like he can hardly move."

Megan looked at Katie and then Mimoso. "Just like I do?"

Katie would have said something but Mimoso decided he'd had enough of this polite behavior. He darted over to Megan and licked her face. Megan took a startled step back but then stuck out her hand so Mimoso could lick it.

Katie decided a formal introduction was called for so she commanded, "Mimoso, sit."

He sat down.

"Shake."

He lifted a front paw to Megan. Megan grabbed the offered paw and shook it.

"Glad to meet you, Mimoso."

The dog barked in reply.

"I think they like each other," Katie said to Kaleb. Looking back to Megan she explained, "He likes to run up and down the beach and will get the ball for you if you throw it."

Holding out a little red rubber ball she asked, "Do you want to play with him?"

Megan looked to her father, who nodded his permission. Taking the ball, she threw it a few feet down the beach. Mimoso took off after it and then returned it to her. Megan continued to throw and Mimoso continued to fetch. Soon the two of them were running up and down the beach.

Turning only slightly, Katie could see Kaleb watching the activity. She sensed that he was getting pleasure from seeing his daughter playing. He really was a devoted father.

Kaleb could feel Katie's eyes on him. He turned to her.

"Aren't you going to be late picking up Roger?"

"Picking up Roger? Why would I be picking up Roger? Your driver is available to you anytime you want him."

"He said he had a date for lunch today and was being picked up at noon. He was really looking forward to it. I hope you're not standing him up."

Katie laughed, "Oh, I had forgotten about that."

Kaleb frowned at her laughter and her words.

Seeing his displeasure she quickly added, "The date isn't with me. It's with my friend, April. They met last night while I was in talking to you. We both have our own rules about not dating tourists, but somehow Roger got her to change her mind. Plus, the way April was acting last night, if I even looked Roger's way she would probably do me some real bodily harm."

Kaleb couldn't help it. A grin spread across his face. He had felt somehow betrayed, both by Katie and by Roger, when Roger had announced that he had a date, and he'd assumed it was with Katie. Now he felt relief. He hoped April and Roger hit it off. He knew Roger could be a real charmer and he didn't want any of that charm turned Katie's way.

"Speaking of lunch, I packed a picnic for Megan and myself. Please stay and eat with us."

Katie looked out to where Megan and Mimoso had stopped and appeared to be watching something in the sand. He was married. She shouldn't have lunch with him. She never dated tourists, and a married man was definitely out of the normal scope of what she considered available male companionship. But it was just lunch with him and Megan, not really a date. He was just being polite and friendly.

As she turned back to answer him, he looked at the wedding ring he wore.

Then focusing on Katie's face he said, "Lucy, my wife, died a little over two years ago and I just never took it off. I'm not sure I'm ready to yet. But I do wish you would stay and eat with us."

Katie was struck numb by his words, but as they gradually sank into her mind, she felt something close to relief. No wife waiting for him at home. That thought had barely formed when guilt set in for even thinking such a thing. It only took a moment more for that big soft spot in the middle of her heart to kick in.

This strong, powerful man had lost the woman he loved. The one he had planned to spend the rest of his life with, the woman who had given him his beloved Megan. Megan's face formed in front of her. Sweet, sad-eyed Megan had no mother to hug her, to kiss away her hurts or to sing to her at night. She tried to imagine what she would feel like if she had fallen in love and had a child with a man and had him taken from her. She wanted to empathize with Kaleb, but she had no experience to compare to what he must feel. Sorrow for these two was the emotion that remained on Katie's face as she stood looking at Kaleb.

Kaleb watched the emotions quickly cross Katie's very expressive face. He didn't know her well enough to decipher all her thoughts, but he could see the sheen of tears in her eyes and read the look of pity she now wore. He had seen that look on the faces of countless others over the last couple of years. It almost made him want to yell at her.

He wanted to scream, "Stop looking at me that way, I don't want your pity!" but he said nothing. His lips pressed together, forming a flat line.

Katie was startled by the look of hostility she saw on Kaleb's face when her eyes again focused on him. Was he angry with her for being there, for intruding when it was Lucy he longed for? She looked out at the ocean, no longer able to meet his angry stare.

"I'm sorry," she stammered. Then pulling herself together she added, "I'd love to stay and have lunch with you and Megan, but I'm sure you only packed enough food for the two of you, so..."

He realized she was giving him a way out and that almost made him angrier.

"We have plenty," he snapped.

His harsh tone caused a little bit of that Irish temper to flare as she curtly replied, "I guess you're stuck with me then."

Her brief show of anger seemed to deflate his. He would much rather have her anger than her pity.

"Well then, let's go see what your dog and Megan have found that has them so intrigued."

The three of them spent about an hour walking along the beach. Deciding they were hungry, they sat on the towels laid out in the sand and devoured the lunch Kaleb had brought. Mimoso begged for a share, but Katie assured them he had plenty of his own food and didn't need to eat theirs. Mimoso settled down beside Megan. Katie and Kaleb shared a smile as they saw Megan slipping him bites of her sandwich.

After lunch, Katie made her excuses and headed home. She wanted to work on her yard. The fencing should be arriving sometime this week and she wanted to start getting it up next weekend. She had hired Raul to help her. He worked as the groundskeeper and general handyman for several of the villas she rented. Before they could install the fence, she needed to get the vegetation cleared.

As she worked in her yard she couldn't help but think about Kaleb and Megan. Megan had seemed to take right to Mimoso, but had spoken very little. She was so good, but that bothered Katie. She was just too good.

She had met a few kids over the years that acted just like Megan. They obeyed immediately and never acted up. She had labeled them as kids with Divorced Parents Syndrome.

She wasn't a psychologist but she had decided these children were really hurt by their parents' divorce, but even more than the hurt, they were afraid. It seemed to her that they were afraid that if they misbehaved or caused any problems their mom or dad might leave them.

Was that what was going on with Megan? If her mom had died two years ago, she would have been about five. Kids that young didn't understand death, and maybe she thought her mom was gone because of something she had done. If that was the case, she was probably trying to be good so her daddy wouldn't leave her, too.

She wondered if she could get Megan to open up a little if she had some time alone with her. The need to comfort and help that was so much a part of Katie was pushing full steam ahead. They hadn't made any plans to see each other again, but maybe she could offer to take Megan for a few hours sometime. Surely Kaleb would want to take in some of the adult activities while he was here. She had gotten the feeling he wouldn't let anyone he didn't know take care of Megan. Of course, there was always Roger. Remembering how April had carried on last night about Roger, she knew that if April had her way, Roger wouldn't have many free nights.

With the decision made to find a way to spend some time with Megan, her thoughts turned to Mr. Dalton, Kaleb. She smiled a little.

He had continued to call her Miss McKay until today. No Miss McKays today, but no Katies either. He just avoided using her name altogether, and she had done the same with him. He had let her know with his little speech about his wedding ring that he was only being friendly. That was good, since he was off-limits to her anyway. Katie was content.

Anyone who knew Katie well would understand her contentment. In a few short sentences, Kaleb had created the perfect atmosphere for her. His heart was completely tied to Lucy, so he wouldn't be trying to push into her own private space. She in turn wouldn't intrude into his, but that left a big open space where she could try to help Megan. If she could help ease some of his pain, that would be all right, too.

Megan and Kaleb spent a little more time wading in the water before they started back to the house. On the walk back Kaleb made small talk about what a good time he had, trying to draw some conversation from Megan. Megan walked along beside him making no comment.

As they neared the house, her little hand stiffened in his grasp, causing him to look down at her. She appeared to be struggling to say something and she finally blurted out, "I want a dog."

She looked at him with a stubborn tilt to her jaw that suddenly turned to what almost looked like fear. He frowned, not because of her request but because of the fear he now saw in her eyes. He quickly changed his expression to one of serious contemplation.

"A dog, you say. You know, I hadn't really thought about getting a pet before, but now that I think about it, it sounds like a splendid idea. Did you know I had a dog when I was growing up? His name was Sir Dudley. He could do all kinds of tricks."

At his words her hand relaxed and a spark of real joy lit her eyes. *So, we're making progress*, he thought.

It was the first real request she had made in two years, and that little bit of stubbornness he had noticed was like a soothing balm to his heart.

Katie and her dog were helping to nudge Megan back to him. He would have Roger get Mimoso a big bone and send Katie some flowers.

He spent the evening talking to Megan about what kind of dog he should get her. Megan went to sleep early, worn out by her day in the sun, leaving Kaleb by himself to do some thinking of his own.

Well, Megan, my girl, maybe this place will give us a fresh start, he thought. Then he looked down at his wedding band. *Why am I still wearing it?* he asked himself.

"Oh Lucy, I still love you and miss you every day," he said out loud to the empty room. He closed his eyes and slouched back in the chair.

He swore he heard Lucy answer him, "I know darling, but I want you to be happy. Keeping yourself locked up in a shell isn't any way to honor the love we had, nor does it help Megan."

He opened his eyes, looking about. The room was still empty. A little shiver worked its way up his spine. He had talked to Lucy other times over the past two years, but this was the first time he had ever imagined an answer. He took a deep breath and relaxed again.

So Lucy, you think I've wallowed in self-pity long enough.

On that thought another face forced its way into his mind; Katie, with her sad eyes looking at him on the beach. Why had he been so angry with her for feeling sorry for him? Hadn't he all but asked her for sympathy when he told her he couldn't take off his ring? Had he wanted her pity or was he just warning her to not get too close? Maybe a little of both.

Then came a thought that really had him confused. *Was he trying to warn Katie to stay away or was he throwing up roadblocks for himself?*

He remembered thinking how nice it was to see such a pretty lady waiting for them as they got off the plane, but then, when she had acted friendly, he had been curt and almost rude. At least he had apologized for that.

No, he really didn't apologize for his rudeness, just for questioning her ability to drive. When he had decided to ask her to dinner he had backed off. Instead, he had extended an invitation that made it sound like he wanted a companion for his daughter or a date for his friend. And then today he had definitely put up a wall to keep himself off-limits. His mind in a whirl, he decided to call it a night. Crawling into bed, his last thought was that if his shell were going to start cracking he would like Katie to be the one to pull away the pieces.

Megan had another nightmare.

Chapter 5

The next two days passed in relative peace. Kaleb and Megan toured the butterfly center and the aquarium at the Xcarat Park, swam in the ocean and ate out at the local restaurants a couple of times.

Roger spent his days on his laptop computer and cell phone handling business. His evenings were monopolized by April.

Katie was shocked on Monday morning at the office when she received a large package of bones for Mimoso and a flower arrangement with a note that just said, "Thanks, Kaleb."

She took them home and set the flowers on her bedside stand so she could see them when she went to bed. Both Monday and Tuesday were very busy at work. She got home late both nights.

Wednesday, things were slowing down at work. By noon the e-mail was answered and no one had stopped by with any problems that she needed to handle. She decided to take her full hour for lunch today.

Telling Sybil, the other woman who worked in the office, that she was going out to lunch, she went into the back room to get her purse. She heard the office door open and could hear someone speaking with Sybil. Coming back into the front room she was surprised to see Kaleb and Megan standing inside the doorway.

"You've got company," Sybil said.

It surprised Katie that her heart gave a little flutter of excitement at seeing Kaleb there.

He really is quite good-looking, she thought.

"Hi there, you two. I see you've met Sybil. Is there something I can

43

do for you?"

Megan smiled at her and Kaleb cleared his throat.

"Yes, we have a problem. We don't speak or read Spanish and we need someone to go with us to lunch to interpret the menu and place the order."

Frowning, Katie said, "You shouldn't have any problem. The waiters all speak some English and the menus are in both Spanish and English."

Kaleb laughed and said, "I know. I just wanted an excuse to get you to come to lunch with us. I figured if we were a little pathetic, you wouldn't be able to turn us down. How about it? I'll even pay."

"Okay, on one condition. I get to order for all of us."

He readily agreed. They walked to the nearest restaurant and found an empty table on the open verandah. The waiter brought menus but Katie waved them away. She spoke Spanish to him, placing their order. Besides the food, she ordered a Shirley Temple for Megan, a Diet Coke for herself and one of the local specialty drinks for Kaleb.

"You have your car and driver here with you, I assume?" she said to Kaleb.

"Yes, of course. Why?"

"The drink I ordered for you has alcohol in it, so I just wanted to be safe. Well, what have you two been doing the last couple of days?"

"Not too much. We went to the park that you gave us information about, swam in the ocean and played on the beach."

"How about snorkeling? There is a lot of beautiful sea life and coral to see. You really should try it. Megan, do you think you would like to go snorkeling?" Megan nodded. Looking over at Kaleb, Katie continued, "Maybe I could get off by four today and take her, if that would be all right with you."

Kaleb let a slow smile cross his face as he answered, "I have two conditions for you before I say yes."

With a speculative look, Katie replied, "And they are?"

"Nothing very difficult; the first is that I get to go snorkeling too, and the second is that you go out to dinner with me tomorrow night."

Katie was pleased that he wanted to go with them. She was sure Megan would feel more comfortable with her dad there, but going out to dinner with him was something else.

Looking at Megan she said, "Megan, we would love to have your daddy go with us, wouldn't we?"

Megan answered quickly, "Oh yes, Daddy, please."

Again Kaleb was taken off guard by Megan's show of enthusiasm and said, "You bet I want to go." Then looking back at Katie, "And dinner?"

"What about Megan? Who would watch her?"

"I already spoke to Roger this morning. He said he and April would plan a fun night for Megan."

Katie looked over at Megan to see her nodding her head, letting Katie know that they had already talked about this before they showed up at her office. This was no spur-of-the-moment decision.

"If those are the conditions for taking Megan snorkeling, I can hardly say no, can I?" Katie's tone of voice made Kaleb realize she would have said yes even if there were no conditions.

They agreed to meet at the dive shop at four-thirty. After work she had to run home and let Mimoso out for a few minutes and change into her swimsuit. If she got held up at work she would get there as soon as she could, she told Kaleb.

When Katie got back to the office Sybil said, "He seems like a really nice man, and good-looking, too. Is he the one who sent you the flowers?"

She hadn't even thanked him for sending the flowers and she had wanted to ask him what he was thanking her for. She would be seeing him again today and would thank him then.

She was excited. She just couldn't help it. Four o'clock seemed like it would never come. Now, when she wanted time to go by fast, everything slowed down to a crawl. There were no problems and few e-mails to answer. By the time four o'clock finally came she had already locked up and was on her way home.

At twenty minutes after four she was parked outside the dive shop. Looking down the street she saw the Expedition pull up in front of a little shop down from where she sat waiting.

Getting out of the car, she walked towards them calling, "Mr. Dalton, Megan, the dive shop is over here."

Kaleb turned. "Megan broke a strap on her sandal, and I thought we would stop and buy her a new pair before we met you," he said, his voice gradually losing volume as she walked closer. "And," he said as she came within a few feet of him, "please call me Kaleb."

"Okay, Kaleb it is." Then she whispered, "Until I met you at the airport, I thought the "K" in K. J. Dalton stood for Katherine or Kimberly or maybe Kristi."

He frowned.

"Not a very manly name for someone as strong and good-looking as me." Then he laughed and said, "So you thought I was a woman, did you?"

Nodding, she replied, "Kaleb does suit you better than any of those other names."

Megan interrupted their exchange with a "Hi, Katie."

"Hi, Megan. Your sandal broke, did it? I know they have some really cute ones here. Let's go find you a new pair." Taking hold of her hand they walked into the shop.

Leaving with a new pair of sandals on Megan's feet, Katie suggested that they let their driver go home. She would take them back to the villa when they finished snorkeling. Kaleb agreed. Collecting the snorkeling gear from the shop, they made their way down to the beach. A few feet from the edge, Katie dropped her gear in the sand.

"We can leave our things here. I'll show you how to use the equipment and we can practice where you can easily stand up in the water, Megan. After you feel comfortable with it, we'll swim out where the water gets deep so you can see all the fish and coral I was telling you about. Right now we need to get your top and shorts off."

Megan started taking off her clothes, revealing a pretty swimsuit with blue flowers.

"I saw people floating on their stomachs with funny things sticking up from their heads yesterday when Dad and I went for a walk. Were they snorkeling?"

"I'm sure they were," Katie said as she loosened the belt on her cover-up and pulled it from her shoulders. Taking her and Megan's clothes, she folded them and placed them in a neat pile on top of a towel she laid out on the sand.

Kaleb had been following close behind, listening to their conversation. He dropped his gear near Katie's and was reaching to take off his T-shirt when Katie removed her cover-up. He had seen her in walking shorts and a loose-fitting sleeveless blouse, in slacks and a lightweight sweater at the airport and a skirt and blouse at work. But when she started gathering clothes and placing them on the towel in her two-piece bathing suit, his mouth dropped open, his heartbeat accelerated and that part of his anatomy that he hadn't used in a long time let him know he was still a man. He turned slightly away, hoping Katie wouldn't notice his reaction. He didn't want to scare her off before he even got to know her. He figured she had to be somewhere between twenty-five and thirty years old. Although he already knew from the things she had said that she wasn't promiscuous, at her age she surely would have had a few intimate relationships, so if she did notice she shouldn't be shocked.

He grabbed the bottom of his T-shirt and pulled it over his head. As he lowered his arms, holding his shirt in front of his waist, he saw Katie staring at him. Her look was searing and her breathing seemed a little fast. She was staring at his chest.

I'm sure glad I've worked at staying in shape, he thought.

As her eyes whipped up to his face, he grinned at her and said, "Katie, are you ready to play teacher?"

She flushed a little at being caught staring but quickly looked away, grabbing a snorkeling mask for Megan. She was too flustered to answer him, so she just pretended she hadn't heard him.

Now, when I'm acting like a starry-eyed teenager, he finally calls me Katie, she thought.

"Kaleb, have you ever been snorkeling before?" she asked while she fastened Megan's mask in place.

"Once, a long time ago."

"I'm sure it's like riding a bike. Once you've done it, you never forget," she said, looking back over her shoulder at him.

She showed Megan how to put the breathing apparatus in her mouth and breathe through the tube sticking up in the air. Putting on her own mask, she led them into the water. After a little practice in the shallow part they all swam out to where the water was about six feet deep.

For two hours they went back and forth from the beach, resting frequently so they wouldn't tire out. They saw rainbow-colored parrot fish, sea turtles, enormous lobsters and barracuda. The coral was beautiful, in shades of red, orange and purple.

Around seven o'clock Katie and Kaleb both decided they had seen enough. Megan had gone out to waist-deep water. Kaleb called to her to come in, saying it was time to go. She slowly walked back to where they waited.

With a little whine in her voice she said, "Can't we stay a little longer?"

Kaleb was surprised by that and wondered if he might be able to get her to flash a little of that temper he knew she had.

"Megan, we've been here long enough."

He said it in a stern but not harsh voice. He saw her look up at him; her eyes narrowed slightly and she started to say something, then she closed her mouth, lowered her eyes and said, "Okay."

Kaleb thought, *Well, a little something is better than nothing.*

Turning his head to see if Katie was following, he saw her watching them with a speculative look on her face. Maybe tomorrow at dinner he would tell her what Megan used to be like.

Thursday evening, Katie hunted through her closet for just the right dress to wear. She wanted to look good—feminine and maybe a little sexy. She had discarded several already when she finally settled on a dark green dress with a double-spaghetti-strap top that flared into a full skirt. The skirt fell just above her knees. The material was soft but not clingy. Finding some short heels that matched the dress, she slipped them on. She left her hair down, curling the ends so it fell in waves over her shoulders. She used little make-up, just some lipstick and light eyeliner. She slipped a ceramic bracelet on her wrist.

Looking in the mirror she thought, *Well, this will have to do.* Then she thought, *What are you doing? You were sure everything was so simple this weekend. You were just going to be friends, and here you are worried about how you look and what he'll think. You have to remember that he's still in love with his wife and isn't ready for any relationship, plus he's a tourist who will be leaving in a few weeks. Now you just remember that,* she told herself sternly as she heard a car pull up in her drive.

Kaleb asked Megan one more time before he left if she was sure it was okay for him to leave her with Roger and April. She'd had a bad nightmare again last night. Some days she seemed to be getting better, and then the night would come and those terrible dreams. He was really getting worried. His hope would grow in the light of day and be crushed in the middle of the night. It was tearing him apart.

Megan insisted that he go. She even gave an opinion on what he should wear. She liked his gray and black pullover shirt with his black slacks. Roger said it was all right but he preferred the shirt-and-tie look. Kaleb thought Roger tended to be just a bit too dressy, so he stayed with Megan's choice.

Kaleb stood before Katie's door, knocked and waited.

"I'll be right there. I have to get Mimoso out of the living room or he'll jump all over you."

A few seconds later she opened the door.

Kaleb looked from her shoes slowly up to her face, letting out a soft whistle as he said, "You look great."

"Thank you."

Then she commenced to look him over as he had just done to her.

"You look pretty good yourself," she said with a smile in her voice.

"I think you are being a little bit impertinent, miss," he said in a very good imitation of a precise English accent. They both laughed.

"Your chariot awaits, my lady," he said as he extended his arm for her to hold.

They went to a quaint restaurant on the south end of Akumal. It was bustling with customers, but they were able to get a table off to the side and away from the main activity. They could see lights reflecting off of the water in the lagoon.

They ordered drinks first, deciding they would like to visit for a while before eating. They both seemed hungry for knowledge about each other.

Asking about his family, she learned that his father had died several years ago and that his mother had remarried and lived in Philadelphia. He had no brothers and sisters, but did have a cousin around his own age that he was quite close to. As children they had played together and had attended the same schools, even the same college. He and his family now lived in St. Louis, so they saw each other much less, but still stayed in close contact.

His grandfather had started Dalton Construction Company in the

1930s, limiting most of his work to the Boston area. Over time he had expanded to include projects in other communities.

When his father had taken over the company, he had enlarged it to include the manufacturing of some building materials because he found he was unhappy with the quality of some of the products they were using. The company had become Dalton Industries in 1975.

As for himself, he had added the development and production of computer programs for use by construction companies. He mentioned that Roger was especially talented in this area and often advised him in the development and production of these products.

He, in turn, found out that she had arrived in Akumal when she was twenty. She had come as a temporary vacation nanny for a travel agency. Liking the area so much, she had found a permanent position as the director of the Lo Ha Kids' Club. Eventually she took the job at the rental agency.

She was born and raised in a small town in California. Her parents still lived there. She had two sisters and one brother. All three were married, and between them she had three nephews and one niece. Whenever she had time for a vacation she usually spent it traipsing from one of their homes to the other. She indicated that they were all very close. About every six months someone in the family usually made it down to visit her.

He noticed how her face lit up when she talked about buying her house. She had purchased it only six months ago and planned to do a lot of remodeling. The construction of a backyard fence was to be her first project. Her other ideas would have to wait until she saved enough money, but she was determined to do them even though she knew it would take her several years.

She talked about how much she liked it here. She told him stories about some of the kids she had cared for, some of the more interesting scuba dives she had done and about the hurricane scares she'd had. Only one hurricane had actually hit, but by the time it came ashore it had decreased to a tropical storm and done little damage.

He asked if she liked meeting new people all the time. She assured him that she did, telling him about the retired couples that were staying at one of the villas right now. She mentioned how energetic and loving they seemed.

They finally ordered their meal. The food was delicious, but they hardly noticed, as they were more entranced with each other.

Eventually they came to the subject of Megan. Kaleb told her Megan had been in the car when Lucy was killed and how he had neglected her for a year. He described what she had been like before the accident — a bright, outgoing child with a stubborn streak a mile wide.

Katie explained her "Divorced Parent" theory and how she wondered if it might apply to Megan. He sat back in his chair when she had finished.

"You know, that could be part of it. If you're right, I wonder how one goes about changing it."

His hand was lying on the table and she reached out and squeezed his fingers in a gesture of sympathy saying, "I don't know."

He pulled her hand into his and laid his other hand over the top. He was rubbing his fingers slowly back and forth, looking into her eyes.

He thought, *You really are something, lady.*

Katie felt the heat of his touch all the way up her arm. They were so lost in each other that the rest of the world seemed not to exist.

Suddenly, Katie felt someone hug her across the shoulder, saying, "Why look, everyone. It's our Katie from the rental agency. We're out partying since this is our last night in town." Glancing down at Kaleb's left hand resting on top of Katie's, she continued, "Oh, you must be Katie's husband. I couldn't help noticing your wedding ring. It is almost the same as my husband's. Lovely, just lovely."

Kaleb kept his left hand over Katie's hand as he stood and nodded to the group of six standing behind her. One of the other ladies in the group spoke up saying, "Why, Katie, I didn't know you were married. I didn't notice you wearing a wedding ring, and I always look at jewelry. It's one of my favorite things."

The rest of the group burst into laughter. She had a ring on every finger, bracelets on her wrists, a long beaded necklace hanging around her neck and big loops dangling from her earlobes.

Her husband spoke up, "Yes dear, we know."

Katie sat still trying to think of what to say, when Kaleb spoke.

"I'm afraid Katie has had to make do with the little ceramic bracelet I gave her on our wedding day," he said, lifting her left arm so all could see. "You see, she is highly allergic to all metals and simply can't wear a ring. I'm Kaleb, by the way, and you must be the fun group my wife told me so much about. We are so happy you've had a nice time in our little town."

All six of the people assured them that they'd had a great time and hoped to return someday. They all kissed Katie on the cheek, saying they were so happy they had run into her, since they were leaving early in the morning and wouldn't have had a chance to say goodbye. After they walked away, Katie let out a long sigh of relief.

Kaleb wiggled his eyebrows and said, "Well, wife, what do you want to do now?"

Katie giggled and said, "You're quick on your feet."

Then they both stared at each other and laughed some more.

When Kaleb said goodnight to Katie at her door he leaned forward, brushing his lips across her cheek, and whispered, "Thanks for a wonderful evening."

Then he turned and walked away.

Megan heard her dad come in. She listened closely and heard her name. He was probably asking if she was asleep and if she had been good while he was gone. She continued to listen but couldn't make out what was being said.

She sat up in bed, pulling her legs up and wrapping her arms around them. She tucked her chin on top of her knees. Then she heard her daddy laugh. She liked to hear him laugh, but he didn't do it very much anymore. Daddy and Mommy used to laugh a lot, but now Mommy was gone and she knew she wasn't coming back.

She remembered lots of nights, when she had first left, lying in bed and closing her eyes and just wishing real hard that Mommy would come into her room and kiss her goodnight. She would even wait for night to come, sitting outside for a long time, so she wouldn't miss the first star to come out. Mommy used to say to her, "Oh look, Megan, there's the first star."

She couldn't remember all the words anymore, but she had known that Mommy had said that if you made a wish on the first star you saw, it would come true. But she had wished for weeks and Mommy never came home.

Now that she was older she understood that when someone died they never came back. She tried to remember everything she could about Mommy, but unless she looked at a picture of her, she wasn't even sure what she looked like. She knew what she smelled like though and how soft she had been when she cuddled her on her lap. She remembered a few other things like the star wish, her mom singing something about her being "sweet as candy and cake" and then leaning over her bed and kissing her, and Mommy brushing her hair.

The only bad thing she remembered was her Mom saying, "Megan, you're five years old now, and too big to still be throwing things. You could break something or hurt somebody."

She knew Mom had been real mad at her then, and she didn't throw things anymore.

Daddy was gone most of the time after Mommy died, and it scared her. Every day she tried to be good so he would want her. Then, suddenly, he started being with her almost every day, especially at dinnertime. She tried so hard to stay good so he wouldn't go away again.

Sometimes it was so hard though. Sometimes she was so mad at her mom for leaving her and sometimes she was mad at her dad because she had to be so good.

She knew Daddy got mad sometimes. She had heard him say bad words and slam his telephone down. Other times she heard him stomp back and forth in his room. It was at those times that she wanted to go in and stomp around beside him. Maybe, some day, she wouldn't be so afraid and she'd do it.

She thought about Katie. She liked her. Katie liked to do fun things. Megan hadn't liked it when Daddy called her Miss McKay. She knew she wasn't anything like the lady who stayed with her at home when Daddy was gone. Daddy always called that lady Miss Lewis.

Miss Lewis was a lot older than Katie, for one thing, and she would always pat her on the head and say, "You poor little dear." Katie had never done that to her.

Miss Lewis always made her eat everything on her plate, too, even the peas that she hated. Grown-ups didn't always eat everything on their plates, so she didn't know why she had to. Just yesterday, when they had lunch together, Katie had told her that if there was anything she didn't like she didn't have to eat it. She had been tempted to leave something just to see if she really meant it, but everything had tasted so good that before she realized it, all the food was gone.

Katie hadn't been mad when she gave Mimoso some of her sandwich. She knew Katie had seen her do it. Maybe, if she was with Katie, she could be a little bit bad and she would still like her.

Yawning, Megan lay back in the bed. She sure hoped she didn't have any bad dreams tonight. Her dad used to ask her all the time what her dreams were about, but she hadn't told him because when she woke up she couldn't remember. Now she could remember a little of them, but when she woke up, he would just keep holding her. It felt so good that she didn't say anything and he didn't ask anymore.

Megan closed her eyes and fell asleep. No nightmares tonight.

Chapter 6

Katie's fencing material didn't arrive by Friday, so no fence-building this weekend. She bumped into April on her lunch break and they decided to invite Kaleb, Megan and Roger to Katie's house for a Saturday afternoon barbecue.

Everyone had a good time, exchanging stories and just getting to know each other better. Katie took them on a tour of her house and explained some of the remodeling ideas she had for the future. Megan spent most of her time playing with Mimoso. She fed him part of her lunch. No one got upset with her for it.

They all made plans to go to Playa del Carmen on Sunday.

Sunday, they trooped from one tourist shop to another, buying all kinds of trinkets. Kaleb bought Megan a sombrero to keep the sun off her face and Katie bought her another pair of sandals with little pink flowers on them. She bought Kaleb a T-shirt with "I Love Akumal" printed on the front. Kaleb made a big deal of buying Katie a cheap, gaudy, plastic bracelet. He told her to keep it in case her ceramic one from their wedding got broken. Later he gave her a finely designed silver bracelet.

Roger and April bought each other silver chains. April's had a little silver heart attached.

When their stomachs started to tell them it was time for food, they bought some butter tortillas, smoked fish and chips and Pepsi. They sat on the beach to eat.

All were tired and ready for bed by the time they got home.

Katie had a busy week at work, but managed to spend her evenings at the villa with Kaleb and Megan. When they had said goodnight on Sunday, Kaleb had asked Katie to come over after work, adding, "I'm a good chef, so you needn't worry that you'll starve."

"Sounds good to me, but I need to go home first and take Mimoso for a walk on the beach. Why don't I stop by your place and pick up Megan and she can go with me, if that would be all right with both of you?"

"Good idea. I know Megan would love it. She really does seem to like Mimoso."

And so a pattern developed. Katie would leave work, pick up Megan and go home. After changing into casual clothes they would take Mimoso for a walk and then return to the villa for dinner.

Megan and Katie enjoyed their time together. Katie told Megan stories about when she was growing up. She related tales about the pets she'd had. Her dog had been named Doctor Fever and would go crazy barking whenever the mailman came to deliver the mail. She told her about the little parakeet she'd had. It was messy and smelly, but if she took it out of its cage it would sit on her shoulder and not fly away. The hamster had been her brother's. He would get loose sometimes and it often took the whole family hours to find him.

She talked about playing dress-up and school with her sisters. Of course, being the youngest, she always had to be the student and never the teacher.

The story Megan seemed to like best was the one where Katie had played maid and servant to her older brother and his friends. She'd fix snacks and drinks and wait on them hand and foot just so she could go into their secret hideout in the field beside her home.

Katie tried to get Megan to talk about herself and gradually got her to say more than yes and no. On one occasion, Katie got her to talk about school.

She confided, "I like story time the best because all I have to do is listen, and practicing my letters is okay, too. I don't like it when the teacher asks me questions because I don't always know the answers."

They were walking on the beach and Katie was holding her hand. She gave it a little squeeze and replied, "I wouldn't worry about that. No one knows all the answers. If you and the other kids knew all the answers, you wouldn't need to go to school."

That seemed to make sense to Megan after she thought about it.

"What about recess? That was always my favorite time at school."
Megan shook her head back and forth.

"I hate recess. I just sit on a bench and watch the other kids play."

"Won't the other kids play with you?"

"I think they would, but I don't want to."

"Why not?"

Megan shuffled her feet in the sand and then mumbled, "I'm afraid I'll get in trouble." When Katie just looked at her, Megan continued, "Lots of times the kids push each other or fall and get hurt and stuff like that. Then the schoolyard teacher takes them in the office. If I ever got taken into the office, I know they would call Daddy. He might get mad at me and go away. I don't want that to happen."

Katie knelt down in the sand in front of Megan. Laying a hand against her cheek she said, "Megan, your daddy would never leave you even if he got mad at you. Your daddy loves you and wants to be with you no matter what you do."

"Are you sure?" Megan asked, her lips trembling.

"I'm very sure," Katie replied, giving her a big hug.

Katie and Megan had fun on the beach, too. They ran with Mimoso and played fetch with him. Sometimes they would splash in the water and have to change their clothes when they got back to the house.

Every day Megan seemed to become more animated. She complained one night about not wanting to go to bed yet. So Katie offered to tell her a story about a little girl who grew up to be the president of Mexico. Another night she announced at dinner that she didn't like her vegetables, so Katie offered her some salad instead.

Roger spent most evenings with April, leaving Katie and Kaleb alone to talk after Megan went to bed. They never seemed to run out of conversation.

One night Katie asked Kaleb what the "J" in K. J. Dalton stood for. Kaleb assured her repeatedly that it didn't stand for anything. Katie couldn't let it rest and started to try to guess what it stood for.

"How about James? John? Jack? Jefferson? Jake? Jerome? Jasper? Judas?"

With each name Kaleb shook his head.

He finally said, "All right, I'll tell you, but you must promise never to tell anyone, not even Roger, and you can't laugh." Katie readily agreed. "Okay, here goes. It's Julie."

"Julie!" Katie repeated and then burst out in gales of laughter.

"You little minx, you promised not to laugh," and in one svelte swoop he pulled her down on the couch and began to tickle her. "I'll give you something to laugh about," he said in a fake gruff voice.

Eventually the laughter faded as Kaleb lowered his head and kissed her. It felt so right. Pulling back, they just looked at each other, both a little stunned at what they had felt.

Katie cleared her throat and with a little smile in her voice asked, "Julie, like in J-u-l-I-e?"

"No, it is spelled J-e-w-l-I-e, as in my mother's maiden name."

She couldn't help teasing just a little bit more.

"I guess Katharine or Kristi may not have been completely off after all."

He just laughed and said, "You do like to play with fire don't you, my Katie girl?"

At another time, Katie brought up the subject of driving. She wanted to know if he was afraid to drive. He thought about it for a long time before he answered.

"No, I don't think so. If you had asked me six months ago or even last week, I would have said yes. Things seem different now. My mind is less muddled. To be completely honest, I've decided it was more the fear that by sitting behind the steering wheel of a car I would feel more anguish over losing Lucy. She loved to drive and she loved her cars. A better way to explain it would be if, say, she had loved to paint. It would have been hard to pick up her paintbrushes or look at one of her paintings. Now I understand that. I'm not really afraid of cars and driving. It's the fear of feeling more pain. Does that make sense to you?"

She nodded and then quietly asked, "Does it still hurt as bad?"

He again thought for a long time before answering.

"No, it is finally getting easier. I don't think about her every minute of every day like I used to. Not that I will ever forget her, nor do I want to, but now I can think of the good things we shared and I'm beginning to look to the future with hope for finding happiness again."

Roger and April joined them for dinner on Thursday, and after

Megan had gone to bed they decided to play cards. April insisted on poker. She said bridge or hearts was just too boring. The ladies wanted to play for pennies, but the men said that was like being back in high school. They wanted to play for real money. April and Katie quickly vetoed that. They finally agreed that whoever lost the most chips in a hand had to do whatever the winner demanded as long as it wasn't immoral or illegal.

They all got into the fun demanding drinks to be served, snacks to be prepared, shoulder rubs to be given. Roger tended to ask for a kiss every time April lost and he won. Katie made Kaleb rub her feet. He had done it grudgingly and promised retaliation.

When it appeared that he was going to be the winner and Katie the loser, he started to voice various options of what he might make her do.

In a haughty tone she said, "If you're not careful, I might make you tell all of us what the "J" in your name stands for."

Roger was studying his cards and without thought said, "The "J" doesn't stand for anything. His parents just named him Kaleb J. Dalton."

Katie looked over at Kaleb. He winked at her. He knew she wouldn't tell.

When he finally won, he asked Katie for a kiss. She leaned across the table and gave him a peck on the cheek.

Several hands later, when Kaleb again won and Katie lost, he demanded a kiss on the lips. Katie leaned in and gave him a quick kiss on the lips.

It took about seven more hands before Kaleb once again won and Katie lost. This time he was much more specific. Katie had to come over to his chair and kiss him on the lips for no less than thirty seconds.

As Katie placed her hands on Kaleb's shoulders, tilted her head and kissed him, Roger and April watched, but as the kiss continued they decided to take advantage of the situation and melded their lips together. Time seemed to slip away and when both couples came up for air they decided the card game was over.

On Friday, Kaleb and Megan went on a fishing expedition. Katie walked Mimoso by herself, knowing they would be late getting back. By seven, when Katie arrived at the villa, Megan was already asleep, worn out by the long day in the sun. Roger and April were out for the evening.

Kaleb suggested they sit on the patio since it was such a beautiful evening. He got them each a glass of wine and joined Katie on the wrought-iron swing that faced the lagoon. The sun was just working its way down the horizon, creating a breathtaking site. Holding his drink in his right hand, Kaleb reached over and picked up Katie's hand. They sat gazing out at the myriad tones of pink and blue in companionable silence.

Katie eventually looked down to where her and Kaleb's hands were joined, seeing the white strip of skin where his wedding ring had so recently been. Kaleb felt the movement and glanced over to see her eyes riveted on his hand.

"You've taken off your ring."

It was a statement, but he could hear the question in her voice. Reclining in the swing, Kaleb lifted her hand, absently kissing her knuckles. He seemed to be trying to organize his thoughts.

"You know I loved Lucy, still do and always will. But I've come to understand that she wouldn't want me to quit living because she isn't here. When I first got the word that she had been killed I was numb. Not really feeling anything. By the time the funeral was over and everyone else went back to their normal lives, I got so despondent that I went to the cemetery and just sat there telling her I wanted to come with her.

"Eventually, I began stopping every day and telling her what was going on in my life. It was my way of trying to fill the void in my soul. I began to push myself and everyone else at work, to try to cram something into that empty space inside of me.

"It was around this time that I started working on a project with Roger. He knew what had happened and at first treaded lightly around me just like all the other employees. Even my old friends seemed to have drifted away like they were afraid to talk to me. Roger, being who he is, took only so much of my abuse. He started calling me on the carpet for my attitude.

"One day, after I had yelled at an accountant because he miscalculated a minor figure on a contract bid, he got bold enough to say, 'Mr. Dalton, it's not his fault that your wife died any more than it is yours. I doubt Lucy would be very proud of you right now.'

"He made me so mad that I went slamming out of the office. I went straight to the cemetery and I started to yell at Lucy. I yelled, 'How could you have left me when I need you so much.'

"I remember repeating over and over, 'Why, Lucy? Why?' with tears streaming down my face.

"Until then, I hadn't realized how angry I was at her. Roger talked to me once about God and eventually I was able to let the anger go. I didn't have to go to the cemetery every day anymore.

"In time, Roger got me to stop thinking only of myself and to start thinking about Megan. For the past year she has become my main concern. I still talk to Lucy sometimes in my mind. That day on the beach, when I told you about Lucy," he glanced at Katie seeing tears on her face and absently wiped them away with his fingers but never stopped talking, "I was so mad at you for feeling pity for me. That night, I thought about the day. Megan had got up the nerve to ask me for a dog. A big step for her and so I was pleased. But she had a bad nightmare and that worried me.

"So I found myself talking to Lucy. I would swear she answered me. It was like it was her turn to be mad at me. She let me know that by clinging to the past I was somehow lessening our love. It's hard to explain, but I started to understand that I really pitied myself. I had, deep down inside, wanted you to feel sorry for me. I stood there telling you my wife was dead, holding out my hand so you could see my wedding ring. It was as though I was saying, 'See, Katie, how much I still hurt. Feel sorry for me. I deserve to be pitied.'

"I was just angry because I didn't want to acknowledge my own feelings. I also understand now what Lucy meant by dishonoring our love. The only way to honor love is by giving it. I had built a shell around my heart so nothing could get in to hurt me again, but when you do that nothing can get out either and eventually your heart will just shrivel and die.

"Taking off my ring doesn't mean that I no longer love Lucy, it just means that I'm opening my heart again."

He looked at Katie then, really seeing her, and this time when he brushed away her tears he knew what he was doing.

"Katie, I want you to know that you have helped me so much by just being here, by listening to me, by teasing me and laughing with me. And this time I don't mind the tears, as long as you are crying them with me and not just for me."

She reached up then, wiping away the moisture that had spilled from his eyes as he had talked.

"Oh, Kaleb," was all she said, opening her arms to him. He moved into them and soon they were clinging to each other. He was drained.

Katie was thinking, *What a wonderful, gentle man. I think I have already lost my heart to him. What would it be like to be loved by such a man?*

Chapter 7

The fencing material had been delivered to Katie's place earlier in the week. Raul and Katie made plans to install it on Saturday. Raul would begin early, doing some of the preparation while Katie was at work. There was plenty to do before he would need a second pair of hands.

Arriving at her house about one-thirty, she was shocked to see Kaleb and Roger carrying part of the fencing on their shoulders as they disappeared around the corner of her house. They had to be helping Raul put up the fence. She was grateful for their help, but she was a little concerned for Raul. She knew Kaleb's business was construction and she hoped he and Roger weren't running roughshod over Raul.

As she approached the backyard, she realized her fear was unnecessary. Having dropped the last piece of fencing to the ground Kaleb was saying to Raul, "Well, boss, what's next?"

Raul grinned at being called boss.

"We need to mix the cement next to set the permanent post."

Katie interrupted, calling out, "What is going on here? Where did you find these two workers, Raul? I sure hope they work cheap."

"They came begging for a job. What could I do? They agreed to work for food. My Maria will be here soon with lunch."

"Wow, you two must be really good workers. Maria doesn't cook for just anyone. You're in for a treat. Maria's food is magnificent."

Katie continued to walk through the yard coming close to where Kaleb stood. Her eyes were drawn to the bare expanse of his chest, revealed by his open shirt.

He really is a superbly built man, she thought.

Looking up, she saw Kaleb watching her. He gave her what only could be called a cheeky grin. She flushed scarlet and turned away.

You better watch your step, she admonished herself. *I think you're getting in way over your head.*

Mimoso's bark brought Katie's mind back to the present. April and Megan were trailing behind as Mimoso ran full throttle toward her. He jumped up to lick her face in greeting.

Kaleb was standing right behind her and she heard him mumble, "Lucky fellow." She ignored the comment, walking off to greet April and Megan.

Lunch arrived and was as delicious as Katie had predicted. When all the food was devoured, Megan and Mimoso played and chased each other around the house. The adults all pitched in to get the fence up.

The gate was the last part to be installed. Kaleb held the gate while Katie slipped the hinge pins into place. It was then that she noticed the engraved name of the manufacturer on the gate frame. It said, "Manufactured by Dalton Industries, Pittsburgh, PA."

Looking up at Kaleb she queried, "What kind of things does your company manufacture?"

Kaleb was surprised by the question. Katie hadn't asked him a lot about his company, and what little he had said was pretty general. He wondered why she was asking now, seemingly out of the blue.

Shrugging his shoulders, he replied, "Some cement, iron and tile products, why?"

From what Kaleb had said before about his company, she had assumed that it was a small family-owned-and-run business that probably included the manufacturing of their own decorative tiles for bathrooms and kitchens and maybe cabinets and light fixtures. She supposed decorative fencing could be in that category, and she had ordered the fencing from an American company. She had known that he had to be financially well-off, if he could take a month's vacation and bring his personal assistant with him. Still, she imagined that he owned a small construction company that built houses in Boston and some of the surrounding communities, using their own products to make the homes special and unique. With a vague sense of unease she wondered just how big his company was.

Glancing back down at the gate she replied, "Because Dalton Industries is stamped on my gate."

He followed her gaze, noting the little circle with a "D" in the middle along with the engraving. He didn't need to read the words to know what it said.

"Well, my Katie girl, you have shown great taste and business sense in buying one of my products. Plus, if you have any problems with the fence, you can always complain to the president of the company."

She laughed and replied, "If I have any problems I'll be beating down your door."

Her mind was focused more on his calling her his Katie girl. This was the second time he had called her that and both times her heart had done a little flip. She thought it might be nice to be his.

With the fence completed, Raul and Maria left for home. Roger and April went to their respective houses to clean up and planned on meeting later. Kaleb and Megan stayed at Katie's for dinner. After eating, Kaleb and Megan headed back to the villa to bathe. Katie agreed to come by after she washed the dishes and showered.

Two hours later, when Katie arrived at the villa, she found Kaleb pacing and repeatedly pushing his hands through his hair.

"What on earth is the matter?"

"There's a problem at one of my construction sites. Roger is trying to find a place in Cancun where we can set up a video conference call."

That was the first Katie realized that Roger was there. He sat at the table, talking on his cell phone and typing on his computer. He snapped off the phone, saying, "We can do it from the Hilton in Cancun. The report coming over the computer does not sound good. I already sent Mr. Carson a memo to stop all work on the project in Riga until you can talk with him."

"What happened?" Katie asked.

"It appears that the scaffolding the men were using to place the steel beams on the upper levels of the office building we were constructing collapsed. The report said that several men were injured and at least three died. It was a hard-won project to begin with, and now this."

Looking toward Roger, Kaleb continued, "We need to make sure the commerce secretary for the Latvian government is part of the conference call. Tell Carson to contact him. We should be able to have everything set up in two hours. See if that will work for them."

Then turning to Katie he asked, "Katie, could you possibly stay here with Megan? I'll probably be gone all night and part of tomorrow."

"Of course; I'll take good care of her. Don't worry about a thing. You go. My car is in the driveway and here are the keys. You'll need it to get to Cancun."

Roger had already closed his computer and was heading for the door. He called back to Katie, "When April gets here, could you tell her what happened and that I'll see her when I get back?"

"Sure," Katie replied.

Kaleb took the keys, grabbed a briefcase and jacket, gave Katie a quick hug and left.

Katie stood, somewhat dazed, in the middle of the living room, trying to digest everything she had just heard. Scaffolding collapsing, men dead and injured in a country halfway around the world, setting up video conferencing in a matter of two hours and expecting a member of a foreign country to participate at his request. It slowly sank in that Kaleb's construction company didn't build tract houses for new developments in and around Boston.

Oh my, Katie thought, *I think you're way out of my league, Kaleb.*

She tried to reconcile this powerful businessman with the man she had come to know. He was the man who had tickled her for making fun of his name, acted the role of husband to help her out at the restaurant, played a silly game of poker. He had worked on her fence like a common laborer, worried and fretted over his daughter and, most of all, cried with her over Lucy.

She tried to merge the images of the kind, caring and loving man with the commanding, forceful figure. She now knew that all these characteristics were part of Kaleb. The attributes that she had discovered this night made her uneasy and wary. She simply didn't know how she felt. She knew she was falling in love with the man she had spent the last two weeks with, but tonight Kaleb seemed a different person. It felt like she was caught in a tidal wave and was being sucked into the raging water with no help in sight.

At that moment, the doorbell rang. April whisked through the door in her usual brisk manner. She was surprised by the news of the accident, but was much less troubled than Katie by the obvious size and scope of Dalton Industries. She said that she and Roger had talked a great deal about his work and she knew the company was involved in several international construction projects.

Katie invited April to stay for a while and keep her company. She got them each a glass of tea and they settled in the cozy living room for some girl talk.

Katie was used to April falling fast for someone and then within a couple of weeks finding something terribly wrong with them. It would be things like they were selfish or they didn't like to do fun things. But often it was even more outrageous things like their laugh was grating on her nerves or they picked their teeth or they wore the wrong kind of clothes. So, she was relieved to find out April was still enamored with Roger, since she could tell that Roger really liked April.

April was quick to expound on Roger's wonderful qualities with very little urging from Katie. She said that besides being handsome and a great kisser, he was smart, kind to everyone he met, easy to talk to, liked to do fun things and, most of all, he truly liked her.

"What do you mean? Didn't all those other guys you've dated like you?"

"No, not really. Oh, they said they did. Some of them even said they loved me, but they didn't. They always wanted to change me. Roger has never said that he likes me, but he doesn't have to. I just know he does. I showed him my work at my aunt's hotel and he said it was awesome. He tells me how gorgeous I am and seems to love my taste in clothes. He laughs at my jokes and is always ready to go along with me when I come up with something new to do on the spur of the moment. When we're out in a crowd, he never appears bothered by my flirting a little with other men. In fact, he will often wink at me as though he understands that it is just second nature to me and that I'm not really trying to come on to anyone. I'm just having fun. I can't say that we are in love with each other right now, but I think our relationship is going to grow."

Then she laughed and continued, "I know that this sounds strange for me, but I believe Roger and I need to take things slow and easy."

Katie blinked owlishly at April. "Is this my quick, rush-into-everything friend? You do seem happy and content though, so more power to both of you."

"What's going on between you and Kaleb? Roger told me about his wife dying. When I first saw the two of you together I figured, 'Perfect, someone else for Katie to help.' But being with the two of you Thursday night and again today, I'm not sure you're here just to help him."

"Oh, April, I'm so confused. I just don't know. I think I might be falling in love with him. Don't you dare laugh! I'm serious and I'm scared to death."

April smothered the giggle that almost escaped when she noted Katie's serious face.

"Katie, falling in love isn't a bad thing. Sometimes confusing, but so exciting. You need to relax and enjoy."

In a fatalistic tone Katie replied, "I guess time will tell for both of us."

April just smiled. They talked a while longer about some of their friends and work. Eventually April said it was time to go, gave Katie a hug goodbye and left for home.

Katie decided she was tired. She grabbed a pillow off of Kaleb's bed and found a blanket in one of the linen closets. She lay down on the couch, pulled the blanket over her and cuddled her head in the pillow. She noticed that the pillow smelled like Kaleb as she closed her eyes and drifted off to sleep.

Kaleb lowered himself into the chair behind the desk in the small conference room the Hilton had provided. Roger sat in a chair to his right working at a computer and phone terminal getting everything set for the conference call. In front of the desk on a table by the wall sat three screens. The speakerphone and cameras showed blinking red lights. A few more minutes and he should be connected to all three screens.

He briefly thought of Megan and Katie. He hoped Megan didn't have one of her nightmares tonight. He had never told Katie about their frequency or how bad they were. He knew he had mentioned that she'd had one but he hadn't gone into any detail.

He smiled briefly to himself when he remembered how easy it had been for him to drive tonight. Of course, he hadn't had time to think about it. He'd just done it. These were only fleeting thoughts, as his mind turned quickly back to the problem in Riga.

The red lights turned to green and the screens came to life. On one screen was the face of Mr. Carson, his site manager in Latvia. The second screen revealed the secretary of commerce in his office in Riga, and the third showed his conference table in Boston. There were four men and two women sitting at the table with files scattered about them.

Kaleb began, "Good evening or good morning to all. I know I'm the only one who can see all of you, but you should be able to hear each other. If any of you have any problem with the reception, let us know. Okay, let's get down to business. Mr. Carson, please update us on the casualties and the condition of our employees."

"Three men were killed instantly and four others are in the hospital. One of those is in serious but stable condition with some internal injuries. He should be going into surgery any minute. The other three have broken bones and may need surgery. Their injuries are such that they should recover completely in time. As per your memo, I have sent a representative to each of the seven men's homes to offer our assistance. Sir, I have also halted all work at the site as you requested."

"Thank you, Mr. Carson. When we complete our call with the others, please remain connected, as I wish to speak with you privately concerning the families of the men who were killed and about the hospitalized men. As to our other employees there, please inform them that the entire project will remain halted until we are able to determine the cause of the accident and we are convinced that all aspects of the construction site are safe. Also tell them that their salaries will continue as normal throughout this time. I would like all foremen available when my team arrives."

Next Kaleb turned his attention to the secretary of commerce.

"Mr. Secretary, thank you for agreeing to talk with me. First, I wish to extend our condolences to you for the loss of your fellow countrymen."

The secretary nodded his head saying, "Thank you."

Kaleb continued, "I am also requesting permission to allow my team of experts to come to Riga to investigate the accident. You, of course, will want to assign your own people to work with mine and oversee their work."

The secretary hesitated only briefly but then agreed, "Yes. That will be acceptable. You will provide me with a list of the people you are sending."

Kaleb agreed and then asked that the accident site not be disturbed and nothing removed until his team arrived. It was agreed upon. He thanked Mr. Zbanov for his time and said he would be in touch. With a farewell, that connection was broken. Kaleb then turned his attention to the men and women in his conference room in Boston.

"Ladies and gentlemen, have you gathered all the files on this project?"

Mrs. Lange, a structural engineer and the coordinator of this particular construction project, became the group spokesperson.

"Yes, sir, we have. As you know, in order to get permission to contract this project we had to agree to purchase at least twenty percent of the building material from within the country of Latvia as per their government's regulations. We have just begun to sort through our records to see from whom the scaffolding was purchased. Our investigative team should be able to test the quality of the scaffolding material, and if the site is untouched, check for any human errors in both the design and the construction of it when it was built.

"Also, sir, this country has had some unrest between the native Latvians and the Russian population, so we will want to make sure there was no sabotage involved. Our investigative team should leave by this time tomorrow. We will know by then who manufactured the scaffolding material."

"Efficient as always, Mrs. Lange. Keep me apprised of all information via Roger. Thank you all for your hard work."

Kaleb then severed that connection.

Turning back to Mr. Carson, Kaleb asked about the families of the three men who had been killed. One was only twenty years old and still lived at home with his parents. The other two had been married. One was thirty-three and left a wife and two children, ages four and nine. The other was fifty-four. He and his wife had never had any children. Kaleb felt a hard knot in his stomach as he listened to these brief details about the men who had died.

Kaleb made it a policy to always insure the lives of all his employees, no matter what country they were in. He told Roger to get whatever information he needed from Mr. Carson and to contact the insurance company.

"Have them send the money to Carson so we are sure the families actually receive it. As to the men in the hospital, be sure we pay all the hospital bills and that they get the best care possible. Continue their salaries until they are able to return to work and give them an additional amount to take care of any other financial hardships their hospitalization may cause their families. I think that should cover it for tonight. Roger and I will stay here until noon tomorrow, which would be about midnight your time in Latvia, if you need anything else. And Mr. Carson, I'm sure you knew these men, so I extend my sympathy to you, too."

"Thank you, Mr. Dalton. Goodnight."

The screen went blank.

"Good work, Roger," Kaleb said, coming out of his business mode. "I'm really beat. I don't suppose you had time to book us rooms here, did you?"

"Now what kind of a personal assistant would I be if I didn't make sure my boss had a bed to sleep in when we're in a hotel? Besides, I want a bed myself. I'm just going to look up the information I need for the insurance company and then I'll turn in. I'll ring your room if anything comes in on the computer or anyone calls before morning."

"Okay. I'll meet you in the lobby about eight for breakfast. See you in the morning."

Chapter 8

The moon shone brightly and the stars were visible on this clear and warm night. All was silent in the villa by the sea. Two people rested in quiet slumber within its walls as the clock on the wall ticked away the hours.

A scream rent the silence, startling Katie awake. It took her a moment to realize it was Megan screaming. She threw off the blanket and ran to Megan's room. She switched on the lamp to see her tossing on the bed. Her eyes were closed but her little arms and legs were thrashing about.

Katie tried to wake her.

"Megan! Megan! Wake up."

Megan continued to scream and twist around, unaware of Katie. Afraid she would hurt herself, Katie crawled onto the bed and, sitting with her back against the headboard, she pulled Megan onto her lap. She put her arms around Megan's, holding them tight. She began to talk softly.

"Hush Megan, it's okay. You're all right. Shush now. I'm right here with you."

Eventually Megan quieted. She turned her head into Katie's chest. Katie released her tight hold and gently rubbed Megan's arms.

Suddenly Megan began to tremble and Katie heard her sobbing, "Mommy, Mommy, I'm sorry. I'm so sorry. I won't be bad anymore."

Megan's tears soaked the front of Katie's shirt. She tried to soothe her.

"Hush now, Megan, it's okay."

At her words Megan jerked her head up and looked at Katie's face.

"You're not my mommy. You're Katie."

Katie didn't know what to say. Megan began to rub away her tears.

"I thought you were my mommy. You smell like her. You don't usually smell like her."

Katie remembered the new perfume she had sprayed on after her shower that evening.

"Oh, Megan, I'm sorry. Someone gave me some new perfume today and I put it on tonight before I came over. I didn't know your mommy wore that kind."

"It's all right. I like the way you smell. Where's Daddy?"

"He and Roger had to go to Cancun to take care of some business. They'll be back some time tomorrow. Is it all right if I stay with you?"

Megan nodded. Then she settled back against Katie.

Katie held her awhile and then asked, "Megan, are you asleep?"

Megan shook her head.

"Do you want to tell me about your dream?"

Megan didn't answer.

Katie continued, "You know, sometimes if you have bad dreams and you tell someone else what they were they don't seem so bad and they never come back."

Megan finally spoke, "I have bad dreams all the time and when I wake up I don't remember them, but tonight I remember."

"Will you tell me?"

Megan barely whispered loud enough for Katie to hear.

"I was sitting in the back seat of Mommy's car. I told her over and over that I wanted to go to McDonald's to get French fries but she said, 'No, not today.' I was mad, so I started to kick the seat. She told me to stop, so I did. But I was still mad, so I threw my new dolly I had just got for my birthday over the seat. Mommy got real mad then and said, 'I told you that you must quit throwing things now that you're a big girl. Someone is going to get hurt if you don't.' Just a few minutes later we hit another car and Mommy got hurt real bad and she died. I made Mommy get hurt and go away."

By this time Megan was crying again.

"I didn't mean to be bad and make Mommy die."

Katie just kept holding Megan, smoothing her hair and kissing her forehead.

"Megan, you didn't make your mommy die. It was a car accident. It didn't have anything to do with you being bad."

Megan sat with her head down. Katie turned her towards her and lifted her chin so she could see her face.

Trying again she said; "Mommies and daddies try to teach their little boys and girls how to act. You wouldn't like it if every time your daddy got mad he picked up a shoe or a plate or a lamp and threw it, would you? Your mommy was just trying to teach you so when you get all grown up you won't still be throwing your things. You can still get mad, and all kids do things that their parents don't like, but they don't go away or die because their children aren't good all the time."

Megan continued to look unsure.

"Megan, does your dad ever get mad?"

Megan nodded.

"What does he do when he gets mad?"

"Sometimes he says bad words in a real loud voice."

Katie couldn't help smiling at that.

"Well, maybe you better not do that. What else does he do?"

Megan was getting into it now.

"He slams the telephone down if he gets mad when he's talking on it, and sometimes I hear him stomp around in his room."

Katie thought for a minute.

"I think the next time you get real mad you should stomp around your room just like your daddy."

A small smile crossed Megan's face.

"I wanted to stomp the other night 'cause I was so tired of trying to be good all the time, but I was scared."

"Megan, nobody, not even grownups, are good all the time. We all try, but we just aren't. I think you should try stomping the next time you feel like it. Do you think you can go back to sleep if I turn the light off? I'll sleep here with you if you want me to. And Megan, I want you to tell your daddy about your dream tomorrow when he comes home. Okay?"

"All right."

They turned out the light, cuddled up together and fell asleep.

Kaleb got out of the car. Stretching, he looked at the villa in front of him.

This place is almost starting to feel like home, he thought.

It was one in the afternoon. His stomach rumbled, reminding him that it was time for lunch.

I wonder what Katie and Megan are doing. Don't just stand here wondering. Get in there and find out, he thought.

His face had a shadow of a beard and his clothes were wrinkled, as he hadn't thought to pack anything when he left last night. He had showered and found a toothbrush furnished by the hotel. Having bought a plastic comb in the gift shop, his hair was at least neat. Smudges could be seen under his eyes, as he had gotten little sleep last night.

Pounding on the door had awakened him about five in the morning. Roger was there. He had received word from Mrs. Lange that the material used in the scaffolding had been their own, but the bolts holding it together had been purchased from a little company in Latvia. Once he was up, he stayed up. He decided since work had intruded on his vacation he would use the rest of the morning to get updated on some of the other projects he was involved in.

Stepping into the villa he heard laughter coming from the patio. He saw April and Megan dodging around Katie. Katie was blindfolded and was taking cautious steps toward the corner of the patio, where a planter sat. She was laughing and saying, "I'm going to catch one of you soon, and when I do you have to give me a big hug and kiss."

April and Megan saw Kaleb at the same time. He motioned both of them to silence. Then he stepped about a foot in front of Katie and waited. Katie moved forward with her arms extended. She felt something in front of her and grasped quickly to the cloth her hand encountered.

"I got you now."

She pulled off her blindfold to see Kaleb standing with his shirt clutched in her hand.

A tingling sensation spread through Katie at the mere sight of him. He appeared to be tired and a little unkempt, but so strong and handsome.

Megan started cheering, "You have to hug and kiss her, Daddy. That's part of the game."

"You're sure I have to, Megan?" he said in a mournful tone, but with a twinkle in his eye.

"Yes, Daddy, yes," Megan insisted.

"Well then, if I must," Kaleb said with a laugh, pulling Katie into his arms and lowering his head. The world seemed to spin a bit off-kilter for both of them, but Megan's giggles and clapping had them stepping apart quickly. Kaleb knelt down and opened his arms to Megan.

"How about a hug and a kiss for your poor old dad?"

Megan went into his arms.

"Daddy, I'm so glad you're home. We were playing blind man's bluff. I never played it before, but it's fun."

Still holding tight to Megan he said, "I played it when I was little, but we never had to hug and kiss anyone when we got caught. We were just blindfolded next. I think I like this way better."

Katie flushed a little, but smiled and said, "Why don't I fix lunch for everyone? You haven't eaten yet, have you, Kaleb?"

"No, and I'm starved."

During lunch, Roger and Kaleb relayed all they knew about the accident in Latvia and what they were doing in response to it. Roger told Kaleb that the insurance company had informed him that the best way to get the money to the victims' families was to set up trust accounts for them in a bank in Riga. They wouldn't send any money though, until the investigation was completed.

"You better contact Mr. Carson and tell him to get the families some money now. Have him tell them that it's from wages still owed."

"Okay, I'll take care of it. I almost forgot, while I was upstairs changing I got a call from Mr. Carson. He said the man who had surgery is doing well and should be back to normal in a few weeks."

Katie was pleased to hear these exchanges. It made her realize that Kaleb respected and cared about his employees.

Another point in his favor, she thought.

After lunch and when the kitchen was put back in order, Roger and April decided to go for a walk on the beach. They invited Megan to go with them, and she agreed. Kaleb started to ask Katie if she wanted to go too but Katie stopped him with a look and a quick shake of her head. He could easily read her unspoken request. She wanted to talk to him alone. He felt a tightening in his chest. Megan must have had one of her nightmares.

Pouring them each a glass of wine, Kaleb took a sip.

Peering over the rim of his glass he said, "All right, tell me what happened."

Katie was struck again by how easily he seemed to read her mind.

She took a deep breath and said, "Megan had a bad dream last night, and from what she told me she has had a lot of them."

Kaleb only nodded, so Katie continued, "I was sitting on the bed holding her and she finally calmed, but then she said, 'Mommy, Mommy, I'm so sorry,' and began to sob."

Kaleb was surprised by this addition to the usual nightmares.

"She's never said anything like that before."

"Probably not; you see, she thought I was Lucy. When she realized it was me, she explained that I smelled like her mommy. One of my clients had left me a bottle of Tresor perfume as a thank you gift and I put some on before I came over yesterday. I guess Lucy must have worn that scent."

Kaleb confirmed that she had. By this time they had both sat down on the couch and Katie picked up Kaleb's hand.

"She told me about her dream, too."

"She did?" Kaleb said in a shocked voice. "My God, I've asked her a hundred times, but she will never tell me."

"That's because until last night she couldn't remember what she had dreamt once she woke up. Maybe the perfume jogged her memory."

"I hadn't even thought of that. Poor thing was so afraid but didn't even know why. What was her dream?"

Had she somehow seen her mother's bloody and crushed face? Dear God, not that.

"Does it have to do with the accident?"

"It does have to do with the accident, but not what you probably think. She didn't see Lucy, if that is what you're afraid of. Right before the accident happened, Megan was acting up and throwing a bit of a temper tantrum. Her mom scolded her and told her she had to stop throwing things or someone would get hurt. She thinks that because she was bad she caused the accident. She thinks her behavior made her mommy get hurt and go away.

"I asked her last night if she would tell you what she had dreamt, and she said she would. She has been afraid to get mad or do anything wrong since the accident. I'm sure she doesn't understand all the psychological reasons why she feels that way, but she's afraid that if she does anything to make you mad you will leave her, too."

Kaleb was stunned by Katie's words.

"What should I do?"

He didn't really expect an answer since his mind was consumed with thoughts of Megan; Megan never complaining, never saying, "No, I don't want to," never demanding anything, always obeying, doing her homework, eating all her food, going to bed as soon as she was told to, trying to be perfect. He was a little startled when he heard Katie answer him.

"I don't know. I told her it was all right to get mad sometimes and that she didn't have to be good all the time. We talked about what you do when you get mad and she told me you say bad words occasionally."

Katie smiled a little but continued, "I told her maybe she shouldn't do that, but she also said you stomp around in your room when you're upset and that sometimes she feels like stomping, too. I encouraged her to do that next time she feels like it. I think she's afraid, but I think she's also mad that her mommy left her."

Kaleb thought back over his own feelings and could easily understand Megan's anger. He pulled Katie's head over onto his shoulder and, rubbing his hand up and down her back, said, "I'll talk to her when she gets back." Then he added, "You didn't know what a mess you were getting involved in that night you picked us up at the airport, did you? But I'm so glad you're here."

Katie whispered, "So am I. So am I."

Katie sat on the couch trying to concentrate on the book she was reading. She had planned to go home and leave Kaleb and Megan alone, but Kaleb had asked her to stay, saying it would give him courage just to know she was in the house while he talked with Megan. They had been in Megan's room for what seemed like hours, but glancing at the clock she knew it had only been about forty-five minutes.

At times she could hear voices and once she thought she heard Megan crying, but now all was quiet.

Please, God, give Kaleb the words he needs to help Megan, she prayed for the hundredth time.

It was then that she heard a peculiar noise. Rising she went nearer the door. It was like someone was pounding quietly on the floor.

Then she heard Megan laugh and say, "Daddy, will you stomp with me?"

A warm, almost giddy feeling filled Katie.

She thought, *I hope you pound hard enough to break the tile. You just let that anger and frustration push right out of your feet.*

Chapter 9

Monday morning dawned with a spectacular sunrise. Roger lay in his bed gazing out the window. He had been awake now for some time watching the sun gradually peek over the horizon, showering the earth with rays of light. He was thinking of April as he watched the sun make its way into the sky.

She was everything wonderful. If you had asked him a few weeks ago to describe the perfect woman for him, he wouldn't have described April. Katie would have been more likely to fit the image. But now, all he could think of was April's laugh, her bright and somewhat slinky clothing, and her energy that seemed to shimmer around her like a constant magnetic field. She kept him off step just a little and he liked that, too.

He knew other men might have been bothered by her flirting, but it was just part of the whole package. There was something in her eyes that assured him that she was just having fun with the others but he was special to her.

If he were to have his way he would pick her up, take her to the nearest minister and put a ring on her finger this very day, but that was one thing he somehow knew he couldn't do.

She was spontaneous and rushed headlong into everything, but deep down inside he realized that if he wanted ever after with her, he needed to take their courtship slow. Maybe it was because everything else in her life was so flamboyant and hurried that he understood that their relationship needed to be gradual and steady to last. Well, slow and steady he could be.

He heard Kaleb moving about in the kitchen and thought, *Enough daydreaming. It's time to rise and shine.*

Once again he looked out the window to admire the beauty as he dressed for the day.

The following week flew by in a flurry of activity. On Monday, as Katie locked up her office for the day, Kaleb and Megan were there to whisk her off to Lol-Ha for an early dinner of pizza and pasta. They ate at a leisurely pace. Katie told them stories about how awful Mimoso had been as a puppy, chewing everything in sight and causing havoc in the little one-bedroom apartment she'd had at the time.

Megan wanted to hear more stories about when Katie was growing up and about her brother and sisters. Kaleb related stories about his own youth. Their tales enthralled Megan.

Several of the locals stopped by their table and Katie made the introductions. They had just decided to leave when Raul and Maria came in. They wound up sitting and visiting with them for another hour.

Kaleb and Megan appeared at Katie's office at lunchtime on Tuesday. They had a picnic basket and blanket in hand. The hour lunch on the beach seemed much too short to all of them.

Kaleb announced that he was taking Megan to the Xcarat Park to go swimming with the dolphins that afternoon.

That evening Kaleb again cooked dinner. After they had eaten they played some games with Megan until her bedtime.

Katie and Kaleb sat out on the verandah. Kaleb told her more about his business and Katie told him about the people of Akumal. They shared their similar views on American businesses coming into poorer foreign countries and the need to pay the native people a decent wage while trying to improve the living conditions and education of all who lived in the area. Katie brought up an article she had recently read. It talked of the need to develop the area along the coast of the Yucatan Peninsula more slowly and to reach an environmental, social and economic equilibrium. Kaleb was impressed by her interest and knowledge of environmental protection and her concern for the native people of the area.

On Wednesday, Kaleb and Megan went on a day trip to visit the Mayan ruins, so Katie grabbed a sandwich and spent her lunch hour working. That evening when she arrived at the villa, Roger and April were there. Megan and Kaleb arrived a half hour later.

Roger had gotten a report from the investigative team in Latvia. They had found that the bolts holding the scaffolding together were inferior and had snapped under the weight of the men standing on them. They had purchased the bolts from a small manufacturing company in Riga. Being concerned that some of the other material they were using might be of poor quality, Kaleb told Roger to have his team check all the material they had purchased from outside sources before resuming work on the complex.

Thursday afternoon, Kaleb came by the office about four.

"I have to go to Cancun again. Would you mind keeping Megan for me? I should be back in a few hours."

"What happened? Not another accident, I hope; and yes, I'd love to keep Megan."

Kaleb shook his head, "No. No more accidents if I can help it. Secretary Zbanov is giving my people a hard time about doing testing on the other material. I need to talk to him face to face, so to speak, and convince him that we are not trying to cause problems. We just want to make sure our employees are safe and that the office complex will be sturdy when it's completed. Their present government is relatively new and as of yet has a very lax building code. I plan to offer him my assistance in gathering information to get a stronger code through his government. I have to be careful though, so I don't step on anyone's toes. I sometimes find myself in the role of diplomat and I'm not always successful."

"I'm sure you can be very diplomatic, and even if they don't act on your ideas right away, I bet that they take what knowledge you share and use it eventually."

"You seem to have a lot of faith in me. I appreciate it. A man needs someone to boost his ego every once in a while," Kaleb grinned.

"You go now, and don't worry about Megan. We'll have a grand time together. Megan, do you want to sit here at my desk with me while I finish up my e-mails?"

Megan followed Katie to her desk and soon the two of them were engrossed in conversation as Katie explained what she was working on. The picture they made, Katie with her head leaning down towards Megan, her blond hair brushing against Megan's own dark curls, while Megan looked up at Katie, interested and eager, made Kaleb smile.

They belong together and I love them both so much, he thought.

That brought Kaleb up short. He loved Megan of course, but Katie?

Then he just shook his head as he walked away and said to himself, "Don't act so surprised, old man. Your mind is just accepting what your heart has known for some time now."

He knew Katie loved him, too. He just wondered if she had realized it yet.

It was late when Kaleb got back. He told Katie that he was pleased with the conference call. Secretary Zbanov had agreed to let his team complete the work that he wanted done. He was a little hesitant about working with Kaleb on a building code but said he would contact him some time after he'd had a chance to think over his offer.

Katie only stayed a few minutes and then left for home. Morning always seemed to come too soon.

On Friday, Katie made arrangements to have all of Saturday off. April had dropped by and suggested that the four of them go cave diving. When Kaleb and Megan stopped by for lunch, they discussed it and Megan agreed to stay at the kid's club while they went diving. She almost seemed pleased with the idea of playing with other kids, a big step for her.

That evening they all met for dinner at the La Buena Vida. April informed them that she had an offer to do a remodel job in Amherst, Massachusetts. The job would probably take four months to complete. The offer had been made two months ago, but April had been dragging her heels. Now, with Amherst so close to Boston, she was ready to go. Roger told everyone that they had discussed it and he was so pleased she was coming. They would be able to see each other on most weekends. Kaleb and Katie were happy for them, but couldn't help thinking of their own situation. The four weeks of Kaleb's vacation were ticking away.

Having taken Megan to the Lo Ha Kid's Club and stayed for a short time to be sure she felt comfortable, Kaleb and Katie made their way to the dive shop. Roger and April were already there. They had the equipment and gear waiting. They all donned their wet suits and then followed the instructor to the waiting minivan that would take them to the cenote.

Both Roger and Kaleb were certified in scuba diving, but neither had ever done any cave diving. April and Katie assured them that they would like it. As they made their way to the diving site, the instructor went over some of the differences in cave diving as compared to regular scuba diving.

Upon arriving at the cenote, they checked their gear one last time before plunging in. The guide led the way with all staying close behind. The stalactite and stalagmite formations were breathtaking. There was no plant or sea life, just cylindrical forms hanging from the roof and columns rising from the floor of the caves. Roger had brought an underwater camera and snapped dozens of pictures.

After they were back on dry land, Kaleb confessed that he had found it a little scary and confining. Roger had loved it.

It was late afternoon when they got back to Akumal. After collecting Megan from the kid's club, they all headed for the villa intent on having a nice relaxing evening. Roger's phone went off just as they arrived at the house.

Roger went up to his room still talking on the telephone. He stayed there for at least thirty minutes and when he returned to the living room his face was marred by a frown.

"What is it?" Kaleb inquired.

"It's the new software. They're having trouble with the application and I think I know what the problem is. I tried to talk them through it but with no luck. I'm going to have to go back to Boston myself and see if I can fix it. I already called the airlines and I can get a flight out about nine tonight."

He glanced towards April.

Kaleb was pushing his fingers through his hair like he always did when he was thinking and didn't like what was happening.

"I hate for you to cut your vacation short, but if you think you can fix it, I don't know what else we can do. That software program is scheduled to be ready for full production in a week."

April walked up to Roger and giving him a shaky smile said, "I'm going to miss you, but we'll see each other in three weeks. You better be at the airport waiting with flowers and candy when I arrive."

Roger appeared a bit puzzled.

"Flowers and candy?" he asked.

"You big oaf, I land on Valentine's Day," she said smartly.

He hugged her then.

"I'll be there with bells and balloons, too."

"I'll leave the phone and laptop with you in case anything comes up," he said to Kaleb as he and April ascended the stairs to his room.

Once Roger had left for the airport, April said, "Okay, you two," pointing at Katie and Kaleb, "go get your dancing shoes on. Megan and I want to pop some popcorn, watch a movie and have some girl talk. We don't need the two of you mooning over each other while we do it."

"What's girl talk?" Megan asked.

"It's when just girls and no guys sit around and talk about things, like what our favorite kind of clothes are, what color of fingernail polish we want to try, how to style our hair and, most of all, who are the cutest boys we know."

Megan made a face. "I don't like boys."

April laughed. "Someday you will, Megan. Someday real soon you will."

Then Megan thought for a minute and asked, "Why can't Katie stay and do girl talk with us? She's a girl."

April whispered, "But then who would your daddy have to dance with? He can't dance by himself."

"Oh," Megan said and then grabbed April's hand and pulled her toward the kitchen, telling her that she liked butter on her popcorn but no salt.

Kaleb looked at Katie.

"Well, I'm game if you are. It will only take me a minute to change. Then we can run by your house on our way. All right?"

"Sounds good to me," Katie replied.

Katie wore a long black dress with a slit up the side. It had a v-neckline with off-the-shoulder sleeves. Little pearl drop earrings dangled from her ears and she chose a pair of open-toed heels for her feet. Kaleb had dressed up in a shirt and tie.

They went to a nightclub in Playa del Carmen. The dance floor extended outside so you could dance under the stars. It was close enough to the ocean that you could see the lights from the town sparkling on the water, definitely a romantic atmosphere.

Katie loved to dance and Kaleb was an excellent partner. They danced to almost every dance. Fast...slow...it didn't matter.

As the evening was wearing down, Kaleb slowly danced Katie out onto the open floor underneath the spectacular moonlit sky. There was a slight chill in the air, so there were few other couples outside. Wrapping his arms around her to keep her warm, he pulled her close. As they swayed with the music they stared into each other's eyes, not even noticing when the music stopped. Kaleb gradually lowered his head and took Katie's mouth in a gentle kiss. Katie closed her eyes, savoring the feel of his mouth on hers. The kiss deepened and passion flared. They used their teeth and tongues. A low moan emanated from them. Whether from him or from her they didn't know, nor did they care.

When their lips finally parted, Kaleb moved to her ear; nibbling on her ear lobe he whispered, "I love you."

Without thought Katie whispered back, "I love you, too."

If either was startled by the admission they never said, for at that moment they became aware of a loud noise coming from the nightclub. Someone was shouting fire and people were pushing and shoving trying to get out of the building.

From where he stood, Kaleb could see small flames leaping in the corner of the room. It appeared that a table had been knocked over and a decorative screen of some kind was burning. The fire looked small and should be easily contained. It was the panicked people that had him worried.

"Katie, go there by that cement planter and stand behind it. As people get near the door tell them to walk slowly down that side path. Try to calm them as they come out or they're likely to trample each other."

Katie did as he instructed. Kaleb went quickly to a second door that opened into the area of the nightclub where tables were set up. People were beginning to push through the open archway that opened onto the outside dance floor.

Katie calmly said, "Please walk slowly down the path. Watch your step so you don't fall. Please, no pushing. That's right, nice and careful." Over and over she repeated the words.

Kaleb pushed open the side door and took in the situation in a glance. He was used to being in command and took charge. His booming voice echoed around the room. People who were grabbing their purses and jackets and rushing in all directions stopped at the sound of his voice.

He ordered, "You people in that half of the room go out the front door, and you people on this side come out this door. Those of you on the dance floor go out through the arch over there. No pushing or shoving, and for God's sake, walk carefully so you don't fall."

As one of the people from the dance floor went rushing toward the tables to get her belongings, Kaleb shouted, "Stop! The fire will be out shortly and you can come in and get your things then."

The woman hesitated, but then shrugged her shoulders and proceeded toward the door. Several of the employees were already grabbing tablecloths and using them to try to smother the fire. Kaleb looked about and noticed a large tapestry decorating the wall behind him. He took hold of one end and yanked but it didn't come down. A man from the crowd moved over to the other side of the hanging.

He said in his accented English, "Two, *sí?*"

Kaleb said, "Yes, two." Then bracing to pull, he said, "Okay," and with a hard jerk on both ends it came tumbling down. They both held onto it as they carried it near the fire. Then motioning the others to stand back, they tossed it over the fire, quickly pulling the top down over the flames and smothering them.

When he was sure the fire was out, he looked about the club. Only he, the man who had helped him and some of the employees were left inside. The manager walked up to Kaleb, praising and thanking him profusely.

Kaleb was a little embarrassed by the praise but said, "You're welcome. You'll have to let the people back in to get their belongings, and if you'll excuse me I have to go find a certain young lady."

Walking onto the outside dance floor he found Katie sitting on the edge of the planter. She had been watching him from where she sat.

"You were wonderful," she gushed.

He flushed slightly at her words.

"I just didn't want anyone to get hurt."

"I know, but you were safe and didn't need to go back in. I'm so proud of you."

This time he turned scarlet at her praise. Reaching for her hand he said, "Come on. Let's go home."

That night as Katie curled up on her side and closed her eyes to go to sleep; she reached up and touched her lips. That kiss had been so...so...fantastic. Then she remembered his words; I love you. Did he mean them? Could he have really fallen in love with her in three short weeks?

She knew she had said, "I love you, too," but she didn't know if he had heard her.

She knew her heart was saying, *I love him*, but her mind kept saying, *Are you sure?* As her body relaxed into slumber, she still thought of his words, but could she believe him?

Kaleb had no trouble going to sleep. He was giddy inside. Katie had said she loved him.

Oh, sweet heaven, what a wonderful gift, he thought and then fell into a peaceful slumber.

Chapter 10

Sunday they spent on the beach sunbathing, swimming, swinging in the hammocks and playing fetch with Mimoso. Kaleb brought lunch and Katie supplied dinner. It was while they were lying contentedly on the beach that Kaleb asked Katie to come to Boston.

"Do you think you could get away for a few days? Maybe you could fly up with April and make it a long weekend. I'd love to show you where I live and show you the sights in Boston. I know I'm going to miss you terribly. If I know when I leave on Friday that I'll see you again in two weeks, it won't be so hard."

Katie had been dreading Friday's arrival. Maybe it wouldn't be so bad if she knew she would see him again soon.

"I'll have to check at work and see how things look for that weekend, but I'll try."

Kaleb leaned back his head and covered his eyes with his arm.

You'll be there, Katie, he thought, *because I already know what I'm getting you for Valentine's Day. The most beautiful engagement ring I can find.*

She confirmed her plans to come to Boston on Tuesday. She would fly in with April but had to return to Akumal on the following Wednesday. He was thrilled.

This week passed much as the previous one had, having lunch together at a restaurant or on the beach, dinners at the villa, playing games and talking with Megan until she went to bed. The rest of the evenings were spent in quiet, relaxing time on the patio. Kaleb would hold her hand as they talked. Kissing seemed to be their other favorite pastime outside, under the stars.

Kaleb told her several more times that he loved her. When he told her, she would lean up and kiss him, and on a couple of occasions when the kissing was more passionate she would return his words saying, "I love you, too." Kaleb didn't seem to notice that she never said the words first.

As the days sped by, Katie's mood was gradually changing. Depression was creeping up on her and her mind was in turmoil. Kaleb kept telling her he loved her, but would he feel the same when he got back to Boston? She was sure that beautiful, sophisticated women would surround him once again when he got home. Was it really love or was he just grateful for her help with Megan and for easing his loneliness? Would he come to realize that she simply wouldn't fit into his social class?

Could she trust her own feelings? Things had moved so fast. She didn't know what true love felt like. She was so unsure and scared.

Thursday came much too quickly. It would be their last night together, for Kaleb and Megan had to leave Akumal by eight Friday morning to catch their flight out of Cancun.

April stopped by Katie's office during the day and said she was going to spend the evening with Megan so Katie could have Kaleb all to herself.

"I think you should get out of here early. Go home and plan a romantic dinner for two at your place."

"I'll have to see what Kaleb wants first."

"I already talked to him and he's all for it. He said he knew you would want to say goodbye to Megan, so he's going to stop by with her around three this afternoon."

Katie laughed. "I think you two are running roughshod over me, but thanks, April. You're one in a million."

It was hard to say goodbye to Megan. She knelt down and hugged her and told her she would see her again in a couple of weeks.

"Now you remember to stomp those feet of yours whenever you need to and don't try to be perfect all the time. You'll remember, right?"

Megan nodded her head and then leaned over and whispered, "I don't feel like I need to stomp as much anymore and I'm not as scared as I used to be."

Then she gave Katie a kiss on her cheek, a big hug and murmured, "I love you, Katie."

Hugging her back she said, "I love you, too, Megan."

Katie knew a part of her self had left when Kaleb and Megan drove away, but she also felt she had received the greatest gift ever when she heard Megan's whispered words.

The table was set. A long white tablecloth hung over the round edges. Colorful flowered plates sat on rich blue place mats. Dark blue napkins were folded and lay on top of the dinner plates. The silverware was stainless steel but had been rubbed with a towel to make it shine. The water goblets were already filled and the wineglasses sat ready to be used. Two crystal candle holders with long white candles sat on each side of the fresh tropical floral arrangement in the middle of the table.

Katie walked from the table into her bedroom. Gazing into the mirror she gave herself the same appraising look she had just given the table. She had on the same green spaghetti-strap dress she had worn the first night she had gone out to dinner with Kaleb. She had brushed her hair until it shined. A small gold chain necklace with a little gold nugget hung from her neck, and the ceramic bracelet circled her wrist. She checked her lipstick and then went to the kitchen to see to dinner.

Caesar salads were chilling in the refrigerator. She had barracuda with a special seasoning sauce baking in the oven, along with twice-baked potatoes with Mexican cheese. She had prepared brown sugar-glazed carrots and picked up fresh bread from her friend at Quz Onda, the local Italian restaurant. The wine was open, giving it time to breathe.

"Well, Mimoso, it's time for you to go out in the backyard."

Catching hold of his collar she led him out the back door.

She felt nervous and giddy, sad and lonely. He would be here soon. She thought she loved him. He was leaving tomorrow. She missed him already.

As she walked to the table she heard the car stop outside her house. He was here. She opened the door to see him standing stiffly on her step. He was dressed the same as he'd been on their first night out.

Great minds...she thought.

His eyes traveled from her toes slowly up to her face and he whistled through his teeth.

"Wow, you look gorgeous."

Her eyes traveled the same path, from his feet to his eyes, and then she said, "And you look extremely handsome."

They both laughed and he took her in his arms for a welcoming kiss. Closing the door they moved into the house.

"Do you want a drink before dinner or are you ready to eat now?"

"The food smells delicious. Let's eat. We can relax with a drink later."

"Okay. I'll get the salads and bread if you'll pour the wine."

As they ate dinner they talked and laughed. Both avoided mentioning that he was leaving in the morning. After dinner they took their glasses of wine and sat on the couch. They couldn't contain their emotions any longer. They both spoke at the same time.

"I'm going to miss you so much," Katie was saying as Kaleb said, "I can't stand to think of the next two weeks without you."

Kaleb removed Katie's glass from her hand, setting it next to his on the little side table. Then he leaned over and pulled her close, kissing her repeatedly with little pecks and then nibbling on her lips. The kiss deepened and passion flared.

He kissed her eyes shut and then kissed a path down her jaw to the pulse point in her neck. He could feel her heart racing just like his. Moving his hands up to her shoulders he lowered the straps of her dress. Reaching behind her he unsnapped the flimsy strapless bra she wore, releasing her breasts for his hands to touch.

He moved back slightly, looking down as he gently lifted one pale, white mound with its rosy nipple. He rubbed his thumb across its tip, watching it swell and harden. Lowering his head he laved the tip with his tongue. Not satisfied, he did the same to the other breast.

Katie felt as though she was going to melt into a little puddle at his feet. She tried to move closer to him. Stroking one hand up and down his back, she used her other hand to sift through the hair at the nape of his neck.

Kaleb slowly brought his hand up her leg, and sliding it under her skirt, brushed his fingertips over her inner thigh. Katie suddenly went rigid. He looked up.

"What is it?" he asked, trying to slow his breathing.

"I've never..." she stammered.

Confusion marred his face.

"You've never what?" he asked.

Katie looked down shyly and just shook her head.

"You've never..." he started again and then he understood, finishing the sentence for her, "... made love."

She nodded yes.

"Oh, Katie, I'm sorry if I frightened you. You know I love you and would never do anything to hurt you."

Kaleb reached down and pulled the straps of Katie's dress up. Then placing his finger under her chin, he lifted her face and gazed into her eyes.

"I can't say I'm sorry there hasn't been anyone else, but you are twenty-seven and very beautiful and giving, so why?"

Katie shook her head.

"I don't know. I guess there just hasn't been anybody I really felt close enough to. Plus, I wanted to save myself as a special gift for my husband."

He liked that idea since he planned on being her husband, but as he looked closer he got a gut feeling that there was something more.

"Katie, if you want to wait for marriage, I think that's great, but is there something more? Are you afraid of the actual act itself? Did something happen to make you afraid?"

"No, no, nothing like that."

"But you are afraid. I can see it in your eyes. What are you afraid of?"

Katie stood then and started to pace around the room.

"I don't know how to explain it. I do want to save myself for marriage, but I'm also afraid, not so much of sex itself but of the commitment that making love represents to me. When I was a teenager I saw several of my friends and even a cousin destroyed by sex. They were so sure that they were in love and then they would wind up pregnant and the guy just walked away. Even if they didn't get pregnant, they would be so hurt. As I got older, I realized that making love in your twenties didn't have the same devastating effect, but a lot of my friends have still been hurt badly. I guess I still carry the fear that if I make love with anyone I'll still get hurt, that the next morning the man will look at me with disgust and I'll feel dirty and ashamed. Making love is so intimate and the ultimate way of sharing.

I'm afraid that I'll find out later that he didn't really love me or I wasn't really in love with him. I'm afraid to trust my feelings, so I have always kept men at a distance."

Kaleb sat looking at her, trying to understand.

"Do you feel that way now? Here with me?"

Katie nodded her head and barely got out, "Yes."

Kaleb felt completely helpless. Didn't she know how much he loved her? He walked over to where she stood and taking her hands in his he held them tight.

"My Katie girl, I shared all my pain and anguish over Lucy with you and my confusion and worry for Megan. I let you see my inadequacies and confessed my mistakes to you. You didn't turn away from me but helped me heal. You broke away the shell around my heart and then you wound me so tight around you that you snapped the chain that held me to my past. The only thing I can give you in return is my love. I opened my heart and let you in. You make me laugh, you bring life to my world and I don't want to go on without you. If you don't love me enough to trust my feelings for you, there is nothing I can do."

Katie stood before him with tears running down her face and with an anguished cry said, "I'm so sorry."

Kaleb caught one of her tears and brought it to his lips.

"Katie, I can see and taste your tears, but mine are all here where you can't see them," he said, placing his hand over his heart. Then he turned and walked out the door.

She stood immobile, listening to his retreating footsteps. She heard the engine of the car start and knew he was gone and would never be back. She was like a statue, her harsh breathing the only sign that she was alive. Suddenly the dam broke and she began to shake and sob. She grabbed at the ceramic bracelet on her wrist; tearing it from her arm she hurled it across the room. It hit the tile floor and shattered into a million pieces.

Just like my heart, she thought.

The noise must have alerted Mimoso to her anguish, for he started to whine at the door. She let him in. He licked the tears from her face but they continued to fall. Somehow she wound up in her bed with Mimoso curled beside her.

Chapter 11

The sun shining through the window onto Katie's face awakened her. She still wore the dress from last night. Her eyes felt scratchy and she knew if she looked in the mirror they would be red and puffy. Her limbs felt like they were weighted down with cement. She didn't think she could move. Mimoso had jumped down from the bed and stood whining to be let out. She crawled from the bed and let him out into the backyard.

Now that she was up she knew she had to shower and get ready for work. Looking at the clock she saw that it was eight. Kaleb and Megan would be leaving Akumal now. The tears started again. At least the water in the shower would camouflage them.

She somehow made it through the better part of the day, only crying when she found herself alone. Sybil could tell something was wrong but decided not to intrude. It was April, bustling into the office, demanding to know what happened that made Katie completely crumple again.

It took her several minutes to be able to talk. April was saying that Kaleb had come home early last night and he looked like hell.

"What happened?" she again demanded.

"I told him I had never made love with anyone and I couldn't do it with him either."

"And?" was all April said. She knew there was more to it than that.

"He said he was happy I had saved myself for my husband, but he could tell I was afraid and he wanted to know why."

"What did you tell him? I've always wondered myself what you were afraid of."

Katie pulled herself together and looked from April's expectant face to Sybil's.

"I'm not going to talk about it now. I have work to finish." She resumed typing on her computer.

April gave up but promised that she was coming by her house tonight. With that, she turned and left.

Katie slumped in her chair. She knew there would be no rest until she told April everything. Would she understand or would she criticize her and judge her harshly?

She just couldn't work any longer, so she told Sybil to lock up when she was finished and she went home. She took Mimoso for a long walk on the beach. It brought back so many memories of Kaleb and Megan, it was almost like a kind of punishment, but she clung to the memories anyway.

When she got back to the house April was already there. She had brought a bottle of wine and had made herself at home. She gave Katie a scrutinizing look, and then a big hug and, handing her a glass of wine, said, "You look like death warmed over."

"Thanks, but I already knew that."

"Drink up and tell me everything."

Katie took a big gulp, choking a little as it slid down her throat. Then she proceeded to tell April all that had been said. April listened intently and when Katie had finished she said that she understood why Kaleb was so upset.

"He truly loves you and you turned him away. What are you going to do now? I can see that you love him."

"I do love him but is it enough?"

Katie then told her about some of the doubts she'd had because of Kaleb's background and how she feared that he just thought he was in love with her because he was grateful.

"That man knows the difference between love and gratitude, and if he said he loves you, you can bet he does."

Katie wasn't completely convinced, but she did start feeling a little spurt of hope. April had asked her what she was going to do. She didn't know, but maybe she could think of something. They continued to talk a little longer, but April could see that Katie was almost asleep on her feet.

"I'll fix us a salad while you go get into your pajamas, and when we finish eating, it's bedtime for you."

Katie did as April instructed and was asleep by seven.

Over the next two weeks, she vacillated between depression and hope. She took to wearing the little plastic bracelet that Kaleb had given her as a joke. It brought her comfort.

April and Katie spent a lot of evenings together. Katie knew that April often talked to Roger on the telephone, but she managed not to ask if he had said anything about Kaleb. She was afraid she wouldn't like what she heard. It was better to just not know. April let Katie stew until two days before they were to fly to Boston.

"Have you decided if you have enough courage to take a chance on yourself and Kaleb yet?" she asked as they were sitting in Katie's house eating dinner.

Katie slowly lowered her fork to the table.

"I've been debating that very thing with myself for the past several days. What if I go to him and he turns me away? But what if he doesn't? I have finally come to understand that I do truly love him and that I need to trust his love, but I'm scared. You may have to prod me with a poker to get me on the plane, but I want you to do it."

April's face lit up with relief.

"I was starting to get worried that you wouldn't have the guts to try. I'll hog-tie you if I have to. There's no backing out now. And before you ask me, I haven't asked Roger about Kaleb, and he hasn't said anything. I want this to be strictly between you and Kaleb."

Her stomach was in knots and her palms were sweaty. She kept rubbing the little gaudy plastic bracelet that she wore. What was she going to say to him? Would he even see her? She was one big lump of tightly wound nerves.

The passengers were disembarking, standing in the aisles to try to be the first off. Katie was willing to wait for the rush to pass, but April wanted to jump over the people in front of her just to get to the door and Roger. Hurrying Katie along, they swept through the ramp to the airport lobby.

Roger was standing as close to the door as was allowed. He had balloons with little bells tied to the ends of the ribbons in one hand, a big box of chocolates under his arm and a dozen red roses in the other hand. When April saw him she went running into his arms and he somehow managed to wrap her in a big hug despite his full hands.

They kissed, completely oblivious to the other people who passed by.

When they came up for air, Roger noticed Katie standing behind April. His face registered surprise, but he only said, "Hello, Katie. I didn't know you were coming."

"Don't worry; I'm not going to intrude on your evening. I just need Kaleb's home address from you and I'll be on my way. How have you been, Roger?"

He gave April an inquiring look, but answered Katie, "I've been fine, but missing April. I'm so glad she's here."

Still holding tight to April, he told Katie the address she wanted as she wrote it down. She asked how to get to where she could catch a cab. She had only brought a carry-on bag, so she didn't need to go to luggage. Katie left the two of them as they reached the lobby. April gave her a reassuring hug and wished her luck.

Katie found a cab and handed the driver the address. She sat in the back of the car looking out the window but not really seeing any of the sights they passed. Her mind was surprisingly calm. She could picture Kaleb in her mind and hear the sound of his voice. Now that she was here she just couldn't wait to see him.

The cab stopped in front of what could only be called an imposing house. It was large and Gothic in style. Getting out of the cab, she handed the driver some money and stood staring at the door to the house. Before he pulled away, he asked her if she was all right and if he should wait for her.

"No, that won't be necessary. I'll call when I need a ride to my hotel," she answered. He just nodded and left.

Katie made her way to the front door and pushed the doorbell. A woman in her fifties answered.

"Yes, miss, is there something I can do for you?"

"Would you tell Mr. Dalton that I would like to see him?"

"Mr. Dalton isn't receiving visitors tonight. Maybe you should come back tomorrow or contact him at his office."

Katie pleaded, "Oh please, I must see him tonight."

There was something in her look that made the woman wonder about her.

"Mr. Dalton hasn't been seeing anyone in the evenings since he got back from his vacation. He spends time with his daughter until she goes to bed then he shuts himself in his study and works until the wee hours of the morning. I don't think he will see you, but I suppose I can ask. Who should I tell him is calling?"

Katie thought for a minute and then reached down and took off the bracelet he had given her. She snapped it in half and handed it to the housekeeper.

"Tell him I want to see him about getting a replacement."

If the housekeeper was surprised, she didn't say so. She took the broken bracelet and nodded.

"You can wait in the parlor while I go check."

Katie entered the house but she didn't notice her surroundings. She was getting nervous again.

The woman returned in a few minutes and said, "You may leave your bag here and follow me. Mr. Dalton said he would see you."

She led the way down the hall. The door to his study was closed. The housekeeper told her to go in and then continued down the hall, disappearing around a corner.

Katie took a deep breath and knocked quietly on the door. She didn't wait for an answer but opened it and stepped into the room. She zeroed in on Kaleb immediately. He was standing in front of the fireplace with his back to the flames and his hands in the pockets of the open cardigan sweater that he wore. His eyes studied her.

"You came," is all he said. She didn't know that in one pocket he was clutching the broken bracelet and in the other he gripped a little velvet box.

He appeared unapproachable and yet vulnerable to Katie. She tried to smile but failed. Taking a few more steps into the room, she felt tears start in her eyes for the pain she had caused this man. It was the vulnerability that she noted that allowed her feet to move slowly, carrying her closer to him until she was within touching distance, but he didn't move. He only watched her.

His face appeared to be carved from stone. She gazed into his eyes and saw so much. There was pain and hurt, longing and desire but most of all she saw love. It was that love that gave her courage.

She reached up and gently laid her hand against his face. He flinched slightly at her touch but didn't pull away or touch her in return. She moved her fingertips in a massaging sort of motion, as though she were trying to smooth away his pain. It took her a moment more to utter any words.

"Oh Kaleb, I'm so sorry."

He was dying inside. When she had walked into the room he had wanted to rush to her and gather her to him and never let her go, but something kept him from moving. And now, as her fingertips caressed his face, he was fighting with all his will not to turn his head and kiss the palm of her hand. He knew it had taken her courage to come here, and now he waited for the words both he and she needed to hear. He could only will her strength to say them. He could see her struggling to form the words and with an ache in her voice she began to speak.

"My grandmother had a teacup that sat on her mantel for as long as I can recall. She always told us it was a gift from Grandpa, and he said the cup represented their life together and it should only be filled with good things. I wanted to fill my own cup with all those things my grandparents and parents had, like love, true intimacy, laughter and trust, but I was afraid, so I let my cup stay empty.

"All my life, I've had this fantasy about a knight in shining armor coming and sweeping the fair maiden away to his castle, where he would badger her and seduce her into loving him. That was my fantasy, but in my real life I always wanted a love like my parents had, the kind that took time and care to form and grow. They had the sort of love where my dad couldn't go to sleep at night if my mom got called into work. He would sit up in his chair and wait for her. Or when one of them had to go out of town they had to call each other every night. One like the three couples you met the first night we went out, where, after fifty years of marriage, they still wanted to dance together and hold hands across the table and touch each other when they passed by. I wanted the kind of love people share that makes them look across the room and read each other's minds. I have always wanted these things and now I have come to realize that in you I have both. You are my knight in shining armor who has swept me off my feet, and you are my true and steady love that will always hold my hand."

By this time a tear had slipped from her eye, making a path down her face. Kaleb couldn't stand any more. He took his hands from his pockets and brushed it away. He opened his mouth to speak but she slid her fingers over his lips to silence him. Taking one of his hands in hers, she placed it over her heart.

"My heart and my soul and my body belong to you. I love you, Kaleb."

Kaleb had listened to her with his heart pounding so hard in his chest he thought it would burst out of him. She had finally found the courage to face her fears and acknowledge the love they shared. He laughed with joy, picking her up and swinging her in a circle. Then he slowly lowered her down his body until their lips met in a kiss that would be remembered always.

Chapter 12

It was high season. The weather was perfect. Tourists were wandering through the specialty shops, drinking up the sun on the beaches, slipping on their wetsuits and collecting their diving equipment. Children's laughter could be heard as they built castles in the sand and chased each other into the still water of the lagoon.

Standing at the open window of her upstairs bedroom, the sights, smells and sounds of this tropical paradise filled her. Katie loved it here. A secret smile crossed her face as she recalled a day only a year ago when she had gazed out on this paradise and wondered what was missing from her life. Now she knew.

Looking down, she saw workers placing chairs around the decorated tables. Over to her left she could see a white carpet runner arranged between rows of white folding chairs. The carpet wound its way to a large trellis that was decorated with countless roses. The trellis was bordered with large floral arrangements of tropical flowers.

She smoothed a hand down the side of the long, rich crimson gown she wore. Glancing at the bed, she saw the small bouquet of flowers lying there. It was April's wedding day. She was so happy for both April and Roger.

She turned back to the window when she heard children's laughter. She loved the sound of children at play. Her mind drifted to her last doctor's visit just hours before they had left Boston to come down for the wedding. She hadn't told Kaleb the news, but she would soon. She was so lost in her thoughts, she didn't hear the door open or the man's footsteps as he crossed the room, but her body sensed Kaleb's presence.

He stood behind her, bringing his arms around her and placing his hands on her rounded abdomen he said, "How are you feeling? Is this little rascal giving you any trouble?"

"None. I haven't had any morning sickness for the past week. I think it's gone for good." Motioning to the view outside the window she said, "Isn't it beautiful?"

Kaleb was nuzzling her neck and just murmured, "Yes, beautiful."

"You're not even looking," Katie admonished.

"I don't have to. The most beautiful thing in the world is right here in my arms."

Katie leaned back into Kaleb. It always felt so good to be held by him. The laughter from outside caught their attention. Megan was racing between the chairs with Mimoso hot on her heels. Several of April's nieces and nephews were running behind, trying to catch them.

"Oh, Kaleb, she's going to be a mess before the wedding even starts, and I thought you locked Mimoso up in the side yard."

"I did. I'll bet Megan had something to do with him getting out. Telling her she didn't have to be good all the time may have been a big mistake."

Kaleb made the statement in an aggrieved tone, but Katie knew he was thrilled that Megan was acting like a normal child.

Megan was excited about the impending arrival of a baby brother or sister. She never had nightmares anymore and was as stubborn as Kaleb had once described. It was wonderful.

Looking out the window, Kaleb commented, "This brings memories of our own wedding."

"A day I will always cherish. It was everything I had always dreamed of. I was so glad my cousin Jessica was able to make it. She's very special to me," Katie replied.

Turning in his arms, Katie leaned up and kissed him.

"I have something to tell you. I haven't had a chance before, but I wanted to tell you before we go down to the wedding. Dr. Kelly listened for the baby's heartbeat last visit and he's sure he heard two. I have to have a sonogram when I get back to confirm it, but I think Megan is going to have two brothers or sisters."

Kaleb could only get out a squeaky, "Two?"

"Yes, dear." Then Katie added, "I love you."

Kaleb repeated, "Two!" Then he started to laugh. "You are definitely keeping my life exciting. I love you, my Katie girl."

Chapter 13

(Boston, MA, about three years later)

Shaking off the water from his umbrella and collapsing it, John turned in to the revolving glass doors. He collided with a woman who had just stepped into the same spot.

"Oh, I'm sorry, I didn't see you. Please excuse me. I should have been watching where I was going."

"That's okay. I wasn't paying attention myself."

"Go ahead. I'll wait."

John stepped back and let her proceed.

"Thanks."

Jessica stepped into the open area and pushed the metal bar in front of her. She wore an English-styled raincoat and black, ankle-high boots. Carrying a briefcase and a little umbrella in one hand, she reached up with the other and shoved her fingers through her hair to try to restore it to some semblance of its former style. The wind had blown it in all directions. She had a meeting with Mr. Kilroy in ten minutes. Maybe she had time to stop by the ladies' room on her way and freshen up. She didn't want to be late. She looked about her and saw a sign and arrow that pointed to the washrooms. She walked in that direction.

John made his way to the elevators. He stood patiently waiting for one to come and noticed the young woman from the door heading across the lobby. He thought she had a kind of classic beauty about her; a little plump, but her features were somewhat aristocratic and she carried herself in a stylish manner. He liked what he saw. He was sick of the toothpick look.

The elevator came and John stepped inside and pushed the button for the fifth floor. It was time for work. He had a meeting with an aspiring writer. He had looked over some of her writing examples and her resume and decided to interview her. He needed someone to give him a woman's perspective on some of the advertising layouts for his magazine. It wasn't what she had applied for, but her writing samples seemed to have a certain sense of female understanding in them.

It was probably a wild idea to even consider creating such a position, and he should probably be looking for a psychologist if he wanted an educated opinion. He often followed his gut instincts though, and there was something that said, "Talk to me," in her writings.

He made his way to his office, grabbing a cup of coffee as he passed the coffee machine. He looked longingly at the donuts but forced himself to forego them. He had to watch what he ate or he would be bulging in no time flat. He was thirty-two and just starting to notice that he couldn't eat everything in sight anymore or he gained weight. He knew exercise was what he needed, but with the new publication just starting to come together he couldn't find the time.

Sitting down behind his desk, he pulled open the folder for his upcoming interview. She was twenty-nine and had graduated from college with a degree in journalism three years ago. She'd had an assortment of jobs before and during college, but the past three years had been spent working for a little newspaper in a small town in Washington. The application didn't tell him why she had moved to Boston, and although it said that she was single he wondered if she had come with a man. That kind of thing happened quite often these days and he certainly wasn't in any position to judge. He had just ended such a relationship himself last year. The buzzing of his intercom alerted him to the fact that it was time to meet this person who had somehow intrigued him with her writing.

"Yes, Miss Fernly?"

"Mr. Kilroy, your appointment is here."

"Send her in."

The door opened and in walked the young woman he had bumped into coming in the building. She had removed her coat and had on a light blue silk blouse tucked into a dark blue skirt. A scarf was arranged around the collar of the blouse almost like a tie, but more feminine.

They were both startled when they saw each other.

"Miss Braxton, please come in and have a seat. It seems I have the chance to apologize again for not watching where I was going."

"Please don't. It was as much my fault as yours."

Jessica moved to the chair placed in front of his desk. She was nervous but tried not to show it. She wanted to appear comfortable and at ease. She really wanted this job. Her cousin Katie had talked her into moving to Boston and said her husband would help her get a job, but she wanted to do this on her own. She had confidence in her writing abilities, even if she was a little unsure in her personal life.

After Jessica was seated, John sat down in his own chair.

"I was just looking over your application and resume, and I see that you have come to us from Washington. You're probably used to the rain."

"Yes, this is typical weather for me."

She rubbed her hands on her skirt, smoothing it, and then realized what she was doing and placed them palms up in her lap. She had read somewhere that to look open and confident one shouldn't clasp her hands together or fidget with them.

"Relax," she told herself.

John asked her some questions about her last job and observed her closely. He wanted to reassure her that she needn't be so worried, but he knew that would only increase her tension. She was quick to smile and John liked that. She was very articulate and answered his questions readily. No rehearsed answers. Another thing in her favor, since the job he had in mind required her first impressions and her honest opinions.

After about forty minutes of conversation John was convinced that he had been right; now to convince her.

"I would like to hire you," he began, "but not for the writing job you applied for."

Her eyes had lit up at his initial words, but now they only asked him to explain.

"I have been considering a new position here at the magazine and after reading some of your work, decided you would be perfect for the job. I need someone to give advice and opinions, mostly on ads that will appear in our magazine, but also on some of the slants our articles take."

It wasn't until after he had said the words that he realized he meant for her to have input on all aspects of the magazine.

Why not, he thought. *Most of our writers are men and they tend to leave the feminine viewpoint out.*

Even the women writers didn't seem to have that flare for getting to the soul of the story he had felt when reading her articles.

Jessica didn't know what to say or think. This wasn't at all what she had expected, a consultant of sorts. Why would he think that her opinions were worth his money? He was looking for a woman's opinion and she didn't think hers coincided with a lot of other women's. She was literally speechless.

"Well, what do you think?"

"I don't know. I haven't had a chance to consider it. It sounds like a great job, but are you sure I'm the one for it? What if I steer you completely wrong? It could mean the financial ruin of your magazine."

"I won't let that happen. Besides, I'm only asking your opinion. I can always disagree and do what I think is best. We can have a three-month trial basis and both see what we think when the time is up. What do you say to that?"

Jessica thought only briefly.

"I guess you have a deal."

The sky was still gray, but the rain had changed to a fine mist when Jessica left the building. She hailed a cab and told the driver the address of her new apartment. Her belongings had only arrived yesterday and she had a lot of unpacking to do. The movers had arranged her furniture, but she had told them to leave the rest, as she didn't know where she wanted everything else placed. She wanted to do it herself so it would feel more like home to her.

As she sat back in the cab she thought, *I have a job. Not the one I had in mind, but it's something totally new and exciting.*

Why did he think she could do it? He had said there was something in her writing that had convinced him. She recalled the samples she had submitted.

One was on a fire that had destroyed the home of a relatively new family who had moved to her town. Half the town had stood and watched as the house burned to the ground. She had been there, too. She had introduced herself to the family as they stood huddled together and informed them she was a reporter. She didn't know at the time if they understood that she was looking for a story, but her easy and empathetic manner had them confiding in her. The story had all the facts, but it also had an element of the feelings of this young family.

The article on the new curriculum adopted by the school board again contained the basics, but after reading it one wanted to keep up on how well it worked. It made the reader understand that it had been approved with the welfare of the children and the community as its main goal.

The last submission had been an editorial she had written after a man had been found guilty of assault and sentenced to two years in prison. He had beaten his girlfriend severely. She could still recall the battered and bruised face and body of the young woman. She had observed her and even talked with her during the trial. The girl's anguished cry when the man had been sent to prison had astonished most present in the courtroom, but not Jessica. She had gradually understood some of the girl's personality and knew she was torn in her emotions. The woman was afraid, but which fear reigned supreme was the unanswered question. Was it the fear of physical abuse, the fear of being alone, or the fear that she had failed in the relationship that had the woman so upset? Her editorial had reflected all of this.

Jessica didn't realize her articles had revealed a lot about her and her ability to express the feelings of others. She just wrote what she observed.

Her thoughts turned to Mr. Kilroy. He was younger than she expected, but easy to talk to and quite good-looking in her opinion.

I wonder if that is an opinion I better keep to myself, she thought with a little smile.

She wasn't sure what his expectations of her were, but she would probably find out soon. She was to report to work on Monday. That only gave her the weekend to get settled into her apartment.

John put his hands behind his head and leaned back in his chair, tipping it so he could put his feet on the desk. If someone had observed him they would have thought he was taking a break, but his mind was rehashing the interview.

A smile crossed his face. He had been wrong, she wasn't a little plump, she was just right. She had curves in all the right places and appeared very feminine in the way she dressed and the way she comported herself. She reminded him of his mother in that respect, and he wondered if she had the same courage and determination that few realized his mother possessed. Her eyes were very expressive and seemed to hold a certain sense of wisdom and compassion he felt one only gained through experience and personal grief.

His brother Patrick would probably think he was crazy for hiring her for the job he had envisioned, but then Patrick thought he was crazy to even attempt the new magazine in the first place. Patrick was in charge of the weekly magazine on business and finance, while he ran the bi-weekly news magazine. It was his mother who had given him the go-ahead to start the new publication. She owned the controlling portion of the business, while he and Patrick each owned twenty-five percent.

He had broached the topic of a new magazine with his brother and mother one night at dinner.

He had explained, "I want a magazine that will appeal to the family. One that takes the news or changing financial information or new laws and lets the common family see how it has affected others or may affect them. I'm not sure I'm explaining myself well, but I can see it in my mind. Something that makes the reader want to know more or learn important things to prevent unwanted changes or make improvements in their lives or makes them understand what the people involved in a story are going through."

His brother had just looked at him like he had lost his mind. His mother had asked a few questions and then said, "I think you should give it a try. Maybe you could start out with just local stories and publish it for the Boston area. If it works we can go national. How does that sound to you?"

That had been three months ago. He had writers from the news magazine doing some crossover writing for him and had hired a couple others to work exclusively for the new publication. He had one person working on getting the accounts for the advertising. It hadn't all fallen together to his liking though, and that is when he came up with the new position. On second thought, he had come up with the idea for the new position after he read Miss Braxton's work.

Her writings seemed to have screamed at him, "This is what I'm looking for."

Maybe he should have just hired her as a writer, but one person couldn't write the whole magazine.

Glancing at his watch, he realized it was time for a meeting with the staff of the news magazine. He slid his feet off the desk and, picking up a folder, left his office to go to the boardroom.

As he walked he thought, *I guess I'll see what comes of my idea next week.*

Chapter 14

Putting the last spoon into the plastic holder in the silverware drawer, Jessica placed her hands at the small of her back and stretched, trying to relieve some of the soreness. She had been unpacking since Friday evening and only had two more boxes to go.

Moving into the living room, she gazed around.

It's beginning to feel like home, she thought.

She opened one of her last boxes and spied the little china cup that had belonged to her grandmother. Gathering it gently in her hands, she looked about for just the right place to put it. There was no fireplace in the apartment, so no mantel to set it on. Then her eyes fell on the glassed-in cupboard built into the wall. She had already put books on the two bottom shelves but the top one stood empty. She lovingly placed it there. Eventually she arranged some pictures of her family around it.

She had always loved that cup. It held a wealth of meaning for her. Unlike most people who celebrate their twenty-first birthdays with friends making the rounds of bars, she had spent her own with her mother and father. When it had come time for gifts, her mother had handed her a little silver wrapped box. Tears had filled her eyes when she saw the little cup.

"It has always meant more to you than anyone else so you should have it," her mother had said.

It was looking at the china cup and remembering her grandmother's words about what it held that had pushed her into going on with her life. The following semester she registered at the local junior college and started the hard road back to living again. She had a lot of schooling to make up for, as she had never finished high school, but five years later she got her diploma.

Now I'm in Boston with a whole new career in front of me, she thought.

The chiming of her miniature cuckoo clock interrupted her thoughts. It was twelve and she was to be at her cousin's house at twelve-thirty.

I better get a move on, she thought.

She loved coming to Katie and Kaleb's house. Their boys were two years old and just starting to talk and Megan, their daughter, liked playing mother to her brothers.

They were thrilled for Jessica when she told them of her new job. Kaleb said he read the magazines that the Kilroy family now published and would look forward to seeing what their new one was like.

"This one is supposed to appeal to the family, so maybe you'll like it, too," she informed Katie.

"You let me know when it comes out and I'll be sure to read it."

They had an interesting lunch with all three children at the table. One glass of milk spilled and one of the boys kept dropping his food on the floor for the dog to eat. After eating, Jessica made her excuses and left for home. She wanted to be well rested for her first day on the job.

John spent his weekend going over some stories that had been submitted by his staff for the new magazine. He would have liked to call Miss Braxton to get her opinion on them, but he didn't even know if she had a phone yet. He would just have to wait until Monday.

Sunday night he had dinner with his mother. He told her about Jessica and the new position he had hired her for. His mother was a little surprised but she knew her son well, and when he said he had a feeling about her, she was sure he was right. As he continued to talk about the new magazine her mind wandered.

Mrs. Kilroy knew her sons well. Patrick was very exacting and precise in both his personal and professional life. He was great with the financial and business magazine. He had married when he was twenty-six and had a very supportive but rather insipid wife, in her estimation, but perfect for Patrick. John, on the other hand, was the risk-taker and the one who showed his emotions. Because he took chances he got hurt more. His instincts were usually good, though, and she trusted him.

When her husband had walked out of their lives, she had been thankful that both boys were quite young, and seemingly not adversely affected. She was also grateful that her grandfather had insisted on keeping the business in her name. She took over the running of the company.

Those first few years had been difficult. She had to run the business and hold her own against those on the board of directors who thought she was incapable. She owned the company, but to succeed she had to prove that she knew what she was doing to the employees and the clients who advertised in the magazine.

It was during those first years that she worried most about the boys. She had to work so many hours she feared they would feel abandoned by her, too. She started to bring them to the office with her during the summer months and had them dropped off at her work after school the rest of the time. As they grew older they began to take an active interest in the running of the company. After college they both asked to become part of the business. She made them earn the money to buy out their shares. The rest would go to them when she retired. She still went to work every day but was considering stepping down in a couple more years. Her sons basically ran the company now.

She sat thinking about the past years, but then realized that John had asked her a question.

"I'm sorry, John, I wasn't paying attention. What did you say?"

"I think you were lost in a daydream. I just wanted to know if you would like to meet Miss Braxton tomorrow. Should I stop by your office when I show her about?"

"Yes, I would like that. You sure are talking a lot about her for someone you just met."

"Am I? I guess she just impressed me."

They spent a little more time visiting, and then John saw his mother yawn and decided it was time to leave.

"I better head home. I'll see you at work tomorrow."

He leaned over her chair and gave her a peck on the cheek.

"Good night, Mother."

As he drove home he thought about his mother. She had worked so hard all her life to take care of him and Patrick. He got angry inside sometimes when he thought about his dad. He had never understood how he could have just left them. He and Patrick were only five and seven when he left. If he ever had children he would spend every minute he could with them. He couldn't remember a lot, but he somehow knew his mom had been hurt and worried. If he thought about it very long he would get so angry that he would have killed the man if he were there. It was better not to think about it.

Chapter 15

The number five lit up as the elevator doors opened onto the lobby of Howard Publishing Company. Jessica stepped out.

She took a deep breath and thought, *It's time to see what you've gotten yourself into.*

She turned left down the hall to the reception area outside Mr. Kilroy's office.

"Good morning, I'm Jessica Braxton and I'm here to see Mr. Kilroy."

"He said for you to go right in when you got here."

"Thanks."

She knocked on the door and walked in.

John had been reading an article and looked up at the knock. Miss Braxton was crossing the short space from the door to his desk. She had on a dark tan skirt with a lightweight cream-colored sweater, a pair of dark brown short-heeled shoes and a gold chain with a decorative pendant around her neck. Little gold loop earrings could be seen dangling from her ears. Her hair was down but curled to allow the earrings to show. John was again pleased with her appearance.

"Welcome, Miss Braxton. Do you mind if I call you by your first name? We're rather casual around here."

"No, not at all, Jessica or Jessie is fine."

"Good. You can call me John."

"Okay."

She couldn't quite bring herself to say John yet. Maybe when she got to know him better it would be all right. He was her boss, and that small-town upbringing made her think of him as Mr. Kilroy.

"I'll have Rita—Miss Fernly, our receptionist—take you down to personnel to fill out all the paperwork we need from new employees. When you're done with that, come back here and I'll show you around the place and introduce you to some of the other staff."

He pushed a button on the telephone and asked Rita to take her to personnel.

About an hour and a half later Jessica found herself back at Mr. Kilroy's office. He put aside the papers he was working on and said, "Let's go see the place and meet your co-workers."

They started with the actual print shop. He explained that the different magazines were printed in different areas of the long room. The noise level was high and it was hard to hear. When they left he asked if she had noticed the people all wore some kind of ear protection to protect their hearing.

They then went to the area where the writers sat. All had computers and Teletype machines. He introduced her to two of the writers who were working on stories for the new magazine. One was a lady about thirty-five. She had worked for another monthly magazine before coming here. The second was a man somewhere in his forties. He had come from a newspaper in New York. Both were friendly and welcomed her. He explained to them that she would be reading their articles and would have input on them.

He also introduced her to a man named Deacon. He was the sports writer for the news magazine. He had been with the company for the past twenty-six years. She was eager to talk with him.

"You must have so many stories to tell. I'd like to come back and talk to you sometime, if that would be all right with you?"

Deacon nodded and then asked, "Are you a big sports fan?"

"No, not really; I just have lots of things I wonder about and know you could answer them."

"Like what?" he queried.

"One thing I've always wanted to know is what is going through a football player's mind when he is injured and taken off the field?"

Deacon just looked at her in puzzlement, so she continued, "Is he worried that this will be a permanent injury, or that it will keep him out of play for too many games and someone else will take over his spot and be better than him? Or what do the parents of famous athletes feel about the publicity and pressure their children go through by being so famous? Are they sorry their kids can't have an ordinary life, or do they see it as just part of what has to be in order to use their God-given talents? I just want to know things like that."

"I don't know those answers, Jessica, but maybe I'll start asking and find out for you. You come back and talk to me anytime you want."

"Okay, I will."

John started to laugh as they left the area.

"What's so funny?" she wanted to know.

"I have never known Deacon not to know the answer to any question about sports before. You have him thinking now."

As they walked down the hall, John turned them in to what appeared to be another reception area. He asked the woman at the desk if Patrick was in. She indicated that he was, so John tapped on the door and ushered Jessica in. Patrick was turned toward the big window behind his desk apparently doing some thinking of his own. He swiveled his chair around and stood when he saw John with a young woman.

"I didn't expect to see you today. Is there a problem?"

"No problem. I just wanted to introduce you to Jessica. Jessica, this is my brother, Patrick. He is in charge of the financial and business weekly we publish. Jessica is going to be working on the new magazine, and I'm showing her around."

"I'm glad to meet you, Jessica. I'm not sure my brother knows what he's doing with this new idea of his, but time will tell."

"I'm pleased to meet you, too. I hope the magazine is a big success, as my job depends on it. I think the concept is imaginative and should appeal to a large segment of the population."

"We shall see," Patrick replied.

After leaving the office, John suggested they take a break for lunch. He said to meet him back at his office at one o'clock.

They spent the rest of the day finishing the tour. It was in the layout department that John asked her for her first official opinion. They were viewing the advertisement layout for a new perfume. It was a full-page ad for a perfume called Allure. The model in the picture was dressed in a red tight strapless dress and looked to be about seventeen. It said something about if you want your man to notice you tonight, attract him with Allure.

"What do you think?" he asked Jessica.

"The dress needs to be a soft color and more of a flowing gown with long sheer sleeves. You'll need to get a model that looks to be at least in her late twenties, too. The words are okay as long as you're implying through the look of the model that the man she's trying to attract is someone special to her. The way it is now, it looks like a commercial for a hooker. This is a family magazine, and if I had a teenage daughter I wouldn't want her getting the impression that she needed to dress like this to get a man. Are you trying to sell the perfume to teenagers or to women?"

After she finished she looked a little surprised by her outburst. In a quiet voice she added, "It's just my opinion."

John looked at the layout and said, "You heard the lady. We better fix it. Now, one more stop before you're free for the day. Come on, I have one more person for you to meet."

John took her to another office. He knocked quietly on the door. A woman's voice bid them to come in.

Ann Howard Kilroy stood by the window of her office. A smile played across her face when she saw her son and his new employee enter.

"I was beginning to wonder if you were going to come. You must be Miss Jessica Braxton. John told me this weekend that he was going to bring you by. Welcome to the company. I hope you'll like it here."

"Jessica, I would like you to meet the real boss of the company and my mother, Mrs. Kilroy."

Jessica was both pleased and surprised that John wanted to introduce her to his mother and the head of the company.

"It is so good to meet you and very nice of you to take the time to welcome me. I'm sure I will like it here. I hope to do a good job and will do my best."

"I'm sure you will. John has good instincts," she said as she smiled lovingly at her son.

I wonder if my son realizes that he is already quite taken with this young woman, she thought.

Chapter 16

The weather in Boston turned from fall to winter over the next few weeks. Those working on the new magazine hardly noticed, as they were so busy trying to get the first edition ready for its debut.

Jessica read over several articles and made suggestions. Mostly she just asked questions of the writers. In a piece about a small private school that had to shut its doors because of financial difficulties, the writer had told her how the parents and teachers felt and what impact it was going to have on the area public schools, but she wanted to know how the children felt.

Another piece had to do with a planned layoff of several hundred people, and she questioned whether anyone had talked to the city government or local colleges and career institutes about retraining these people. If there were plans, shouldn't they be included in the article for those who needed the information?

She seemed to be able to get to the heart of an article and ask the questions that would make the piece different than just reporting a story. The layout department began to ask her advice. She always asked to whom they were trying to sell the product before she gave her opinion.

Deacon and she became friends. He even submitted an article he had written to John for the new magazine. He had looked up the parents of two native Boston individuals who were sports celebrities. One was a famous basketball player and the other a tennis player. He asked them the kinds of questions Jessica had asked him. John accepted the article for his first publication.

Included in the first issue was a portion geared to younger children. The writer interviewed a hundred kids to see what they thought of the Boston Little League program. It included their likes and dislikes, but also their fears about playing the game and what winning and losing meant to them.

The day the first magazine rolled off the press they all celebrated, but the real test would be when they got the input from the community. They only printed a limited number and within a week it was sold out. The company received numerous calls both to praise the magazine and to order future publications.

Since it was to be a monthly publication, the celebration was short-lived. It was time to start all over again. The second issue came together easier than the first, as everyone had a better understanding of what John had envisioned. Jessica continued to read over the articles and check the layouts, but her input became less and less needed.

By the third publication, Jessica asked John if she could write some articles herself. He agreed.

"Don't get too bogged down, though, in case I need you. We're considering going national in three more months, and that will mean taking on several more writers and increasing our advertisement base. I'll need your help then."

Jessica was comfortable in her job and liked the people with whom she worked. She started to socialize with some of them. Often after work they would stop by a pub for a glass of wine and a bite to eat. She went shopping or to an occasional movie with some of the other ladies. She had been asked on a couple of dates but turned them down. She didn't want to mix her love life with her work life.

John and Jessica worked well together. They would spend hours going over articles and debating the merits of one versus another, but it was never an argument. It was one trying to convince the other of their point of view.

It was a Friday afternoon in January when John first asked Jessica to dinner. She would have turned him down, but then he said, "I want to finish going over this last article for Monday's issue and I'm starving. How about it?"

"I guess that would be okay. Just let me run back to my office and get my coat and purse."

They rode the elevator down to the basement of the building and he helped her into his car.

"Is there any special place you like to eat?"

"I haven't eaten out often enough here to have a special place."

"I get to pick then. I guess I'll have to do something about you not getting out very often. Have you taken the time to see any of our museums or art galleries?"

"I'm afraid not. I try to get to the gym near my apartment at least three times a week and have gone to a few movies but that's about it."

"I need to start doing that, going to a gym I mean. Which gym do you use?"

"I only live a few blocks from here so I use the one on 23rd Street. It's called The Better Health Gym. Not real imaginative, but it has everything I need."

He drove them to a little Italian restaurant near the office. As they entered, the maitre d' greeted John and asked if he wanted his usual table.

"Your own private dinner place?" she asked.

"It's close, the food is good. I cook, but not that well."

"I'm not a bad cook, but cooking for one and eating alone isn't much fun. It's usually a salad or a bowl of canned soup for me. This should be a treat."

"I'll make you a deal. I'll provide the company if you'll do the cooking. I'll even do the dishes. You do have a dishwasher, don't you?"

Jessie laughed. "I do not. You'll have to wash them all by hand."

John pouted and said, "I don't want dishpan hands, but I guess I'll suffer through. When do you want me to come? Tomorrow night?" he asked hopefully.

Without thinking she said, "Sure. Why not."

They had a leisurely dinner. He asked about her family and learned that she had two older brothers. Her parents had been forty and forty-four when she was born.

"I was a surprise to them. I'm sure I was the reason they didn't get to retire young, but they've been retired for several years now. Since I moved, they've decided to sell their house and are moving to Scottsdale, Arizona. My dad wants to play golf and they want to be where it's always warm. I'm glad I moved. I didn't realize they were staying there because of me. What about you? Is there just your brother and your mother?"

"They're it, except for my brother's wife Jill. I don't have a father anymore. My mother's grandfather started the business and left it to my mother when he died. Her parents have their own investment company. My mother was Ann Howard before she married. She's worked a lot of years to keep the business going and will probably retire soon. I wish she would do something fun and relaxing for herself."

Jessica wanted to ask him when his father had died, but decided he would have offered more of an explanation if he had wanted to tell her, so she didn't ask.

They continued to talk and learn more about each other. A friend of John's came in and waved as he was seated. John told Jessica that he had gone to college with the man, Brad.

"He's a lawyer here in Boston now."

The lady with him was the model type, slim with long legs and long straight silver-blond hair.

"Is that his wife?" she asked.

"No. He's not married, and the lady with him is Sophia. She does modeling for a local advertising agency."

"Oh. Is that where you know her from?"

John flushed a little and said, "No. I used to date her. We broke up over a year ago. I guess Brad is probably more her type."

Jessie wondered if he still felt something for her, but that was another question she wouldn't ask.

After they finished the meal they realized they hadn't even looked at the article.

"We can go over it tomorrow night at your place," John said.

"I guess so. Do you have something special you like?"

"Anything home cooked is fine with me. The only thing I don't like is Spam."

"Okay, I promise not to make fried Spam," Jessie said with a laugh.

As they left the restaurant, Brad called to John, "Hey, aren't you going to say hello, and introduce us to your friend?"

Reluctantly John took Jessica's arm and steered her over to their table.

"Hi Brad…Sophia. This is Jessica Braxton. She works with me at the office."

Both acknowledged Jessica with a nod. Jessie said, "Hello. It's nice to meet you both. This is such a lovely little restaurant, isn't it?"

Sophia just smiled but Brad commented, "You're coming up in the world, John. She not only looks good, she talks, too."

Sophia punched Brad in the arm and then giggled and said, "Oh Brad, darling, I can talk."

Brad just rolled his eyes and patted her hand.

"We have to be going. It was nice to see you both."

John turned and led Jessica away. He was mumbling to himself but Jessie heard him say, "I wonder what I ever saw in her?"

For some reason that made Jessie feel happy.

Jessie hadn't accepted a date with any of her co-workers because she didn't want to mix business with pleasure, and here she was cooking dinner for her boss. As she seasoned the pot roast, she was still shaking her head over how it had happened. At least she didn't have to eat alone and John was excellent company.

Since it was her home she decided she could be casual, so she wore a pair of slacks and a loose-fitting scooped-neck top. She checked her makeup and fastened some earrings in her ears. A quick brush through her hair and she was ready. He said he would come around six.

Glancing at the clock, and seeing that it was close to six, she decided to put the bread in the oven to warm. Everything was ready.

The doorbell rang. She answered it promptly. He was dressed in a pair of slacks and a sweater. He had removed his coat while coming down the corridor. It had begun to snow and there were still snowflakes clinging to it.

"Here, let me take that for you. I'll just hang it here on the coat rack. Didn't you wear a hat? It's cold out there and you have snowflakes in your hair."

"I don't ever wear a hat and it's not snowing very much. Something sure smells good."

"Don't think you'll get out of doing the dishes by complimenting the cook. I even saved the pots and pans for you."

John laughed and said, "Okay, but it was worth a try. I'm starving. I haven't eaten all day in anticipation of this meal. Is it ready?"

"Yes, it's ready. Come on in and have a seat. I'll dish it up and we can eat."

"I'll help. That way I can sneak a taste before we sit down."

He followed her into the kitchen. The kitchen was small and they found themselves bumping into each other at every turn.

"This kind of reminds me of the day we met," John commented.

He didn't mind that he had to touch her at every turn. In fact, he started to exaggerate his movements just so he could come into closer contact with her. She finally caught on and shooed him out of her kitchen.

He pouted and said, "I was just having a little fun."

"Don't give me those little puppy dog eyes. You sit there until the food is on the table."

The meal was quiet and relaxing. The conversation was interesting and easy. They both felt comfortable. Time seemed to fly by. After the meal was completed John stacked the dishes and carried them into the kitchen. She heard the water start to run and then stuck her head through the doorway.

"It's a lot easier if you just stick them in that dishwasher to the right."

John glanced down to where she was pointing. There sat the dishwasher.

"You little imp. I thought you said you didn't have one."

"I thought you couldn't miss it when you were in here 'helping' me."

"My mind got distracted with other more interesting things," he said in a suggestive tone, giving her a wicked look from her head down to her toes. Jessica blushed.

"I'm sorry I told you it was there," she said in a haughty voice.

John just laughed and asked if she wanted to come help him.

She shook her head no and said, "I don't think I'd be safe."

After John got the dishes in the dishwasher, they settled in the living room and finally got around to looking over the article. After a lengthy discussion they came to an agreement.

John walked over to her bookcase and looked at the pictures of her family. He asked her who was who and commented on how young and attractive her parents still looked.

He was saying that he supposed it was time for him to leave when

Jessica looked out the window and saw the snow coming down so thick you couldn't see the streetlights below.

"Oh, John, it looks terrible outside. We better turn on the television or the radio and see what's happening before you try to drive in that."

The local television channel was giving warnings about the blizzard-like conditions outside. The radio was more specific in its appraisals, saying all the side streets were closed and even the main roads were being used only for emergency vehicles. They asked that people stay where they were and only go out if absolutely necessary.

John said, "Well, I guess you're stuck with me for the night. Do you have a guest bedroom or is the couch going to be my bed?"

"Sorry, only one bedroom. I'll get you a blanket and a pillow."

"I'm not tired yet. How about you?"

When she shook her head he suggested that they pop some popcorn and watch television.

"I'll go get the popcorn made and you pick out something to watch."

They settled on the couch with the bowl between them and blankets over their laps. He had found an old John Wayne movie that they had both seen before, so talking filled most of the time.

Another hour had slipped by and Jessica yawned, "I think I'm going to call it a night."

She had no sooner gotten the words out when they heard a terrible crash from outside. Both sprang to their feet and ran to the window. A car must have hit the street light on the corner. The snow was coming down so heavy that you could only see what appeared to be headlights. John was already grabbing his coat.

"You call 911 and stay in here so you don't freeze."

He disappeared out the door. Jessica ran to kitchen and picked up the phone. It was dead. She knew that John had a cell phone, but she didn't know if he had brought it with him or not. She went into her bedroom and got her coat and hat. She pulled the hat over her head and went out the door. When she got to the street she realized that the snow was coming down so heavy that she wasn't sure where to go.

She called out, "John, can you hear me?"

"Yes, I can hear you. What are you doing down here? I told you to stay inside."

She was following his voice and walked into the car.

"The phone is dead. Do you have your cell phone with you?"

"No, I left it at home. I don't think anyone is hurt bad, but we need to get them out of the cold. Ma'am," he said to the driver, "let me help you get out of the car. Are you hurt anywhere?"

The driver seemed to focus and assured them that she was all right, but she was concerned for her two children in the back seat. Jessie opened up the back car door and saw a little boy about four strapped into one of the seats and a car seat with an infant in the other. They both looked fine.

"They're okay. Let's just get you unbuckled and up to my apartment before we all freeze."

She took the hand of the little boy and helped him out. His mother was already standing outside the car and pulled him close. Jessie then reached in and lifted out the baby.

"Do you have a diaper bag with you for the baby? We'll need to bring it with us."

"It's on the front seat."

John reached across and picked it up.

"All right—Jessie, you keep hold of the baby, and you hold on to your little boy. Everyone stay together and we'll be inside before we know it. I'll lead the way." He turned to the lady and said, "You hold onto my coat, and Jessie, you hold onto her."

They trooped slowly towards the apartment and were relieved when they got back inside.

Once all were warm again, they asked the woman her name. It was Molly and her little boy was Tommy. The little baby was a girl. She was Rebecca. Once they were safe Molly started to cry.

"I was so scared while I was driving. We were coming back from a visit with my mother and I didn't realize how bad it was until we were in the middle of the storm. I didn't know what to do and then I saw the post coming at me. I think I panicked and hit the gas instead of the brake. Thank you so much for coming and getting us. I don't know how I can ever repay you."

She was sitting on the couch with her son tucked under one arm and her baby in her other arm.

"You don't have to repay us. Do you have a husband at home who is going to be worried about you?" Jessie asked.

"He should be at work now. He works the night shift at the factory, but I don't know if he got there before the storm started or not. I need to call him."

"The phone isn't working. I wonder if someone else in the building might have a cell phone." Looking at John she said, "Do you think I should go pound on some doors and find out?"

"I'll do it. It's getting kind of late, but if I see any lights on I'll ask." About ten minutes later he came back.

"The lady down the hall has one you can use, but you'll have to go there to use it. I think she's afraid I'll steal her phone."

Jessica held out her hands.

"Here, I'll hold Rebecca and you go call your husband. Tommy can stay here with me."

After John and Molly left, Jessie sat on the couch cuddling the baby and talking softly to Tommy.

"Do you like your little sister?"

He shrugged his shoulders and said, "She's okay, but I wanted a brother. When she gets bigger I can play with her, but not yet 'cause she's too little now."

Jessica savored the feel of the warm body in her hands as well as the one curled into her side.

This feels so good, she thought. Her mind drifted to another little boy and she wondered where he was and if he was safe and warm.

Molly's husband was at home and happy to hear from her. She had their only car, so John said he would take them home once the roads were cleared and the storm had stopped.

Jessie insisted that Molly and the children take her room for the night. They fixed up a large cardboard box she still had from her move to act as a crib for the baby, and Molly and Tommy shared her bed.

After they got everyone settled, John and Jessie cuddled up beside each other on the couch. Jessie laid her head on John's shoulder and tucked her feet up on the couch. She fell asleep in that position, but John gradually stretched out and pulled her close to his side. He kept her head on his chest and put the pillow under his own. Then he tucked the blanket around them and fell asleep.

Jessie came awake slowly. She felt something warm beside her and tried to cuddle even closer. Her hand moved and she felt a hard male chest. She could feel the hardness even through the sweater that covered it. She opened her eyes and looked up into the smiling face of John.

"Oh my," was all her lips were capable of forming.

John had slept very little. The feel of Jessie next to him was almost torture, but one he didn't mind enduring. In her sleep she kept cuddling tighter and tighter against him. She was looking up at him now and he couldn't stop himself, he lowered his head and kissed her. She uttered a little sigh and relaxed into the kiss. It only lasted a few moments before warning bells sounded in her head and she struggled to a sitting position. She shoved at him to move but he didn't, so she shoved harder and he fell off the side of the couch.

"What was that for?" he said in confusion.

She just gave him an exasperated look and climbed over him.

Looking out the window she announced, "The snow has stopped. Everything looks so peaceful and calm now. Come see, John."

He climbed to his feet and went to stand beside her. The ground was a blanket of white and the tree branches hung low with snow and ice clinging to them.

It really is a beautiful sight, but much prettier because I'm seeing it with you, he thought.

They were able to get Molly and her family home around ten that morning. A tow truck would pick up the car later in the day. John checked the car and didn't think the damage was too severe, which was a relief to Molly and her husband.

Chapter 17

By Monday morning the roads were all passable and the city had returned to normal. Ann stood at her window looking down at the traffic and the miniature people moving about. She was only fifty-two and didn't know what she wanted to do with the rest of her life.

Her sons were grown men and didn't need her looking over their shoulders. She should sign over the rest of the company to them, but then what would she do?

Most women her age had a husband with whom they could travel or go to the movies or out to dinner. She had not dated anyone since her divorce. Most people didn't even know she was divorced. She had continued to wear her wedding ring and no one ever asked. The divorce papers had come in the mail ten years after her husband left, and she had signed them and put that part of her life to rest.

She had always wanted grandchildren, but John wasn't married and Patrick and his wife, Jill, had been married for eight years and had no children. She didn't know if that was by choice or not. She hoped John would find someone soon, since she knew how lonely life could be. She had thought that Jessica might be the one, but as far as she knew they only had a work relationship.

Thinking of Jessica, she decided that maybe she would ask her to have lunch some time. She seemed to have good insight and the ability to look at things in a critical manner. She knew if she talked to her sons about her future they would want her to retire and play. She wanted something more.

She stepped back to her desk and picked up the phone.

"Would you connect me to Jessica Braxton's extension please?"

Jessica answered on the second ring. She was surprised to hear Mrs. Kilroy on the line.

"Lunch today? Yes, that would be fine. Where do you want to meet?"

They met in the lobby and walked a block to a small café. The place was bustling with lunchtime customers, but they were able to find a small table for two. The waitress took their orders and brought them each a cup of coffee.

"How have you been, Jessica? I haven't had much of an opportunity to speak with you."

"I'm doing well and am so happy that the magazine seems to be off to a good start. Have you seen the latest copy?"

"It's on my desk but I haven't looked through it yet. John said that you're writing some yourself now. That's really what you like to do, isn't it?"

"Yes, that's my real love. Researching and getting to know what motivates the people involved in a story is like viewing a new masterpiece every day. What about you? Do you like your work?"

Ann looked down at the cup of coffee she held and thought about her answer. Glancing back up at Jessica she said, "I have been doing this for a long time, and now I think it's time for me to move on. I know I'm good at organizing things and keeping the business running, but my sons can do that now. I want to find something else to spend my time on, I just don't know what."

"What do you like?"

"That's just it, I'm not sure. I like children, and creating things, and music and laughter. Those are pretty broad things to try to base a new career on. I have plenty of money, so I don't need a job but I need something to do."

Jessica studied her for a moment and then said, "Are you asking me what you should do?"

Ann laughed, "I guess I am."

"I'm flattered but I need a little time to think. Let's see, you like kids and music and laughter and want to create. My first thought is that those are the qualities of a good mother, but you already are that. Do you just like to listen to music or are you talented in that area?"

"I play the piano quite well and have a fair voice. Do you have something in mind?"

"This is only a thought, but on one of the stories I investigated I met a group of community leaders who were concerned about the children and teenagers in their area of the city. These are considered underprivileged children. They need someone to work with the kids to help build their self-confidence and teach them to participate in wholesome group activities. You're good at organizing and leading, so maybe you could start a theater group for young children and teens. That would include what you like, too."

Ann's face was wreathed in a joyous smile.

"That sounds like hard work but so much fun. Do you have the name of someone in the area that I could contact to look into the possibilities?"

"I talked to several people, but there was one man who seemed to be in charge. I think his name was Robert Grayson. I'm sure I have his telephone number back at the office. I can get it for you."

"That would be great. If you see John, don't say anything to him about this. I want to look into it and see what I think before I make any final decisions."

They spent the rest of lunch making small talk, and it wasn't until they were leaving that something was said about the past weekend's storm and Jessica told Ann about the car accident outside her apartment.

When Ann returned to her office she was smiling. She was excited about the possibility of getting involved in a theater group, but also because John had been with Jessica outside of work.

Maybe both of us will have a new beginning, she thought.

That afternoon Ann called Robert Grayson. They agreed to meet at a restaurant for lunch the next day. It was that evening that Ann took off her wedding ring.

If I'm going to start a new phase in my life I think I will start it as who I really am, she thought.

The next day Ann walked into the restaurant and gave the waiter her name. He led her to a table where a man sat sipping a cup of tea. He had a full head of gray hair and when he looked up she noticed his gray eyes. He appeared to be in his fifties and when he stood to greet her she realized he was a least six feet tall.

Robert stood. A very attractive woman had approached his table.

"Mrs. Kilroy? I'm so pleased to meet you. Please have a seat." He held the chair for her as she sat and then moved back to his own. "I must say I was surprised to receive your phone call."

"I got your name and telephone number from Jessica Braxton. She met you when she was researching a story for one of our magazines."

A look of comprehension crossed his face.

"That's where I know your name from. You're the Mrs. Kilroy from the Howard Publishing Company. I read your news magazine and like the new one that just came out. What can I do for you?"

"Why don't we order and I'll try to explain."

After the food was ordered, Ann told him what she wanted to do. Robert was surprised and a bit unsure.

"Have you ever done anything like this before? These are good kids, but a lot of them have either been neglected or have had very little discipline in their lives. Their parents are either working all the time or are absent from the home for other reasons. These aren't kids from your typical middle- and upper-income families. They can be tough and hard to manage and you appear to be a bit on the soft side."

That last comment had Ann straightening to a position of stiff irritation and her eyes shot daggers across the table.

"Mr. Grayson, I had two children by the time I was twenty-one and by the time I turned twenty-six my husband was gone and I became the sole owner and president of Howard Publishing Company. I am not looking for a place to invest a little money and an hour a week to fill an altruistic whim. I am looking for something to sink my teeth into and a way to make a difference."

Robert was impressed. Maybe he had misjudged her. She looked feminine and soft, but her eyes spoke of courage and strength. He was going to like getting to know her.

"In that case, let's take a tour of the area after lunch and let you see what you may be getting yourself into."

They drove slowly through the streets of the neighborhood. The houses, for the most part, were in need of repair and children were playing in the streets with no supervision. Ann was touched by what she saw.

"Are there any buildings near here that could be used as a theater and practice hall?"

"I haven't changed your mind?" Robert asked.

She glared at him.

"Okay. There is an old school gymnasium one block over. I don't know who owns it, and it would take a lot of work to make it useable, but we can drive by and see what you think."

"Let's go."

They parked on the street in front of the building. They walked around as much of it as they could. Part of it had a tumbled down metal fence around it and all kinds of refuge had been dumped behind it.

"I'll have to get someone to come look at it and see if it's worth fixing or if it would be cheaper to just tear it down. I wonder if the city owns it or if it belongs to the school district. This is a good location though, since the kids could easily walk here. Don't you agree?"

"It is a good location. Are you sure you want to try this? You could get the place all fixed up and the kids still might not come."

"Why are you being so negative? I thought you wanted activities for the kids in this neighborhood."

"I do. I just don't want you to have any misconceptions. You aren't from this area or this background, and people don't always do what we want. I don't want to see you disappointed."

"If I'm disappointed that will be my own problem. I've had disappointments in my life before. Just because you are born into a family with money doesn't mean life always goes your way."

"No, but money helps."

"Sometimes."

Chapter 18

The moon shone on the white snow, giving light to the night. Jessica lay in her bed wiping a tear from her cheek. She didn't cry very often anymore, but sometimes something would trigger her emotions and the tears would start. She had met a young teenage girl today who reminded her of herself back when she was fifteen. Thinking about her had brought memories flooding back.

Jessica was content with her past and had only occasional doubts about the decision she had made, but the hurt and loneliness never went completely away. She prayed every day for her little boy. She just hoped the girl she had met today didn't make the same mistakes she had.

Jessie could recall how alone she had felt when she was a teenager. Her brothers were already grown and out on their own. Her parents were very loving and tried to help her through those rough teenage years. She had thought she was all grown up, though, and knew more than her mother and father. They were so old-fashioned in her mind and didn't understand how much she loved her boyfriend. They tried to keep her from seeing him, but she always found a way around their rules. He was only a year older than her and didn't have any more sense than she did.

Now she could look back at that time and understand that he had walked away from her and the pregnancy because he was afraid and scared just like she was. He was really only a child himself.

It had taken her a long time to come to this point in her mind. She was no longer ashamed and she hoped she had made the best decision for her child. Now she wanted to find someone to share her life with and have a family of her own.

John Kilroy came to mind when she thought of the future. Could they bring each other happiness? He was such a kind-hearted man. He treated his employees with respect and was willing to help others. She liked the way he laughed and the way he looked.

"I promised myself not to get involved in a work relationship though, and here I am thinking about the boss," she said to herself.

The boss, John, was lying in his bed thinking about Jessica. "Jessica" fit her at work, but in her apartment "Jessie" seemed to fit her better. He could remember her chasing him out of the kitchen when his hands and body became a little too obvious, and then that kiss. It was short, but it had surprised him in the thundering emotions it had provoked.

He liked her quick mind and generous attitude. He especially liked her rounded hips and the fact that the calves of her legs actually had a curve. Her lips were full and her eyes gave away all her emotions.

Next weekend he would take her out somewhere nice and show her some of the sights of the city. He wanted a serious relationship. He was tired of playing the field. A wife and children sounded awfully good to him. Maybe Jessie was the one for him.

John started a serious courtship of Jessica that week. He took her to dinner at a new restaurant called Grill 23 on Friday night. The steaks were especially good and they ended the meal with one of the establishment's special desserts. On the way home they stopped at a small dance club, had a glass of wine and danced their first dance together.

On Saturday they wandered through the little shops in one of the tourist areas. The air was cold but there was no snow. They ate at a tiny café that was decorated as an old English tavern, warming themselves by the fire in the open hearth. He asked if she had ever ice-skated and she said no. They made plans for him to teach her the next weekend.

On Sunday they spent the afternoon at his apartment. He had a fireplace and had a roaring blaze burning in it. They both had work to finish for Monday, so the day was quiet as they worked in companionable silence. Jessie cooked dinner and John did the dishes.

For the next month they continued to do things together on the weekends. It was during the month of February that the decision to take the magazine national was made. The first edition was planned for June.

It was Patrick who hosted the celebration dinner. John asked Jessie to go with him. Their mother Ann was there and she brought Robert Grayson with her. It was the first time the men had ever seen their mother with a date. They were surprised, but hid it well.

Ann hadn't told them of her new venture and introduced Robert as a friend. She was spending less and less time at the office, but everyone was so busy they hardly noticed. Robert was a high school principal at one of Boston's inner-city schools. He was easy to talk to and blended well with the group.

Jessica hadn't met Jill before and found her to be pleasant and a bit shy. She took great pains to be friendly with her and by the end of the day they had established a tentative bond. Jessica asked her to join her for lunch sometime so they could get to know each other better. They agreed to meet on Wednesday at the little café near work.

Glasses of champagne were passed around and Patrick made the toast, "To my little brother and his great vision, and to Jessica, who helped him bring it to life. May we sell many copies!"

Everyone cheered and drank to John. Jessica was pleased that Patrick seemed genuinely happy with the success of the magazine. He had been the doomsayer at the start, but was quick to change his opinion.

She had a chance to talk with him privately and asked him what he really thought about the magazine.

"I think it is very good. I may not always agree with my brother, but I love him. I take a certain pride in watching him succeed. We didn't have a father around when we grew up, and I always felt like I had to play that role at times for John. Now I can feel the pride of a father, too. You're good for him as well. I hope things work out for you both. You do care for him, don't you?"

"Yes, I care a great deal."

On Wednesday, Jill and Jessica met for lunch. Jill was much more outgoing with only Jessica present. The more Jill relaxed the more she shared. She told Jessie that her mother-in-law and brother-in-law made her nervous.

"They're such strong and commanding people. I feel inadequate around them."

"Oh, I'm sorry you feel that way, but they really are just ordinary people who have a lot of responsibility."

"That's what Patrick tells me, but it doesn't help."

"Maybe you should think of a situation where they would look silly or not be in control, and then when you get nervous around them you could just picture them that way and it would make things easier."

"What kind of situation?" she asked puzzled.

"I don't know. Something totally out of character for them."

Jill got a smile on her face. "Like John trying to walk in high heels or carrying a purse? And Ann," she hesitated, "I can't think of anything for Ann."

Jessica had the feeling that Jill had thought of something for Ann but was either too shy or too embarrassed to say it.

"I'm sure you'll think of something. Next time you're with them try it and see if it works."

Jessie was feeling pretty relaxed in Jill's company, too, and asked her about John.

"Has he had a lot of girlfriends?"

"He's dated several women, and I think he was serious about a couple of them, but they didn't last."

"Why do you think he was serious about a couple of them? Was he engaged?"

"No. He lived with one girl right after he got out of college, but then she got a job in California and left. He moved in with another lady about two years ago, but that only lasted about two months. None of us know for sure what happened. He just said he had made a big mistake. He never brought her to any family gatherings, so I don't know her."

"I'm sorry. I shouldn't be asking you for information. If I want to know something I should ask John."

"You do like him though, don't you?"

"Yes."

Jessica had planned on asking about Mr. Kilroy, Sr., but decided she had done enough prying for one day.

Chapter 19

It was the middle of March when John asked Jessica to go to New York with him for a few days. He asked her at work and made it a business arrangement, so she said yes.

He had several meetings set up with various companies that he hoped would advertise in his new magazine. He also wanted Jessica to check out a high-profile legislative battle that was going on over a new proposed state tax on services, excluding medical, dental and legal. The whole country was watching to see what the outcome would be.

Jessica went to a couple of the meetings with John, but on the second day she excused herself to go sit in on the meeting of the legislature to get a better handle on what they were proposing and why. She hoped to get interviews with some of the legislators themselves.

At lunchtime she made her way to a coffee shop a few blocks from the state house. She listened to the conversations around her and heard many opinions on the new tax proposal, mostly negative.

Being an unknown reporter, her attempts at getting an interview with the legislators failed. She decided to go to some other area of the city and see what the common people were thinking. She took a cab and handed the driver an address of a restaurant she had picked out of the phone book.

As she rode along in the back seat she noticed the clean, well-kept properties gradually changing into older and more dilapidated buildings. Maybe she had made a mistake. She didn't know New York at all and this was probably the wrong way to see it.

She asked the cab driver how much further, but he just nodded and said in broken English, "I get you there," and pointed to the paper she had handed him with the address on it.

When the cab finally stopped it wasn't as bad as she had imagined. It would probably be considered a lower-middle-class neighborhood. She walked into the restaurant and found a table. The waitress wore a pair of slacks and T-shirt with an apron tied around her waist.

"What can I get you, honey?" she asked.

"Just a hamburger and a cup of coffee."

She looked about the dimly lit room. At one table sat a couple probably in their sixties, at another was a woman with a boy about ten and a little girl around six. The table nearest her had two men talking about last night's basketball game. She wondered whom she might approach about the tax proposal. Then she wondered if these people had even heard about it and, if they had, if they had any idea what it could mean to them.

She had decided to ask the sixty-year-old couple first and was just standing to walk over to them when the door burst open. Two young men around fifteen or sixteen years old came rushing through the door. They both had guns in their hands. They had some kind of scarves around their heads and matching coats with a snake on the sleeve. Other symbols were plastered all over the jackets.

They ordered everyone to the center of the room, shoving tables and chairs back. They had everyone sit down in a close circle. One of the boys told the waitress to call the police.

"Call the police?" she asked.

"Yes, we want to talk to them."

The waitress dialed the number. One of the guys grabbed the phone and started talking.

"We want our pals you busted last night brought down here to us, and a car and some money."

There was a pause as the boy listened to the voice on the other end.

"Jake and Henry Stanz and Bobby Jefferys. We want $50,000 in cash, too. There are people here, and someone's gonna get hurt real bad if you don't do what we say."

He slammed the phone down then and looked to his partner.

"I'm sure the cops will be here real soon, so stay close to the people. They won't shoot us if we're near the people."

Sirens could be heard wailing in the background. The mother of the two children was pulling them close to her side. Jessica was scared. Reporting on stories like this was one thing, but being part of the story was another. She was finding a whole new respect for the survivors of trauma and crime.

The phone rang, startling everyone, even the two criminals. The one that appeared to be in charge grabbed the receiver.

"Yeah?" he said, and then listened. "What do you mean you can't just give us our buddies? You're the cops. You locked them up and you can let them out. Do it soon."

He slammed the receiver down once again. He looked at the people sitting on the floor.

"I sure hope they change their minds, or else somebody's going to be real sorry."

The little girl began to cry. Her mother tried to comfort her, but she wouldn't stop. The one in charge grabbed the girl and shook her.

"Stop that noise or you'll make me real mad."

The girl sniffed but stopped crying. Her brother sat staring daggers at the teenager who had touched his sister.

There were all kinds of noises coming from outside the restaurant. No one knew exactly what was going on. The uncertainty of the situation was the worst part. Even the criminals became more restless as the minutes ticked by. The phone rang again.

"Give ourselves up? Are you crazy? We want our pals, a car and some money."

The person on the other end was talking and the teenager was listening.

"No, we haven't hurt anyone yet. Hey, Sam, they say to give ourselves up and they'll go easy on us. They don't understand that we don't got nothing to lose. You better do something real soon or these people aren't going to walk out of here alive. Get us the car and the money and we'll see."

The phone was again hung up. Jessica could see that they were getting desperate. She was worried about what they would do next. One of the teenagers kept rubbing his hands through his hair and rocking back and forth on his heels.

"Maybe we should show them we mean business," the one called Sam said.

The one in charge looked over the group of people and then

reached down and grabbed the little boy. He pulled him to his feet and put the gun to his head.

"You were looking so bad there a few minutes ago, but not so brave now, are ya?"

His mother started to cry, telling him to let her son go. Jessica couldn't take it any longer. She got to her feet and said, "Use me instead."

About that time the elderly man started to moan and hold his chest. He had turned pale and slumped against his wife.

"I think my husband is having a heart attack. Somebody do something," his wife cried.

Sam spoke up, "Jesus! What do we do now?"

The other young man just shrugged his shoulders. "If he dies it's not our fault."

"The police won't see it that way. They'll say it's your fault because you didn't get him help. Maybe you should let most of the people go and just keep one of us," one of the men in the group said.

"Maybe we should think about this," Sam whispered.

The other teenager still had a hold of the young boy, but shoved him back down and pushed his hands through his hair.

"I just wish they would get here with a car and some money and we could get out of here."

Another of the group spoke up and said, "I don't think you would get very far. The cops aren't going to let you just drive away and do nothing. Why don't you just give yourselves up before you get into more trouble?"

He waved the gun in the faces of those on the floor.

"I'm not gonna let them just take me to the clink and get nothin' out of this."

By this time the wife of the sick man was crying and begging them to let her take her husband out to get help. The little girl had started to cry again, too. The situation was getting tense, and then the phone rang again. Everyone jumped at the sound.

"Let it ring. I gotta think for a minute. Everybody just shut up," the teen ordered.

He was looking over the group of people and once again zeroed in on the boy. Jessica was afraid he was going to use him, so she spoke up again.

"I'm a reporter for an important magazine. Why don't you just use me for your hostage and let the rest go?"

The teenager let the boy go and walked over to Jessica.

"You really a reporter like you said?"

She reached into her purse and pulled out the pass she had used that morning to get into the legislative hearings. It said, "Jessica Braxton, Reporter," and had her picture on it.

"Yes, I'm Jessica Braxton. Why don't you let the rest of these people go?"

"What do you think, Sam? We got ourselves a real reporter. If we let them take that guy out," he said pointing to the older man who was sick, "they can't blame us if he dies."

"It's all right with me, long as we still got a hostage," Sam replied.

"Okay, you guys get him out of here and the rest of you go, too. You come over here," he said to Jessica and waved his gun at her.

Jessica walked over to where he stood. After everyone else was out she tried to calm herself and then started to talk to the two teens.

"You know they aren't going to let you just walk out of here. This was a pretty dumb thing to do. I bet you both have a mom who is worried sick about you."

"My ma don't care nothin' about me, but Sam's mom might be. He's got an okay mom. She don't hit him or nothin'. His dad's real mean though, huh Sam?"

"He's just mean when he's drinkin'. Kinda like your ma," Sam added.

"If they aren't going to let your friends go what are you going to do and where will you go?"

"I don't know. We thought Henry could drive and we could go to Canada or some place."

"I got an idea. Maybe I can write a story for our next issue. You can tell me all about what rotten deals you've had and I can get it printed so everyone in the country can read about it. That won't get you out of this, but at least everyone will know why you did it and maybe even make you famous. What do you think?"

Both of the teenagers looked at each other and then Sam shrugged his shoulders and said, "It's okay with me. We ain't hurt nobody, so they won't keep us locked up long. I'd kinda like to see my name in print."

"Yeah, that would be bitchin'. I'll call the cops and tell them to give us a little more time or we'll kill her. That should keep 'em out of here for a while."

After he made the phone call he said, "Okay lady, you get this all down and then you make sure it's in that magazine."

Jessica felt a wave of relief. Finding some paper and getting a pen from her purse she said, "Okay, let's get started."

It took them two hours before they were sure they had told Jessie everything they wanted her to know. She assured them again that their story would appear in the magazine, and they all walked out of the restaurant together. The boys were quickly handcuffed and hauled away.

A crowd had gathered and all cheered when Jessica walked out. Then she heard a roaring bellow.

"Jessica Braxton, you scared me half to death."

The crowd seemed to part under his forceful advance and a little quiver of fear went through her. Then she saw him and went running into his arms. It felt so good to be safe and secure in his embrace. Her whole body began to shake and she began to cry.

"I was so scared. I was afraid they were going to shoot that little boy. Oh John, just hold me tight. I need you."

"Hush, Jessie, it's okay. I'm so relieved that you're all right. I was so afraid, too. I couldn't believe it when I heard your name on the television. They had been reporting on this standoff and then the next minute I hear everyone's been let go except one reporter by the name of Jessica Braxton. My heart stopped. I got down here as fast as I could."

He stood holding her for several minutes. Then the news people started to put microphones in her face and started to ask questions. John shoved them aside and took her to the cab he had come in.

"Get us out of here," he told the driver. "Take us back to our hotel."

He sat holding Jessie close and smoothing his hands up and down her back, trying to rub some of the fear away. When they got to the hotel, John went to Jessie's room with her.

"You go in and take a nice hot bath. I'm going to sit right here and wait for you. The hot water will calm you down and make you feel better. When you come out we'll talk."

While Jessie was in the bathroom, John sat trying to calm himself.

He couldn't remember ever being so afraid. He wondered what he would do if something happened to her. He realized that she had become an important part of his life.

Is this how love feels, he wondered? *It just sneaks up on you and suddenly you can't imagine your life without the other person in it.*

He was sure he had never felt this way before.

Jessie came out of the bathroom all bundled up in her long terry cloth robe. She looked all pink and soft and sexy. John watched her to see if she was still dazed from her experience, but she seemed to be back in control.

"Do you mind telling me what the hell you were doing down in that part of town in the first place?" he almost yelled.

He was still scared and it came out as anger. Jessie understood that he was just worried about her, so she didn't get mad at his bellowing.

"I was hunting for a story. I didn't realize I was heading into a bad part of the city, and no one knew this was going to happen."

"What story could you have possibly been after down there?"

"I just wanted to see what ordinary people thought about the proposed tax bill. I tried to tell the cab driver to turn around when I saw the area wasn't the best, but he didn't understand English very well, and then when I actually got to the restaurant it didn't look too terrible. It really wasn't a bad little place."

"You went to a part of town you knew nothing about to try to follow some harebrained idea you had for getting a story?"

Now he was making her mad.

"It wasn't a harebrained idea. It was a good idea and still is. I just should have checked with someone before I picked out an address from the phone book."

"You what? You just randomly picked an address out of the phone book? Do you know how bad some parts of this city are? I just can't believe you did that."

Jessica knew she was in the wrong but she hated to back down. She finally got out, "I'm sorry; I'm usually not so reckless."

"Oh Jessie, I'm sorry I've been yelling, but you scared me half to death. I just need you in my life and I don't want anything to happen to you."

He had moved up in front of her and pulled her into his arms. He lowered his head and the kiss spiraled from comforting to passionate.

They were both breathing hard when their mouths finally parted.

"I think you better say goodnight. I'll be fine now," Jessie said with a little quiver in her voice.

"Are you sure you want me to go?" John asked.

"Yes. I'll be fine now.

Chapter 20

Their first fight came about a week after they returned from New York. Jessica had written the story she promised the two teenagers in New York and brought it to John in his office.

"I want you to take a look at this and see if you think it will fit into the first national publication of the magazine."

"What story is it?" John asked without looking up from the paper he was reading.

"It's the story I promised the two boys in New York that I would write."

"You are kidding, right?"

Jessica shook her head and looked at John with a puzzled expression.

"Why would I be kidding?"

"I have no intention of printing a story about those two young men. They threatened several people's lives, including yours. Why would I want to give them even a single word in my magazine?"

"But I promised them I would get their story printed. That's the only reason they let any of us go."

"That may be. But you don't have to keep promises you made to criminals under duress."

"They were so young, and from what they told me they have had a really hard life. The gang they belong to is like their family."

"Don't give me a sob story. They knew what they were doing, and you did believe them when they threatened to shoot that little boy. Didn't you?"

"Yes, but I promised them."

"Jessica, forget that promise. I am pulling rank. It is my magazine and I told you in the beginning that if I disagreed with you I would use my own judgment. In this case you are wrong."

"You just don't understand. I made a promise and the story is good. At least read it."

"No. That's my final answer. Don't argue with me any more."

"You are being so stubborn. You make me so mad!"

With that Jessica turned and stormed out of the office. John just shook his head. Didn't she understand that those teenagers could have killed her and everyone else they were holding hostage? They may have had a bad life, but they were old enough to know right from wrong and to make choices. She would just have to get over it, because he wasn't going to change his mind.

Before Jessica left work she called Katie and asked if she could stop over for a few minutes. When she got to Katie's she told her about the story and that John had refused to put it in the magazine.

"I think you're wrong and John's right. We were all so upset when we heard what had happened. To think you want to somehow glorify them in an article is way beyond my comprehension," Katie informed Jessica.

"I don't really want to glorify them. I just feel sorry for the life they've had, and I made them a promise."

"Well, whatever the reason, you're still wrong. Maybe you could write an article on why young people join gangs and warning signs for parents. You could use some of the information they gave you and do other research but leave their names and anything to do with the hostage situation out of it."

"I guess I could try something like that. I'll have to think about it. You really think John is right?"

"Yes. By the way, are you seeing a lot of John? Is it turning into something serious?"

"Yes, and I think it could."

"I want to meet this guy. Why don't we plan an evening together? Would you like to bring him over here for dinner this Saturday? We can think of something to do after the kids go to bed, or if you want I can get a baby-sitter. What do you think?"

"Why don't I see if he's free for dinner Saturday and, if he is, I think

I would just like to stay here and give you a chance to get to know him. I'll call you tomorrow and let you know what he says."

They talked for a few more minutes and then Jessica left for home. She decided she needed to call John and let him know that she had been wrong. Maybe she would rework the information into a different article altogether like Katie suggested.

That evening when the phone rang, John was pleased to hear Jessica's voice.

"I had to call and apologize for today. You were right and I was wrong. Forgive me?"

John was relieved.

"I'm glad you understand. I would hate for those two jerks to come between us. I still shudder every time I think of them holding a gun on you. Don't ever do anything like that again; my heart couldn't take it."

"I'll try not to. I wasn't real happy myself. I didn't do it on purpose, you know."

"I know, but I just want you safe. Have you had dinner yet?"

"Yes. I'm in a pair of sweats and wrapped up in a blanket. I'm going to watch that Mel Gibson movie they're showing on HBO."

"Why don't I come over and watch it with you?"

"Are you sure you want to go out in this cold weather? I'd love the company if you want to come."

"I'll be there in a few minutes. You want me to bring anything?"

"No. I'll make us some hot chocolate and put out a plate of snacks. You just bring yourself. See you in a little bit. Bye."

They spent the evening cuddled together on the couch, watching the movie, talking and laughing, snacking and drinking hot chocolate. They even managed a few intimate moments in each other's arms. Before John left for home he agreed to go to dinner at Katie and Kaleb's on Saturday night.

Dinner at the Daltons' was a unique experience for John. He had never been around young children before. Family dinners for him consisted of only adults, and conversation often centered on the business. The twins tended to play with their food and laugh and giggle over silly things. Megan was very proper for a young girl but quite outspoken.

Conversation consisted of the kids' latest accomplishments and mishaps. It seemed the boys had discovered the cupboard where the rolls of toilet paper were stored. They had managed to string the paper throughout the hall and into several bedrooms before they were found out. While Katie was relating the tale one of the boys spoke up.

"I peeped in my potty today."

Kaleb quickly praised him, "That's very good. You keep doing that. You are such a good boy."

Megan informed everyone that she was taking piano lessons and wanted to play for them after dinner.

"She's doing so well," Katie replied.

Katie and Jessica filled each other in on the latest news from their families, and Kaleb asked John about the magazine business.

As the chatter continued, John noticed Katie and Kaleb grabbing glasses that were about to be spilled or silverware that was poised to drop on the floor. On occasion he heard "Don't play with your food," or "Sit up and eat."

John was enjoying all the talk and confusion around the table when Megan spoke to him, "Are you going to marry Jessica like Daddy married Katie?"

All conversation stopped. Jessica flushed a light shade of red. After a brief pause Katie spoke up, "Megan, you don't ask those kinds of personal questions."

Megan didn't seem to hear her and just looked at John with the question still in her eyes. John glanced up to see Kaleb watching him and waiting for the answer. John turned back to Megan.

"Jessica and I are still getting to know one another, but if we decide to get married, would that be all right with you?"

Megan smiled at him and said, "I think so. I like you."

Everyone seemed to relax after that answer, and the meal continued. After dinner Megan played two short pieces on the piano and all congratulated her on her ability. When it was time for the boys to go to bed they wanted Jessica to tuck them in. John went with her and sat listening while she told them a story to put them to sleep.

After all the children were asleep, they played some billiards and visited. The men won but the ladies were able to make them work for it.

On the way home John told Jessica how much he had enjoyed the evening. He also commented on how well she handled the children and what good parents Katie and Kaleb were. He was thinking how much he wanted a family of his own and then he remembered Megan's question about getting married. He glanced over at Jessica. She was gazing out the window at the passing city lights.

I think maybe we should talk about marriage, he thought.

Chapter 21

It was the first part of May when Ann and Robert walked out of the title company with the deed to the property held firmly in Ann's hand. She was beaming.

"I'm so excited! Now I can start repairing the building. Do you think I can get it ready to use by summer break? I would love for the children to have a place to come while they're on summer vacation."

"Since you already have a contractor who has gone over the property and knows what needs to be done, I would think he should be able to tell you how soon the work can be completed. You know I'll help you any way I can."

"I know. You've been such a big help already. I especially thank you for lining me up with the drama teacher at your high school. He'll be great when I actually get ready to work with the kids. I have a couple of other friends who are interested in helping me. One of them taught music when she was younger, and another is very talented in arts and crafts. She used to work in our layout department. Both of them are looking for something fun to do now that they're retired. I think it's time to talk to my family and let them know what I plan. I'll invite them over for dinner on Saturday. Would you like to come?"

"Sure, I'll be there. I have to get back to the school now. I'm very happy for you. You know I really admire you, don't you?"

Ann smiled and said, "You're good for me. It's nice to have a man around to keep me on my toes and to build up my ego."

Robert leaned over and gave her a quick kiss and said, "I hope to be around a lot more in the future."

"I think that would be really nice," Ann replied.

It was Friday, May 3. John took Jessica to the same little Italian restaurant they had gone to on their first evening together. They ate slowly and talked and laughed. Spring was in the air and so was love. They had continued to see a lot of each other over the past several weeks and were definitely a couple in everyone's mind.

After dinner, John took Jessie to the Isabelle Stewart Garden Museum. It was considered one of the best indoor garden museums in the world. It had an Italian motif with a four-story-high glass ceiling that brought the outside in. The garden bloomed year round. It was a very romantic place.

Its beauty amazed Jessie. She had never seen anything like it. She turned in a circle, looking up at the ceiling.

"This is unbelievable. It's like walking in the garden of paradise."

John pulled her over to a little stone bench and had her sit down. "I have something to ask you."

He cleared his throat and then sat down beside her. He lifted her hand and looked into her eyes.

"I've never done this before and I want it to be perfect. I brought you to this place for a special reason. I love you and want to spend the rest of my life with you. Will you marry me?"

Jessica was overwhelmed, thrilled and happy. Tears came to her eyes.

"Oh John, I love you, too. Yes, I'll marry you."

He was smiling and pulled out a small velvet box from his pocket. Opening the lid, he revealed a solitaire diamond mounted on a gold band. It was exquisite in its simplicity.

"It's perfect. Can I try it on?" Jessica asked.

John laughed, "You can not only try it on, but you better wear it from now on."

It fit her perfectly. They sat in the garden for a long time talking about the future and starting to make wedding plans. They were both so happy.

They decided they would tell his family at the dinner party his mother was having the following night. Jessica wanted to call Katie and Kaleb as soon as they got back to her apartment. He agreed.

Patrick and Jill lay in their bed holding hands. Both wore big smiles.

"I can't believe it. Only two more months and we'll be parents. I'm so happy," Jill gushed.

"It's hard to believe, but it's real. I'm so glad we decided to adopt. I know we both wanted our own flesh and blood, but maybe this is God's way of making sure that little baby we are getting gets a good home. I will always be grateful to the mother for making this decision. It must be hard for her, but she is so young and it wouldn't be fair to the baby for her to keep it. We are so blessed to be getting him or her."

"Two months, I can hardly wait. I need to decorate the room across the hall, make it a nursery. Patrick, do you want to go looking in the shops tomorrow with me to get some ideas?"

"I'd love to. Don't forget we have to go to Mother's for dinner tomorrow night. Do you want to tell them all when we are there?"

"Oh, yes. I think that's a good idea. Do you think they'll be happy for us?"

"Of course they will. I know Mother has wanted grandchildren for a long time. Maybe she'll think about retiring now." Patrick turned to Jill and pulled her close. "Have I told you lately how much I love you and how happy you make me?"

"All the time, but I love hearing it anyway. I love you, too, Patrick."

They kissed and shut off the lights.

Robert was helping Ann set the table.

"Calm down, honey. These are your kids you're having over for dinner."

"I know, but I'm still anxious. I hope the boys are happy for me and don't give me a hard time about this."

"They love you and want whatever you want. They will be fine. Here, let me get that plate down for you."

"Thanks, Robert. It's so nice of you to help me. Do you mind setting those wine glasses on the table while I check the meat in the oven?"

"Sure thing. Everything smells good. What did you find out about the building? Are they going to be able to have it ready by the end of June?"

"It will probably be around the first of July, so I'm thinking of having a community party at the site for the Fourth of July. What do you think?"

"That sounds like a great idea. I should be free the week before that to help you get it all set up. I think I hear someone coming to the door. You all set?"

Ann smoothed her hand down her skirt and gave Robert a big smile.

"All ready. I'm so glad you're here to give me support."

The doorbell rang and Ann answered it. Both Patrick and Jill, and John and Jessica were standing at the door.

"Hi, come on in. I thought we could have a drink in the living room before dinner. Okay?"

Everyone followed Ann into the living room. Robert was there and played waiter to all, so it was he who noticed the diamond on Jessica's finger first.

He smiled and said, "Very pretty."

Patrick was standing next to Jessica at the time and asked, "What's very pretty?"

"I think he's admiring the ring I gave Jessie," John replied.

"Well, it's about time. Hey everybody, come see the ring on Jessie's finger. Congratulations, little brother. It's about time you settled down, and I couldn't be more pleased that he picked you, Jessica. He's been sowing his wild oats for a long time now, but I guess he knew what he was waiting for."

The room erupted in congratulations. Ann was the first to reach John and gave him a big hug.

"I'm so happy for you. I knew she was something special the first day I met her in my office." Then she turned to Jessica and gave her a hug, too. "You are perfect for my son. I'm thrilled that you'll be part of the family."

Jill added her best wishes and gave each of them a hug.

"I'm so glad you're going to be my sister-in-law. John did well. The ring is gorgeous. Have you set a date yet?"

Jessica laughed. "I think I did well, too."

She gave John's hand a tight squeeze and he leaned down for a quick kiss.

John answered Jill's question, "We're thinking that the first part of August would be good. We just want a small wedding with our immediate families there, so it shouldn't take us too long to plan. Jessica wants a church wedding, so we need to look into that first."

Everyone had his or her opinion to add to the planning of the wedding.

Robert spoke up then, "With everybody's help you may be able to move the wedding up to next week." That brought laughter to all.

It was after they were all seated for dinner that Jill whispered to Patrick that they should share their news.

"Do you want to tell them or do you want me to?" Patrick asked.

"You go ahead. I got to tell my parents on the phone last night."

"Okay." Patrick raised his glass of wine and said, "I'd like to make two toasts. The first is to John and Jessica. May all your hopes and dreams come true and may you always place your love and trust in each other."

Everyone took a sip and then waited for the second toast.

"This toast is to honor a soon-to-be member of this family. Jill and I are adopting a baby, and he or she should be with us in about two months."

The silence was deafening for about one second as everyone digested what they had just heard, and then everyone started to speak at once.

"Oh my, that's wonderful."

"I'm going to be a grandmother."

"You're going to have a baby. I'm so happy for you."

After all calmed down, Patrick explained that they had been working with an adoption agency for almost a year and now they were finally going to get a newborn baby. The mother was very young and had decided to give the baby up for adoption. The actual due date was July 7.

Jill talked about the nursery they were going to make out of their spare bedroom and all the things they needed to buy. Jessica said they would have to go baby shopping and wedding shopping together.

It was while they were having desert and coffee that Ann finally got up the nerve to make the announcement that the dinner was being held for in the first place.

"It seems that everyone has had a life-changing piece of information to share tonight, and I have one of my own to tell all of you. I have decided to cut down to part-time at work for the next year and then I am going to retire next May."

"That's great, Mom. I've been hoping you would stop working so hard," John said, smiling at his mother.

"I agree with John. You've worked so hard ever since we were little kids and you deserve to have some time for yourself," Patrick added.

"Well, I'm retiring from the family business, but I have already begun work on another project. I have bought a piece of property in the north part of Boston. It has an old gymnasium on it and I am having it refurbished. It is going to be a community theater for the children and teens in the area. I plan to run the theater. It is my hope to have it open part-time by the beginning of July. The contractor thinks he can get it done by then and I want to open it with a Fourth of July party for the community."

Jessica was beaming at her future mother-in-law, but Patrick and John were both frowning.

"A theater? Mother, what are you talking about? That's one of the poor neighborhoods in Boston. Why would you want to start a theater in that area?" Patrick asked.

"That's why I'm starting it. It's a poor neighborhood, and the kids and teens that live there need something to do with their time so they don't get into trouble, something they can enjoy while they are learning to work with other people. I want to do this. I think I'll be good at it, and it will give me a real purpose in life. I'm not so old that I just want to fade away."

"But is it safe for you? Plus, we wanted you to retire so you could take it easy. This sounds like more work than what you're doing now," John said.

"It's as safe as possible. This particular neighborhood isn't a hardcore criminal area, it's just poor. Didn't that lady you helped in the blizzard last winter live in that area? They're just poor, not bad."

"I guess you're right about that, but I still don't see why you are doing this. You should be taking it easy and going on trips and shopping with your friends and stuff like that."

It was Jill who finally put an end to the objections. She stood up and looked around the table.

"I have something to say," she said in a loud voice, for Jill. Everyone stopped talking and looked at her. No one had ever seen her speak out before, so all were silent.

"I think you two," she said pointing at John and Patrick, "should be telling your mother how happy you are that she has decided to do something that will make her happy and at the same time help other people, especially children. You should be offering to help her as much as you can."

Jill flushed a little at her own words and then looked at Jessica and then at John's feet that were stretched out by the side of the table. Jessica almost burst out laughing. She could read Jill's mind at that point and knew she was imagining John walking around in high heels with a beaded purse clutched in his hand.

"I guess my wife is right. I'm sorry, Mother. We should have been happy for you right off the bat. When do you want us to come see the building? Is there something we can do to help you?"

"I'm sorry, too," John added. "You just took us by surprise. This has been one heck of an evening. A year from now all of our lives will be different."

Ann was pleased and also thought that maybe she should get to know Jill a little better. She glanced speculatively at her and thought, *I dismissed you as weak and mediocre, but I think I was wrong.*

The evening ended with best wishes and congratulations all around. Ann sighed after everyone left.

"I'm so happy about John and Jessica, and I'm going to be a grandmother. Can you believe it, Robert?"

"Your face is all aglow. You have a wonderful family, Ann. You are very lucky."

"Yes, I am. I'm lucky to have you for a friend, too."

"A friend I am, but I hope to be more than that to you someday. You are a very special lady. I've been alone for a long time. My wife died ten years ago, and I haven't had anyone else special in my life since then. Is there a chance that you may eventually feel more for me than just friendship?"

"It's been even longer for me. My husband walked out of my life when I was twenty-five, and except for my boys there has been nobody else. I think I forgot how it felt to have a man around, but I do like having you here and I think it feels like more than friendship already."

"Ann, I'm glad to hear that." Robert pulled her into his arms and gave her a gentle kiss.

"Oh my," Ann said. "I had forgotten what that felt like. Let's try it again."

Robert just laughed and said, "Your wish is my command."

He lowered his head and this time the kiss lasted a good deal longer.

Chapter 22

The following week flew by in a flurry. The magazine was set to go national the first of June. Most of the articles were already written and the layouts for the advertisements were in their final stages. There was room for one more feature article, and several people were working on different stories hoping theirs would be the one to get in the first edition.

Jessica had been working on one about gangs and why young men joined them ever since the incident in New York. She had read a lot of material and even went to the local juvenile hall to interview other gang members. She hadn't completed the article yet, but she got John to agree to read it when she finished.

Jessie and John had decided to have dinner at her house on Friday night. John said he liked her small kitchen. They were constantly bumping into each other as they prepared their meal, sometimes by accident but mostly by design.

After dinner they sat on the couch, supposedly to watch television, but little watching got done. They were talking of the future and kissing and making out. They had never taken their physical play beyond the superficial. John had been surprised at Jessica's seeming lack of sexual experience. She was very responsive and never held back, but she never took the initiative and seemed not to know a lot about the art of making love. He'd had two live-in relationships himself and several other sexual partners over the years, so this was new to him.

"Jessie, I'm not sure how to ask you this, but I have to confess to having had several sexual relationships with other women in the past, and I get the feeling from you that your sexual experience is rather limited. Are you still a virgin?"

Jessica turned bright red.

"I guess that was poor of me to ask. I didn't mean to embarrass you, but I don't want to rush you into something you're not ready for."

Jessica looked down at her hands and then looked up into his eyes.

"No, I'm not a virgin, but I have only had one short sexual relationship in my life. I got pregnant and had a baby. I gave the baby up for adoption."

The words had barely left her mouth when John was standing up shouting at her, "You what? You gave your baby away? What kind of woman are you? How could you do that? How could you give your own flesh and blood away?"

Jessica started to speak but John cut her off. He was pacing by this time and looked at her with disgust.

"I thought you were the woman I wanted to marry and have children with, but you're pitiful. You couldn't even love your own child."

He reached down, pulled the diamond ring from her finger, and stuck it in his pocket.

"I don't know how I could have been so wrong about you. I thought I loved you."

He walked to the door and then, before he walked out he looked at her in total loathing.

"If you were a doormat you wouldn't be good enough for me to wipe my feet on."

With that parting comment he walked out the door. Jessica sat on the couch with tears streaming down her face and sobs shaking her whole body.

Then an inner calm seemed to come over her. She was hurt and crushed by John's reaction, but for the first time since she had given her baby up for adoption she was totally sure of her decision. She had always carried around a certain amount of doubt as to whether she had done the right thing. There was no longer any doubt in her mind. She had loved her baby enough to do what was best for him. If the rest of the world didn't understand that, it was their problem.

John's betrayal was hard to accept. She did love him. Why had he reacted so badly? She didn't know, but it seemed like the newfound faith in her decision about the baby also gave her a faith in the love she and John shared. She wasn't about to give up on him yet.

She spent the weekend locked up in her apartment. She cried often and worried about John. She thought about calling him but didn't. She decided he needed time. She also worked on the article about the gang members. By Monday morning she had it perfected.

It rained most of the weekend, which suited John's mood just fine. He didn't want to see anybody and he didn't answer his telephone the few times it rang.

He kept going over her words in his mind. She had a baby and gave it away. His dad had at least been there for a few years of his life before he walked out. She hadn't kept her baby at all. How could people do that? He thought he had known her so well. Did he still love her? He wasn't sure. He knew you couldn't just turn love off and on at will.

He wondered what she was doing all weekend. He had seen her crying and wondered if she was crying now. He felt bad about some of the things he had said, but he just couldn't understand at all how she could have given her baby away.

Monday morning he went to work as usual. He wondered if she would show up. She did.

She sent the copy of the article she had been working on to him in his office and he read it. It was good as usual but he wrote "REWRITE" across it.

She made her usual rounds in the layout room and read over some other articles that were sent to her office. When she got her own article back with the word "rewrite" on it she just smiled and started it over.

She didn't see John all day. She didn't try to avoid him, but he obviously was avoiding her.

The next day was a repeat of Monday. The article came back with the same word, "REWRITE."

On Wednesday, she personally took the article to John's secretary and said she would wait to see what he thought. Miss Fernly just nodded and took the article in to him.

Jessica sat in the reception area until John's intercom came on.

"You can get this article and send it back to Jessica," he said.

Miss Fernly went into the office and came back a few minutes later.

"I told him you were waiting for it, but he said to just give this to you and tell you that you could go home for the day. He said he didn't need you for anything else. Is there something going on with you two? I hope you aren't fighting. You're so good for each other."

Jessica just looked at the paper with the word "REWRITE" on it and smiled at Miss Fernly.

"He's just trying to sort out a few things. It's just taking longer than I had thought it would. I'll see you tomorrow."

This time when Jessica rewrote the article she put it back the way it was on Monday, but she added a couple of lines in the middle of the paper. She wrote, "I love you and miss you a lot. When are you going to talk to me?"

When John got the article on Thursday morning, he smiled to himself when he realized it was her first draft, but as he read he lost his smile when he came across her addition. It sobered him immediately. What was she trying to do to him? He wrote "REWRITE" on it and sent it back. Again he said that she should go home, that he didn't need her the rest of the day.

He could hardly wait for the article to get to him on Friday morning. He was like a starving man waiting for a morsel of food. Friday's copy of the article contained more words meant only for him. She told him that she had hated eating alone again last night and that she was getting really lonely.

Over the weekend Jessie went to dinner at the little Italian restaurant that she thought of as their special place. She ate alone. John had been heading there when he caught sight of her entering and turned around and went home.

Jessie had several phone calls but she let the answering machine pick them up. Katie had called and wanted to know if she and John could come over for lunch on Sunday. Jill called to see if next Thursday would be a good time to go shopping for baby things and wedding dresses. Jessie ignored the calls.

John spent his weekend moping around and ignored a call from his mother and his brother. He rented some movies and tried to watch them but he couldn't tell anyone what he had seen. What was he going to do? He knew he couldn't keep this up. He was wishing it were Monday so he could at least see what she had written to him this weekend.

By Monday when he went to work he looked like he hadn't slept and his temper was short. People around the office had figured out that something was wrong. Gossip ran wild. Some of the people in the layout department had noticed that Jessica didn't have her ring on. Everyone was speculating. Eventually word made it to Patrick. He was upset, but since John hadn't confided in him he kept his mouth shut.

John read hurriedly through the article Jessica had again sent him. In the middle of the paper he found what he was looking for. She told him about going to the restaurant without him and how sad that had made her. She talked about not being able to sleep at night and asked him how he was doing. She asked if he missed her as much as she missed him and once again she said that she loved him.

The routine from last week started all over again. Rewrite and I don't need you the rest of the day.

By Wednesday, the whole office was upset. John was snapping at the employees. Jessie was never there to give her input, and the magazine was due to go to press. When Patrick again got wind of what was going on he called his mother and filled her in.

Ann was worried. What could possibly have happened? She knew John loved Jessie. Why would Jessie break off the engagement? She decided that even though she shouldn't get involved she was going to. She called Jessie's office and found out that she had already gone home for the day. Well, she would just go to her apartment and find out what was going on.

Chapter 23

The doorbell rang, startling Jessica out of her stupor. She had been sitting at her computer trying to decide what to add to her article that might get John snapped out of his mood and over to talk to her. She prayed that it was him at her door.

She flew to the door and opened it. Ann was standing there. Jessie's look of disappointment had Ann frowning.

"Sorry I'm not whoever you were hoping for."

"That's okay. Come on in. I'm surprised to see you. Did John ask you to come over?"

"No, I haven't spoken to John. It was Patrick who called me." She looked down at Jessica's hand and noticed that the ring was indeed gone. "Why did you break off the engagement?"

Jessie gave her a sad smile and said, "I didn't. Your son broke the engagement."

"Oh Jessie, I'm sorry. Why would he do that? I know he loves you."

"Why don't you come in and have a cup of coffee or tea with me? It's a long story, so you might as well make yourself comfortable."

Jessie got them each a cup of tea and they sat at the dining room table. She began by telling Ann about getting pregnant and giving the baby up for adoption. Ann sat and listened to her entire story. Ann had tears in her eyes by the time Jessie finished.

"I only got out that I had been pregnant and had given the baby up for adoption when John reacted. He was very angry with me and wouldn't listen to me. He told me I was a terrible person and that he didn't know how he could have thought he loved me. He pulled the ring off my finger and left. I have been sending him little messages every day in an article I've written for the magazine, but he just keeps sending it back. I don't know if he reads them or not. I don't know what else to do. I'm trying to give him time."

Ann frowned and said, "I think I know what the problem is, and I'm to blame. His father walked out on us when John was just five years old. Neither he nor Patrick ever asked anything about him or what happened. I thought they were just not affected by it, but it appears I was wrong. Now it's my turn to tell you my story and then I think I better talk to my sons."

When Ann completed her tale, both women were crying out of empathy for each other.

"I'm going to go talk to my boys, and you are going to stay right here. If my son doesn't come over tonight you just keep sending him your messages, because I know he will come around."

Ann got up and gave Jessie a big hug. The doorbell rang again.

"Seems like you have more company. I'll just be on my way, and don't you worry."

Ann opened the door and waved goodbye as Katie walked in. Katie saw Jessie with tears still wet on her cheeks.

"What is going on? Who was that and why are you crying and why haven't you answered my phone calls?"

Jessie laughed, "One thing at a time. That was Ann Kilroy, John's mother. I'm crying for several reasons and I haven't answered your calls because I was too upset. Sit down and I'll fill you in."

Jessie told Katie about John's reaction when she had told him about the baby, and then she told her about Ann's visit and what she had learned about John's father. Katie was furious at John.

"How could he have been so stupid?" she asked.

"Now Katie, don't say too much. I still love him and I know he will come to understand once he gets everything straightened out in his mind. I just need to give him time, and then when he comes around, I'll forgive him."

"I know you love him but I just hate to see you hurt. If he were here I would give him a punch in the nose for you. Is there anything I can do to make it easier for you right now? You know we all love you."

"There's nothing you can do. Just don't tell your mother or it will get back to my folks and I would rather this just stay between us. John will come around."

"Okay. I can't stay. I have to pick up Megan from piano lessons. If you need anything you let me know."

Ann went directly to Patrick's office. He was on the telephone and waved her into the chair in front of his desk. After he hung up the phone he said, "Well, that was quick. Did you find out what is going on?"

"I did. But first I need to talk to you about your father."

"What does this have to do with Dad?"

"I have never told you or John anything about your dad. I think it is time I do. Do you remember anything about him?"

"I have some memories. Most of them aren't real pleasant. I remember him being real moody and locking himself up in that upstairs bedroom for what seems to me was days. I don't know if it was really that long, but it seemed like it. I also remember sometimes he would yell over nothing and then the next minute he would want us all to go do something fun even if it was late a night."

"Your dad was sick and I couldn't help him. You never asked about him though, so I didn't say anything."

"I'm not asking now, so why are you telling me this?"

"Because I think it plays a part in why John broke off the engagement with Jessie."

Ann continued and told him the entire story about his father and then told him Jessie's story. When she finished she told him how badly John had reacted and what he had said to Jessie. Patrick was livid. He and Jill were adopting a baby from a young woman who found herself in a similar situation, and John was condemning Jessie for her sacrifice.

Patrick stood up and said, "Give me five minutes before you come down to John's office to talk to him."

With that he stormed out of his office and down to John's. He didn't bother to knock, but swung the door open and marched up to John's desk. John looked up and saw Patrick's angry face.

"What's the matter with you?" he asked as he stood up.

Patrick didn't even hesitate; he just brought his arm up and aimed his fist at John's face. John saw the punch coming and tried to duck. Patrick caught him in the left eye. John staggered back in his chair.

Putting his hand over his eye he said, "What the hell was that for?"

"That's for being a son of a bitch and hurting Jessica. You better get your head back on straight."

Patrick turned then to see his mother coming through the door. John said, "I don't know what's going on. Patrick just hit me."

Ann just shook her head at Patrick. "Did you really hit him?"

"Yes, and don't go feeling sorry for him. He deserved it and I feel a lot better."

Ann said, "Well, I'm glad one of us feels better. Now if you will close the door as you leave, I would appreciate it."

As the door closed, Ann walked around the side of the desk and perched herself on the edge next to where John sat.

"Let me see," she said. He lowered his hand. "Ouch, it looks like you're going to have a black eye. Does it hurt?"

"Yeah, it hurts."

Ann reached up and grabbed his right earlobe and pulled.

"Well, good. You deserve a little pain for what you did to Jessica."

"Mother, will you let go of my ear before you pull it off. I'm not a little boy anymore."

Ann released his ear but continued to frown at him.

"I guess I should talk to you and see if I can make things better. I need to apologize for twenty-seven years of silence about your father."

John was truly puzzled now.

"Why do you want to talk about my dad now?"

"Because I think you have things mixed up in your head about your father leaving you. I'm going to tell you everything. I should have explained things to you long ago, but I didn't"

Ann moved to the chair in front of John's desk and began, "I was eighteen and your father was nineteen when we married, both of us much too young, but at the time we didn't think so. I begged my father to let me marry and he finally said yes. Patrick came along a year later. Your father had started to work here at the company for my grandfather by then.

"He started having big mood swings. Sometimes he was really happy and acted like everything was great, and then he would get depressed. At first I thought it was just the responsibility of having a family and pressure from working for my grandfather and trying to meet his expectations. A little over a year after I had Patrick, I found myself pregnant again with you.

"Your father was getting worse. He would go into deep periods of depression and wouldn't go to work for a week at a time. I finally convinced him to see a doctor. He was diagnosed as a manic-depressive with paranoid tendencies. The doctor put him on medication and it helped. The problem was that he wouldn't always take his medicine. We muddled through for a couple more years.

"By the time you were three, things were pretty bad. I kept at him to take his medicine. I even tried putting it in his food. Sometimes that worked but sometimes it didn't. Other times I would just lay it by his plate in the morning. Sometimes he would take it, but other times he would get mad and throw it across the room.

"Your grandfather knew about the problem. He had always intended to leave the business to my husband and me. Being the astute person he was, he left the business in my name only. Your grandfather died when you were four years old. That left your father to run the company. He simply couldn't do it. Between the pressure of the business and not taking his medication, he couldn't function anymore. He would lock himself in the upstairs bedroom for days at a time. I would beg him to unlock the door and let me in. He never really harmed himself or any of us, but I was always sick with worry. One day he just couldn't handle it anymore and he left.

"I hired a private investigator to find him. I sent him letters begging him to come home or at least go to a doctor and get help. After two years of this I got a court order for him to appear in court so I could try to get him committed for treatment. The day of the hearing he appeared in court all smiles, and he had a psychiatrist with him who said he was under his treatment and that he was fine since he was on medication.

"He never came back, and for eight more years I had private investigators keep track of him. I would send him money for medicine and wrote him frequently. It seemed every time I contacted him he would disappear again.

"Ten years after he left I received a packet in the mail. It was divorce papers. He had filed for a divorce and wrote me a letter saying that he wanted to be free and he didn't want me to try to find him ever again. I finally gave up. I signed the papers and sent them back to the lawyer. A few months later I got the final paperwork. I put it in a box in my closet and I haven't heard from or seen your father since.

"He was a sick man, but I couldn't help him because he didn't want my help. He didn't leave you boys because he didn't love you. He left because he didn't know what else to do.

"Do you understand now? I'm sorry I didn't tell you all of this sooner. Neither you nor Patrick ever asked anything about your father, so I just let that part of my life go."

John was truly stunned by what his mother had told him. He didn't remember anything about his father. He was a little upset that his mother hadn't shared any of this with him before, but as he thought about it he realized when his dad left he was much too young to understand, and since that time he had never once even mentioned his dad to his mother. He guessed he could understand how she would think he didn't care and that he never gave his dad a thought. All that anger he felt toward his father was already starting to fade.

"I wonder if he is still alive," John said.

"I don't know. We could always hire a private investigator to try to find him if you want."

"I don't know what I want at the moment. I'll have to give it some thought. What does Patrick think?"

"Patrick remembers some things about your father and wasn't really surprised when I told him everything. I think he was old enough to realize his dad was sick and he just let it go."

"Why are you telling me this now? Does it have to do with Jessica?"

"Yes. I went to see her. You have everybody in the office upset and speculating about the two of you. I decided to go to her and see why she broke off the engagement. I found out you're the one who ended it."

"Did she tell you why?"

"Yes, she did. I figured your feelings about your father deserting you probably accounted for some of your reaction. I think you should talk to her and let her tell you her whole story before you judge."

"I take it Patrick has already heard most of her story and that is why he hit me. I guess all of you think I should forgive her."

"I don't think you need to forgive her. She didn't do anything to you that she needs forgiveness for. I think you better be praying she forgives you."

What did his mother mean? She was the one who gave away her baby. He needed to be forgiven for what? And then he remembered some of the hurtful things he had said to her. He guessed he would have to do some soul searching and then decide what to do.

As his mother sat watching him, his door once again came crashing open. In walked Kaleb and he looked ready to kill.

John just moaned and said, "Not again. I don't think I have ever had two black eyes at the same time."

Kaleb nodded to John's mother and said, "Would you mind if I have a private word with John?"

Ann looked at Kaleb and answered, "That depends on what you have in mind. You see, I'm his mother and I do love my son, even if he is a little weak in the mind."

Kaleb laughed then. "Very nice to meet you, Mrs. Kilroy. I'm Kaleb Dalton, and Jessica is my wife's cousin. She is very special to us."

"I understand now, but I don't know if a second black eye will do any good. My other son already beat you to the punch, no pun intended."

"So I see. Well, John, I guess this is your lucky day. Just make sure you get things straightened out or I'll have to come again or worse yet, Katie will come herself. You wouldn't want that to happen."

John moaned, "Does the whole world know about this?"

"No, just those of us who care. I'm sure you'll do the right thing. See you for lunch on Sunday."

With that Kaleb left.

John's mother smiled at him and said, "I'm leaving, too. You better decide how you're feeling about all this and don't let Jessica wait too long. The longer you wait the more you'll have to crawl. Bye, dear. Have a nice evening."

Chapter 24

A book lay open on her lap, but Jessie couldn't concentrate. She kept looking at the clock wondering if John would come over tonight. It was seven o'clock and she had already had a salad and taken a shower in hopes that he would come. She wanted to look her best for him.

When the doorbell finally rang she was a bundle of nerves. She ran to the door, took a deep breath and opened it. John stood outside with a big bouquet of roses in one hand and a little velvet box in the other. She just drank in the sight of him. That was all she really wanted, just to look at him.

After a few minutes, he said, "Are you going to let me in?"

"I don't know. I've been waiting a long time for you to come, but now that you're here I'm not sure what to do with you."

"How about a kiss and then we'll talk? I've missed you and I don't think I would have made it if you hadn't written me all those little notes the past week and a half. I hated the weekend, when I knew you wouldn't be sending me any hidden messages."

"So you did read them. I didn't know if you even looked at the article since I didn't change it."

"I read every word just because I knew you wrote it."

"Then what took you so long?"

"As everybody has been telling me all day, I'm a little stupid and weak minded. Can you forgive me?"

"I should make you beg, but I won't. I love you too much for that. My God, what happened to your eye?"

"It came in contact with a fist."

"You got in a fight. With who and what over?"

"It wasn't a fight. My big brother just thought I needed to get my head back on straight and he tried to straighten it for me."

"Patrick did that to you? First Jill stands up to both of you at dinner and now Patrick punches you. Those two are not at all like I first thought they were. Does it hurt a lot?"

"It hurts. I think you need to kiss it and make it all better. And you need to let me get out of the doorway and set these flowers down."

"Okay. You can come in and set the flowers on the table. I'll go find a vase for them."

"Hurry back. I can't wait much longer."

Jessica returned from the kitchen with a vase filled with water. She put the roses in and stood back to admire them. John came up behind her and put his arms on her shoulders and turned her to him. Then he lowered his head and kissed her. He was like a man out in the desert who had just found water.

When he finally lifted his head he asked, "Will you put this back on? I'm so sorry."

She stuck out her hand and said, "Please, you put it on since you took it off."

"Gladly."

He slid the ring back on her finger and then kissed her fingers one by one.

They moved into the living room and John said, "I'm sorry for all the awful things I said to you. I should have let you tell me what you wanted to the other night. I know my mother told you about my father. She came to the office today and told me everything about him. I've been carrying around a lot of anger towards him and I took it out on you. I'm willing to listen now if you want, but you don't have to tell me anything if you don't want to. I trust that whatever happened and whatever you decided at the time was what was best."

"Thank you for that faith in me. I want to tell you, though. We can't share the rest of our lives together without you knowing my past. It's part of who I was and who I am now."

She walked over to the built-in cupboard and took out the little china cup. Then she sat down on the floor and motioned for John to sit beside her.

Holding the cup lovingly in her hands she began her story, "This little cup belonged to my grandmother. My grandfather gave it to her before they were married. He called it his Promise Cup. He said it was full of their hopes and dreams and love. I always loved this cup.

"I told you once before that I was a surprise to my parents. I came along twelve years after my youngest brother. My brothers were grown and out of the house long before I reached my teen years. My parents loved me and tried to raise me the best they could, but I was headstrong and thought they were old and just didn't understand about being young.

"I thought I was in love when I was fifteen. His name was Michael and he was everything a fifteen-year-old thought was manly. He played football and had a car. He was sixteen and very good-looking. All my friends were having sex with their boyfriends and I thought it was the thing to do.

"We only had sex three times and then he dumped me. It wasn't all that great, but what can you expect when you're that young. Well, two months later I started feeling sick in the mornings and my period hadn't come. I was in a panic. I went to a clinic in town and the doctor ran a test and called me a few days later. He told me I was pregnant.

"I can remember being so scared. How could I tell my parents? I told Michael first, and he just said, 'So, what do you want me to do about it? I suppose I can help you get an abortion if you want one.' I couldn't believe he could be so unfeeling at the time.

"Next I confided in some of my girlfriends. They all encouraged me to get an abortion. One of them had already had one and said it was easy. I knew I could never do that, so I finally decided I had to tell my parents.

"They were shocked. They never suspected that Michael and I had sex. They cried, both of them. I felt just awful. I had never seen my dad cry before. It took them a while to come to terms with it, but then they were there for me. They told me I could do whatever I thought best. The only thing they wouldn't let me do was have an abortion, which I had already decided against.

"They said they would help me raise the child if I wanted them to. I was going to turn sixteen two weeks after the baby was due. I was a sophomore at the time. My mother was fifty-six and my dad was sixty. I gave it a lot of thought.

"Throughout this time I continued to go to school and finished my sophomore year. The baby was due the last part of August. I wore baggy clothes and watched my diet, so it wasn't real obvious.

"By my sixth month I decided that the best thing for my baby was adoption. I couldn't provide for him and I thought it was totally unfair to ask my parents to raise this child. My child deserved a mother and a father and people who could give it love and a normal home. It was not an easy decision. I prayed and thought about it constantly.

"Two months before he was due, I went to the local jewelry store and had a little pin made. I saved my own money from gifts and odd jobs to buy it. I had it made out of silver and it said, 'Fill This Cup With Good Things,' and then I had a little silver teacup made just like this one and had it suspended from the writing. You are the only one I have ever told about the pin. My parents don't know about it. It was the only legacy I could pass on to my son.

"When I talked to the woman from the adoption agency I asked for only two things. I wanted the couple to be of the same religion as myself, and I asked that before my baby was given to them, I could have ten minutes alone with him.

"My baby was born on August 22. He was beautiful. When it came time for his new parents to take him they brought him to me for my ten minutes. I remember removing his blankets and taking off all his clothes so I could be sure he had all his fingers and toes. He was perfect. He had blond hair and a round face. He was so small and smelled so good.

"After I checked him out, I redressed him and then I took out the little pin I'd had made for him and pinned it to his T-shirt. It was the only gift I ever got to give my child. I held him then and cuddled him and told him how much I loved him.

"When the nurse came to get him, handing him over to her was the hardest thing I have ever done. It was because I loved him so much that I had to give him to someone who could take care of him."

There were tears rolling down Jessie's face as she was talking. John kept catching them and brushing her face with soft kisses. He held her in his arms as moisture seeped from his own eyes.

Jessie got hold of her emotions and then continued, "After he was gone it was like I was dead inside. School started a few weeks after that, but it was hard to even think. I only passed a couple of my classes and the teachers were at me to stop daydreaming and pay attention, but I just couldn't.

174

"Everyone knew I had given my baby away and they didn't understand. They either ignored me like I had some kind of disease or they said cruel things to me. The guys started to come on to me like I was some kind of whore. By the second semester I dropped out of school. I took a couple of classes as home study and got a few more credits, but my heart wasn't in it.

"I lived in a small town, so it wasn't just the kids at school who knew I'd had a baby, it was everyone. The boys and young men who lived in the town, even those in their early twenties, started to try to pick up on me. I was so dead inside though, that they couldn't even get a rise out of me. When someone would say something to me, I would just look through them. I guess that must have really bothered them, because before too long everyone started to call me Crazy Jessie.

"My parents were really concerned about me. They didn't know what to do. My dad had a friend who was a veterinarian and he asked him if he could use me to help him at his clinic. I went to work for him and that helped. Animals don't talk, and they're so helpless that it gave me a sense of being needed. I gradually started to get better.

"It was on my twenty-first birthday that my mother gave me this cup as a present. As I held it in my hands I knew my grandmother was watching over me and that she would want me to start filling it up again with good things. That was when I decided to go back to school. I had to finish up high school and then go to college. It took me until I was twenty-six to get it all done, but I did it.

"I went away from home for my four years of college, but when I finished my parents urged me to come home. They said the local newspaper was looking for a reporter. I think they were still worried about me. I wound up taking the job and moving back home.

"Things were different when I got back. The people my age had grown up and they treated me fine. Michael still lives there and is married and has a couple of kids. He stopped me one day as I left work and apologized for the way he had treated me those many years ago. He said he was scared at the time and didn't know what to do.

"He also thanked me for not having an abortion. He said now that he had his own children he didn't think he could have lived with the idea that he had helped me kill one. I was very touched by his words and it made me realize just how young we both were when the whole thing happened.

"With a little blush he also confided in me that after he found out I was pregnant he never had sex with anyone until he married, he was so afraid of getting someone else pregnant. Shock therapy, or something like that, it seems.

"There hasn't been a day since I held my son for those brief moments that I haven't thought of him and said a prayer for him. I got over the shame I felt about getting pregnant years ago, but I have always wondered if I had made the right decision. The other night when you were mad at me it seemed like something inside of me just finally said, 'Quit worrying about it. You did the best you could for your son at the time.'

"I know now that it was the right decision and I will never question it again. I will continue to pray for him and I will always love him, but I know he is better off with his family than he would have been with me."

John brushed away her tears and pulled her close.

"I think you are the most wonderful person ever created, and I don't deserve you. You should have given me two black eyes and a few broken bones for what I said to you the other night. I don't see how you can forgive me, but I'm glad that you have. I know our children can't replace him, but I'm planning on giving you so many you won't have a chance to be lonely."

Jessica laughed then and said, "That is the nicest thing anyone has ever said to me. How many children do you think we can manage?"

"At least a dozen, I would think."

"That might be a few too many, even for us. How about half that many?"

"Hmm, we'll see. I think you're going to find that making them can be lots of fun. That is if this old body of mine can stand up to the demands I have a feeling you're going to make on it."

"Well, you did say the other night that you have had lots of practice, so I hope you're a good teacher. My own experience is very limited."

"I'm more than willing to teach you, but I think we'll wait until after the wedding band is on your finger next to that diamond. I like the idea of our wedding night really being our wedding night. How does that sound to you?"

"It sounds perfect, but maybe we can move the date up. August sounds so far away."

"Anxious for this poor old body of mine, are you? If it wasn't for our families I'd say let's go find a minister tomorrow. Let's talk to them and see when they can come?"

"You have a deal. The sooner the better. We have to get the magazine out, too. Is everything ready and have you decided on the last feature article yet?"

"I sent your story into the print shop before I came over. It's all there and they'll start printing it tomorrow. I may have been a bear at work the last few days but I still got things done."

"Then I guess there's nothing that should hold us up. It's too late to call my folks tonight, but I'll call tomorrow and see what they say. John, I really do love you and I'm so glad you got your head back on straight. I was starting to get worried."

"If I ever act like such a fool again you have my permission to just take me out and shoot me. Okay? I love you more than I could have ever imagined loving anyone."

"Even that model Sophia? I'm far from the model type."

"Are you hunting for a compliment? I love your type. The first day you came into my office I couldn't help but notice how sexy you were and so feminine. I like your curves and the fact that you're not just skin and bones. You're soft and smooth and perfect."

"You've convinced me. I may not be perfect but I'm perfect for you."

"That you are."

Chapter 25

(Six years later)

John pulled Jessica closer and smoothed his hand down her stomach.

"Good morning, Jessie, and how are you feeling this morning?"

"I feel wonderful. Nobody woke up last night and the bed is so warm and snugly. I think I could just stay here all day."

"I think that sounds like a wonderful idea, but our guests are due to arrive in a few hours and they might frown on us still being in bed with no food prepared. Plus, I think our little ones will be upset if we don't give them any breakfast."

"It's still early. Maybe we can practice some more of your lessons before we have to crawl out of bed."

"I knew you were going to be a demanding wife. My job is never done, it seems."

"Well, I'm trying to get this all down perfect, and the only way I know of doing that is to practice it over and over again."

John laughed and said, "If you get much better at this I'll have to start having you give me lessons. I think you've come up with some creative moves of your own."

"I just don't want you to get bored with me. Some of those romance novels I've read have given me inspiration."

"Remind me not to complain about that stuff you read ever again."

A half hour later they both looked to their bedroom door as it gradually opened. Two little faces appeared in the doorway.

"We're hungry. Can we have waffles this morning?"

"Why don't you come in here for a minute and get under the

covers with your mother while I get dressed? Then I'll go down and fix them for you."

The children ran to the bed and jumped in. They loved to cuddle with their parents in their big bed.

Johnny, the oldest, asked his mom if he could feel her stomach. He had felt the baby kick the night before and he wanted to feel it again.

"You can try, but he's been real quiet this morning."

"Can I feel too?" his little sister asked.

"Here, let me put your hand right here. Oh, did you feel that? I think he's saying hello to you."

Little Christine laughed. "That felt funny."

"Well, Mommy has to get up now. We have lots of company coming today and I have a lot of things to do. You two go to your rooms and pick out something to wear and I'll be there in a minute to help you dress."

"I can dress myself," Johnny said.

"I guess you can. Well, hop to it."

The children went running out of the room. John came out of the shower and got dressed.

"You take your time. I'll go get Christine dressed and then we'll go down to the kitchen and I'll start breakfast."

He gave Jessica a quick kiss and looking at her stomach said, "We need to design a pin for this new one if we want it ready before its born. It will have the birthstone for August, of course, but do you know what you want it to say?"

"I've been thinking about it but I haven't decided yet. Since we're both in the writing business we should be able to come up with something clever."

"Maybe we'll have time to work on it this weekend. I better get downstairs and start breakfast. Take your time coming down."

Jessica took a shower and got dressed. She and John had been married for six years now, and she loved being a wife and mother. She was pregnant with their third child. John was keeping his word about giving her lots of children.

As she dried her hair she thought about the rest of the family. Her parents were enjoying good health and loved living in Arizona. Her older brothers were going through the teen years with their own children.

Katie and Kaleb remained close and had another little girl. They were coming this afternoon, along with John's family.

Patrick and Jill had been able to adopt a second child, and Jill seemed to have lost all her shyness. Motherhood had made her more confident and she radiated with happiness.

Ann was now Ann Grayson. Her theater had taken off and was known throughout Boston for its quality children's productions of old and new plays. Several of her students had received scholarships in the past couple of years from drama and music departments in various colleges. This year her big accomplishment was that one young man received a scholarship in journalism. He had written several productions for the theater, and Ann had submitted a couple of them to Boston College to try to get him in. He was thrilled when he received notice that he was accepted on a full scholarship.

Jessica still thought often about her other son. He would be twenty in August. She still prayed every day for him and hoped that his life was wonderful and that his parents were proud of him. Her last thought before she left to go down to breakfast was that her little cup was full and overflowing and she hoped his was, too.

Chapter 26

(Santa Barbara, CA. That same year)

It was a hot day in August and the sand on the beach felt warm as he walked lazily along the shore. Occasionally the waves would lap up and wash over his feet and ankles. The seagulls screeched out their calls and the sunbathers rubbed suntan lotion over their bodies. Children ran in and out of the water throwing large beach balls to each other. Kevin was just one of many enjoying the California sun.

He was home on summer vacation from college. He had to be at the restaurant for the dinner crowd, but his shift didn't start for another three hours. Working the evening shift gave him plenty of time to bask in the sun. This was home and he missed it when he was away, only three more weeks and then back to Boston College. He was already dreading the coming winter in Boston. This was his last year though, so he knew he would stick it out. Once he was done with college he planned on returning to California.

His father was a graduate of Boston College and had really pushed him to go there. He had balked at first but eventually had given in to his dad's wishes. It was a good college and he had enjoyed his years there. The weather was an entirely different matter, however. Snow was not his thing. Ocean and sun and warm weather were what he had come to expect as normal.

He walked a ways further down the beach and then swam out into the water. Relaxing on his back he allowed the waves to carry him back to shore. He did this several more times before returning to the parking lot and his car. *Time to go home and get ready to go to work,* he thought.

Evenings at the restaurant this time of year were always busy. His dad and mom owned the business, and he had spent many an hour there helping ever since he could remember. He liked waiting on the people, but stayed as far away as possible from the kitchen. The kitchen was his mother's domain, and that was just fine with him.

He was getting his degree in archeology and hoped to eventually get his masters and doctorate and then teach and, if he were lucky, he would get to take part in some research and archeological excavations.

By five o'clock he was seating customers and taking orders. The place was already packed with diners. Tourist season was especially busy, but then they were busy year round. Their specialty was seafood, although they had other things on the menu.

Kevin had grown up in Santa Barbara, this wonderful city by the sea. He was an only child, but his mother was of Italian descent and had been one of eight children. His grandparents and most of his aunts and uncles and cousins all lived in the area. He had never been lonely or alone when he was growing up. He loved the large intimate family that he was a part of and could hardly go anywhere in town without running into a relative. He missed them when he was away at school.

Chapter 27

(Boston, MA, nine years later)

The wind blew the snow in swirls around him as he made his way to the car. It was extremely cold tonight and the sidewalk was slick with ice and snow. Kevin hoped the roads were cleared so he could get home without any trouble. Sometimes he couldn't believe that he was living in Boston.

When he graduated from college, he got his masters and after that it only seemed sensible to continue on and get his doctorate. Getting his doctorate in Scotland had been great, but when he began to look for a teaching job, Boston College had seemed a likely place to start. He had come to love Boston College, and teaching at the school was great, but he still hated the weather.

He would only be here until June, and then he was getting a chance to work with some very experienced people in Mexico. They were doing a dig in an area in the Yucatan Peninsula where the Mayan ruins were located. He was taking a leave from teaching until the following spring semester. He could hardly wait. The weather would be hot and the ocean would be near, even if it wasn't California.

His parents were proud of him and thrilled that he was Dr. Kevin Mackenzie, but they wanted him to come back to California. They visited him as often as they could, but since he was their only child, they wanted him near.

Kevin started his car and waited for the windows to clear before pulling out of the parking lot. He drove slowly as he felt the car slide a few times. He made his way from the side streets to a main thoroughfare. The traffic was moving much faster there and he picked up speed. When he pulled off onto another side street leading to his house he noticed a car on the side of the road and a young woman standing at the back with the trunk open. Her emergency lights were flashing.

Being a gentleman, he knew he should stop and help, but he hated the idea of getting out in the cold. He pulled off slightly ahead of her car and, opening his door, he pulled his collar up around his neck and walked back to her.

"Is there something I can do to help you?"

The lady looked up and said, "Thanks for stopping, but I'm fine. I already called AAA and they'll be here shortly. I was just getting a blanket out of the trunk to keep myself warm until they get here. I'm not sure what happened, but the car just sputtered and died. I just had it serviced last week, so I can't imagine what the problem could be."

"It's freezing out here. I can wait with you if you want to sit in my car where there's a heater."

She gave him a grateful look but then seemed to think it over and replied, "I'll be fine. Thanks anyway."

"I'm not a weirdo or a criminal. I promise to be a gentleman."

Megan was a very cautious person.

"I don't want to keep you, and help should be here soon."

She glanced over her shoulder as if she expected the tow truck to be coming at that very moment.

"It could be a while yet before they get here, and my mom taught me to be a gentleman no matter what the circumstances. I would feel really bad if I read in the paper that a young woman was in the hospital with frostbite she got waiting for help to come when her car broke down."

She laughed then. "You got a point there. Okay, you've convinced me. I'm a black belt though, so be forewarned."

It was his turn to laugh. "No way am I going to have you demonstrate your abilities to me. Come on, I'm freezing myself."

They hurried to his car and got in. He had left it running and it was nice and toasty inside. After they were both warm, Megan took off her gloves and loosened the knitted scarf around her neck. She still had a knit hat pulled down over her ears, but without the scarf up around the lower half of her face he could see her features. She was really quite striking. She had large eyes, high cheekbones and full lips. Her hair was pulled back at the nape of her neck, but with the hat on he couldn't tell anything about it except that it was dark. The actual color was hard to see in the interior of the car.

They hadn't spoken since getting into the car, and Megan felt uncomfortable with the silence.

"Do you live near here?" she asked.

"I have a house just a few blocks away. My name is Kevin Mackenzie. I teach at Boston College."

"Really? I went to Boston College. I don't remember seeing you there."

"I've only been there for the past two years. I got my Ph.D. in Scotland and then came back here to teach. I hate the winters here and sometimes I wonder why I ever chose Boston. I'm from Santa Barbara originally, and this is a far cry from the warm California sun I'm used to. I really miss it. It's a wonderful place."

"I've only visited California and have never been to Santa Barbara. I've lived most of my life here and can't say I love the cold, but it just seems normal to me. I'm Megan Dalton. I graduated from Boston College three years ago, so I guess that's why I never heard of you when I was a student."

"What did you get your degree in?"

"I got it in criminal justice but minored in business. I find that I'm using my business more than the criminal justice part of my degree. I actually work for my father."

"The name Dalton seems familiar to me, but I can't place it."

Before Megan could reply they saw the lights of the tow truck through the back window of the car.

"Well, thank you, Mr. Mackenzie. It was nice of you to stop. I really appreciate it. If I ever get over to the college, I'll look you up."

She got out of the car and pulled her scarf back up around her face and put on her gloves. She waved to him as he pulled away.

Nice man, I wonder if I will ever see him again, she thought as she walked back to her car.

The man in the tow truck was just getting out and she gave him all the information he needed. She planned to ride with him to the garage and then call her parents to pick her up from there.

Kevin was happy to get home. He fixed himself a nice warm bowl of soup and sat down to grade some papers. He couldn't get Megan off his mind. There was something about her name that struck him as familiar. Then it suddenly dawned on him, Dalton Industries was a large business in Boston, and if she was connected to that Dalton, he had met her father. Kaleb Dalton had donated a large sum of money to Boston College and had been the guest speaker at one of the graduations he had attended last year as a member of the faculty.

There's probably no connection, he thought with a shrug.

Chapter 28

Megan sat watching her father walk back and forth in the library. She smiled to herself when she recalled how, when she was little, she used to think that when he paced he was stomping out his anger. She now knew that it was really a frustrated, worried pacing that he did.

He looked over at her with a frown and said, "I know we have been over this before, and it won't change anything, but I really wish you would give up your job with the DEA. Why can't you just work for the company and be happy?"

"Daddy, you know how I feel about that. I love my work and I hope I'm doing some good."

"I know, sweetheart, but I worry so much about the danger you put yourself in."

"I'm very well trained and can take care of myself. Besides, I have all kinds of responsible and trustworthy people working beside me. I'm not out there all on my own."

"The DEA is lucky to have you. I feel bad that I can't share this whole situation with Katie." Putting up his hand to stop any comment she might voice, he continued, "I know, we agreed to keep it just between the two of us, and that is the way it will stay, but I think Katie might be able to talk some sense into you."

"She wouldn't be able to change my mind, and telling her would only worry her and could cause her harm if she accidentally said something to the wrong person. I'm much safer with you being the only one to know that I don't just work for Dalton Industries."

"I know you're right, but I still worry. When do you leave for Akumal?"

"I have three more days here. I have to be on a flight leaving the thirty-first. I'll be staying at the house in Akumal and I'll be putting in some time at the water purification plant you're building, so you need to give me some information on that so it will appear that I have a legitimate reason for being there. A lot of drugs come through the coast there and straight up to the U.S. The fact that Mexico and the United States now have a joint program to stop the flow of drugs gives us a whole lot more freedom and authority in that part of the world. We have a better chance of stopping it there than we do once it hits the U.S. border."

"I know, but I still can't help worrying."

"I'll be very careful, I promise."

Megan had been recruited by the Drug Enforcement Agency before she ever graduated from college. She had so many things in her favor. Not only was she one of the outstanding students in the criminal law department at Boston College, but she spoke Spanish and French fluently. She had learned Spanish from Katie, her step-mom, when she was young and also from spending several months a year in Akumal, Mexico. Her family owned a villa there. She had studied French since she was in seventh grade and had a natural ability when it came to foreign languages. She had also picked up some German, Italian and Mayan over the years, although she wasn't fluent in these languages.

The fact that her father owned a large construction company that built throughout the world was also a plus. He had been willing to provide a cover for her, even if it worried him.

She had gone away to study with the agency for nine months before they actually had her work on any of the undercover missions they were involved in. Her new assignment definitely used all the skills she had brought with her to the agency. She didn't tell her father everything about this particular mission since she knew it would only worry him more.

The agency felt certain that there was someone of importance involved in the transport of drugs from South America to the Mexican Riviera and then on to the United States. Drugs had been entering Mexico along the coast of the Yucatan for years, but it had been a haphazard operation up until the past year. Now it was highly successful and organized. They were not only concerned about this new development and who was involved in creating this cartel in Mexico, but they also suspected that one of their own agents might be part of it. Megan had only worked for the agency for the past three years and was not well known to most of the other agents. That fact, and her ties to Akumal, made her the perfect candidate for this particular mission.

One agent she had met briefly, early in her career, was going down as a consultant on the plant her father was building. He had a chemical engineering degree and was using Dalton Industries as his cover so he could stay in close contact with Megan without causing any questions to be asked. He had come to the agency from another law enforcement organization four years ago. His name was Richard Trent. He was in his forties and his knowledge of chemicals and proper mannerisms had earned him the nickname of Professor amongst the other agents.

Two other agents were working in the area and it was one of these that they feared was working against them. Megan would stay unknown to them. She had read over private folders on these two agents and knew a lot about their personal habits. She had also reviewed the work they had done and found it hard to believe that either of them would double-cross the agency.

One man was in his mid-thirties and had been with the agency for the past nine years. His name was Josh, but he was better known as the Bum. Although, from his picture, he appeared to be average in looks and he maintained a rock-hard body from vigorous exercise. He was also an actor of sorts. He had infiltrated several organizations by playing different roles. Sometimes he was the wino who just hung around, or else he was the tough guy trying to push his way into an established drug ring. On one occasion he had played the part of a semi-retarded person who did odd jobs in a sleazy bar in the heart of New York City. On this mission he had cast himself as a rich beach bum, down in Mexico to have a good time.

The Preacher was the agency's name for Stuart Grover, the other agent. He had the gift of gab. He could talk his way in and out of most situations and loved to quote the Bible. He was small in stature and forty-two years of age. He often did his job by playing the con man. Criminals seemed to take to him. They took it in stride when he cheated them at cards or ripped them off in some other manner. They thought of him as one of their own and just simply liked him.

Megan was known in the agency as the Gypsy because of her ability to go to many places throughout the world with no questions asked.

Maybe her superiors were wrong and no one from the agency was involved. She hoped that was true, but she would do what she could to find out the information they were looking for.

On Sunday she boarded her flight to Cancun. She carried a briefcase full of facts and figures on the water plant. When she arrived she would rent a car and go to the villa in Akumal.

The flight took several hours, with one plane change in Houston, Texas. She planned on going over some of the information her dad had given her and then hoped to get a little sleep before she landed. She loved Akumal and hated to think that someone was using that little town as their illegal drug headquarters.

Looking at the papers in front of her, she sighed and thought of the first time she had come to Akumal. She had just been a young girl then. The place had seemed so quiet and peaceful, and that was where she and her dad had met Katie, her stepmother. That had been a wonderful time, and they had continued to visit Akumal frequently during her years growing up.

Akumal and the whole Yucatan Peninsula had grown since that time. The Mexican government had put more restrictions on the area, hoping to have it develop at a slower pace to keep the environment sound. The government had been partially successful, but building had continued as the demand from tourism had increased.

Many new villas and hotels had sprung up along the coastline. The hotels had been restricted in size and had been forced to build back from the actual beachfront property, but many private villas did not have the same restrictions placed on them.

Rich Mexicans, as well as wealthy people from the United States and Europe had built homes close to the beaches. The water treatment plant her father was building was an attempt at improving the water supply for Akumal and its surrounding area. A large sewage treatment plant had already been built.

Megan had taken a night flight, so as the plane started to lose altitude she could see the sun just coming up over the horizon. It was a breathtaking view. The ocean was a pure shade of blue and the sky glowed with various shades of red and orange. She hated to think that there was something rotten in this paradise.

After clearing customs, she picked up her car from the rental lot and started out for Akumal. She hadn't been to Mexico in the past couple of years and was surprised by the construction she saw as she made her way along the coast. Akumal had grown, but was still relatively small. As she drove into town she noted several new villas and one new hotel.

Once she got settled and took a short nap, she would go to the construction sight and make her presence known. She also had friends and acquaintances to visit. Her intent was to make everyone think she was here to check on the progress at the water plant and at the same time have a vacation. She was often viewed as the rich pampered daughter of Kaleb Dalton with no real responsibilities, a role she could easily slip into.

By afternoon, Megan was at the construction site. She checked in with the director of the project and had a tour of the site. She asked some questions about the take-up system and made some notes. She was introduced to Mr. Trent and informed that he was there as a consultant concerning the chemicals and filters necessary for the purification of the water. She told him she would like to meet with him some time later in the week to go over his recommendations.

That evening Megan slipped on a chic black cocktail dress, sheer nylons and black sling-back heels. She completed the outfit with diamond earrings and necklace. She let her long dark hair down and brushed it back from her face. Just a touch of makeup and she was set to go to the newest restaurant and nightclub in Akumal.

On her arrival, several people she knew greeted her. She was asked to join a group of diners. One of the women, Beth, was an aunt to an old friend of Katie's and the owner of a hotel in Akumal. Megan had known her since she was a little girl but the other people at the table were strangers.

Beth introduced them to Megan. One couple, Mr. and Mrs. Cowen, were in their late fifties and had built a villa in Akumal as a retirement home. A gentleman by the name of Rex Higgins was introduced as a sales representative for a new satellite company looking to invest in the area. He was around forty and nice looking. He explained that his wife was unable to join him this trip as they had children in high school and she needed to be at home with them.

One other man joined them shortly after Megan arrived. He was introduced as Josh Brown. Beth explained that he was staying at her hotel and was in Akumal for an extended vacation.

He had laughed at his introduction and said, "I'm still trying to decide what to do when I grow up. Maybe I'll write a book some day about my various travels."

It had taken Megan only a glance to recognize him. She thought of him as The Bum. She took note of the others at the table wondering if he suspected someone there of being involved in the drug cartel or if he was still fishing for information. Too bad she couldn't ask him.

Megan observed everyone at the table carefully. The Cowens seemed friendly, but Mrs. Cowen appeared to dominate her husband. He spoke little and always deferred to her. They still had their home in New Mexico and spent part of their time there. When Megan asked if they had any children, Mr. Cowen began to say something but he was interrupted by Mrs. Cowen, who said, "No, we have none."

"You can have my two if you're in the market for some. They run my wife ragged," Mr. Higgins said with a laugh.

"Teenagers can do that," Beth said, smiling at the table at large.

"What brings you to Akumal?" Josh asked Megan.

"I came down to check on the construction my father's company is doing. I think he just got tired of me sitting around the house and decided to put me to work. He does that every once in awhile. I've been able to go to a lot of different places around the world. He gets tired of my loafing, and off I go to some other destination. I especially like coming to Akumal, though, as he owns a villa here and I get a chance to get a great tan."

Beth frowned at her answer but said nothing. She knew Megan was a hard worker and that her dad kept her busy. She doubted if Megan had done any loafing in her life except on vacations.

They all made small talk as they ate their meal. As they sat back to have an after-dinner drink a woman clothed in a short, bright red dress came in and headed straight to their table. Everyone appeared to know her but Megan. As she drew nearer, Megan thought she looked as though she was in her early thirties, but wasn't sure. She could be older, but the way she was dressed and her makeup made it hard to tell.

"Hello, everyone. I thought I might run into someone I knew if I came in here. I've been shopping all day and I found some great bargains."

She made the rounds of the table giving everyone a kiss and a hug.

When she got to Megan she said, "And who is this pretty little thing?"

"I'm Megan Dalton, and you are?"

"Megan, such a pretty name. I'm Victoria, but everyone calls me Vicki or Tory. Oh look, there's Stu."

She waved to the man who had just entered the restaurant. He made his way slowly over to the table. Vicki flung her arms around Stu and gave him a kiss when she reached them. He gave her a smile and a pat on the bottom.

"Now behave yourself, Vicki. You don't want to corrupt this sweet young thing. You know what the Bible says about leading others astray," Stuart said as he winked at Megan.

Vicki grinned and replied with a little laugh, "Oh, you charmer. Have you met Megan yet?"

"No, I haven't. Nice to meet you. I'm Stuart."

"Nice to meet you, Stuart. Why don't you both get chairs and join us?" Megan replied, realizing this was the other agent.

Well, the whole gang's here, she thought to herself.

Vicki and Stuart seemed to monopolize the rest of the evening. Stuart told outrageous stories and Vicki flirted with all the men at the table. Mr. Higgins seemed the most interested. Mr. Cowen would blush every time she turned her attention to him.

After another hour of small talk, everyone decided to leave or go do other things. Mr. Higgins and Vicki were going to go dancing, and Beth excused herself to go home. Stuart had already made his way to the bar and was talking with some locals that were gathered there. Mrs. Cowen said she thought it was a nice evening for them to take a walk on the beach, and Josh said he was heading back to his hotel.

Megan decided she would go home and do some checking into the people she had met tonight. She stopped by the restroom on her way out. As she came out of the restroom she noticed Vicki talking with Mrs. Cowen just a few feet away. The men must have been in the washroom.

Megan was about to tell them goodnight when she heard Vicki say, "I'll meet you at nine in the morning and we can go see the progress they're making at the dig. I'll drive."

Mrs. Cowen said, "That should be good. I know that Vince plans to go on a fishing trip and he's leaving at eight. Pick me up at our house."

Ordinary plans for visitors, nothing suspicious in that, Megan thought.

She left the restaurant and was going to her car when Josh materialized out of nowhere.

"Hi, I thought I'd wait and see if you'd like to go to another club and go dancing or something? I don't know too many single women here, except for Vicki, and she really isn't my type."

"Any other time and I would say yes, but I came in on an all-night flight and I'm really beat. Can I take a rain check?" Megan replied.

"Sure thing. How about Wednesday night? I have plans for tomorrow and don't know what time I'll be back in town."

"Wednesday sounds good. Do you want to meet here or somewhere else?"

"I'd be glad to pick you up at your place if you tell me where it is."

"I'm staying at the family villa. Why don't you just take my telephone number and give me a call on Wednesday. We can make plans then. Okay?"

"Fine with me. What's the number?"

"I'll write it down for you. Here. I'll see you Wednesday then. Goodnight."

Megan went home and thought about all the people she had met. The two agents were exactly as she had imagined them to be. Rex Higgins was definitely a jerk, but was he smart enough and base enough to be a drug king? Then there were the Cowens. They appeared to be a normal couple, even if he was a bit henpecked. Victoria was typical of many others who had come before. They came to the resort areas looking for a wealthy man to latch on to.

She could hardly keep her eyes open and decided to get a good night's sleep and then tomorrow she would do some background checks on the people she had met. Her bed was calling her.

Chapter 29

Megan was up early and working on her computer. Logging into the agency's database she first pulled up what she could find on Rex Higgins. He was from Riverside, California, and was involved in satellite communications. He also had a criminal record. He had been found guilty of embezzlement ten years ago. The conviction had been in Idaho, and it appeared that he had only gotten a slap on the wrist. He paid a fine and didn't do any jail time. Shortly after that, he moved to Riverside and married a woman who had two children. He had been working at the satellite company since then and was listed as a vice president in charge of marketing. She wondered if the company knew of his criminal record; probably not.

The Cowens were a big surprise. Ruth Cowen had served as a senator from New Mexico for one term. That had been twelve years ago. An investigation had been launched into her campaign finances at the beginning of the campaign for re-election and she had dropped out of the race. Once she quit, the investigation was halted.

A couple of years later, she resurfaced as a lobbyist for a large real-estate conglomerate. The company sold everything from vacation condos and tract homes to retirement home developments. They had holdings in several countries outside the U.S. She had been in Washington, D.C., representing them for four years.

Mr. Cowen had been employed as an insurance salesman for a small company in New Mexico for twenty years. He had retired two years ago.

The information she had looked at also indicated that they had one son, born in 1972. No other information was given about the son. Mrs. Cowen had indicated that they had no children. Megan could only speculate on why they had lied.

Since she didn't know Vicki's last name, she couldn't look her up. She would have to find out who she was and then do some checking.

Having stored the information away in her head, she erased it from her computer memory. She had been taught early on that you didn't leave anything around that someone else could find and question you about.

Megan had to go back to Cancun sometime in the next few days and check in with the Mexican agency that had given them the go-ahead in this investigation. They had been the ones who first became aware of a change in the situation and had asked the United States for help. She hoped they had some more information to give her.

The Mexican Coast Guard had intersected several shipments before they reached land and had been able to get some information from a couple of the people transporting them. It was through these people they had learned that there was now an organized group in charge, but the informants didn't know who they were or how the drugs got from the coast to Mexico City or the U.S.

Time to go visit some of my old friends, she thought, *and see if there is any gossip about the drug cartel.*

Some drugs had been crossing through the area for years, and maybe the locals didn't realize that things had changed. It would be interesting to find out.

Kevin couldn't believe it. He was really in Mexico and on his way to the archeological dig. He had loved taking part in excavations when he was a student and he was looking forward to the next six months. He would be here until the middle of December. One of the people from the dig had picked him up and was taking him to the site. He had a duffel bag full of personal belongings, a small amount of cash and that was it. He would be living in a tent at the dig site. His food would be furnished.

The past two weeks he had spent with his parents in Santa Barbara. His mom had been happy to have him home but was sorry that he could only stay for a short time. Most of his relatives couldn't understand why he would want to go live in a tent in the jungle and dig up old things from the ground. They told him he should be finding a nice girl and settling down and having babies. He had laughed and told them he would keep his eyes open for a nice jungle girl.

As they drove, Kevin noticed construction going on at various locations along the way. Jake, his driver, explained that the coastal area was constantly growing because of tourism. About an hour out of Cancun, they passed a little town called Akumal.

Glancing out the window, Jake said, "That's the nearest town to our site. You can go there on Saturday nights to get a change of pace. The people are friendly, and they have some nice restaurants and nightclubs. We usually take one of the vans so anybody who wants to go can. They have some nice hotels that don't cost a lot, so we usually stay the night and then spend the day on the beach before we head back on Sunday evening."

"I'll see. Right now all I want to do is get to the site and start to work. To be part of a dig is the best thing I can think of."

"It is fun, but a lot of backbreaking work. I've been here for three months and I like getting away for a few hours every week. I taught at Portland College before I came and I can tell you that for the first few weeks I was plenty sore. You get used to it though."

"I've been working out at the gym for the last few months, but I know this will use muscles I don't know I have. It's good to know that in time my body will adapt."

They were riding in a Landrover and soon were driving over some pretty rough roads.

"Now I know why you used this big car to pick me up," Kevin commented.

Before long they were pulling up in a clearing where several large tents could be seen. Some were closed, but the biggest had its flaps up and people were working over tubs, sifting dirt through wire mesh.

"Some articles we find are big enough that we see them in the dirt and have to brush it away with small paint brushes, but a lot of the dirt is carried up here and we sift it to see if anything is in it. We've found several small objects that way. Come on, I'll show you where you'll be bunking and then I'll take you on a tour to see the place and introduce you to everyone."

"Sounds good to me."

Kevin grabbed his duffel bag and followed Jake to one of the tents. He was shown his cot and Jake suggested that he change into cooler and more appropriate clothing before they continued the tour. He put on some khaki pants and a cotton long-sleeve shirt. He also pulled a wide-brimmed hat from the bag. He had received a list of necessary clothing items before he came.

After he was changed, they went to the big tent and he met two of the other workers. He was also shown a bulletin board that was kept in the main tent.

"Every night you check this board to see what your assignment is for the next day. We all do some of everything."

"Professor Parker is in charge and he's down at the main site. I'll show you there, and he can decide where he wants you to help for now."

They walked for some distance and passed two others pushing wheelbarrows full of dirt up to the main tent. Everyone seemed friendly and welcomed him.

When they arrived at the actual site, Kevin observed several large stone Mayan statues sitting on stone steps, but the work was going on a few feet from them. The statues had been there for years and would remain as they were. The excavation was taking place deep in the ground. He could see at least six holes with their sides reinforced with wood planks and ramps leading down into them. Some people were shoveling dirt into little wooden boxes with what appeared to be small toy shovels. Another man was lying on his stomach brushing dirt away in slow even strokes. Archeological digs were painstakingly slow and had to be done in a meticulous fashion.

"I think Professor Parker is over on hole number three. It's this way," Jake said as he headed to one of the work sites.

Kevin walked beside him until they reached the ramp. A man in his fifties was walking out.

"You must be Kevin Mackenzie. I'm Max Parker. You can call me Max," he said as he shook Kevin's hand and gave him a big smile.

Then turning to Jake he continued, "How long will it take to break him in to the rigors of this life, you think?"

Jake laughed and said, "If enthusiasm has anything to do with it, not long."

"Oh, so you're one of those who can't wait to get in the dirt. That's good, because we have a lot of dirt. Come on down here and I'll show you what I'm doing. Thanks for picking him up, Jake."

Kevin liked Max right off. He was a big hulk of a man and had the same twinkle in his eyes that he always saw when he looked at his dad.

As he followed Max down the ramp he called out, "Thanks, Jake, it's been great so far."

Over the next three weeks, Kevin got sore muscles as had been predicted. He also got to do anything you could think of to do with dirt, including shoveling it, brushing it, carrying it, pushing it, sifting it, lying in it and breathing it. He loved every minute he spent at the site.

The only people who didn't work with the dirt were the cooks. They were local people hired to feed the others. Their clothes were taken to Akumal by the cooks once a week and returned to them clean each Tuesday morning.

Sundays they were free to do whatever they wanted. Kevin turned down the chance to go into town. He read anything he could get his hands on about the Mayan culture and spent many an hour talking with Max about what they had already found and what they had learned from their discoveries.

Whatever artifacts they found were shipped either to the university in Mexico City or to the Institute of Archeological Studies in New York City. Each item would be studied and then dated and categorized. How best to preserve it would then be determined. Finally, it would be stored or placed in a museum in Mexico according to whatever the Mexican government decided.

By the fourth week, Kevin was considered a veteran. His body was used to the work and he had adjusted to the heat and humidity of the climate. His co-workers started to call him Professor since he spent all his free time reading or trying to learn more by picking the brains of those around him.

Chapter 30

Strolling along the main street of Akumal, Megan saw several people she knew. She stopped and visited with everyone. A Mexican husband and wife that were family friends, Raul and Maria, invited her to their home for lunch on Friday and she accepted. Another woman she had played with as a child told her to come by anytime so she could meet her two little boys.

Megan eventually found herself at Beth's hotel and decided to stop and visit for a few minutes.

Beth had her come into her office and then said, "Okay, young lady, I want to know what's going on with you. What was all that blarney you were spouting last night about loafing and your dad making you work?"

A sigh escaped before Megan could stifle it.

"I really can't tell you, but please keep my secret. All I can say is that it is important that the people we were with last night believe I'm a rich spoiled brat. You know I wouldn't ask you to play along with me if it weren't important."

Beth studied her face for a minute and said, "All right, for now, but if you are in some kind of trouble or if you need anything you will let me help, right?"

"You can count on it. Now fill me in on all the latest gossip."

Beth laughed, "Now why would you think I know any gossip. I'm an old lady and don't get around much anymore. Well, let me see. I'm trying to think who you know and if there is anything new with them. Manual and Rosa are expecting another baby in November. That will be number three for them. We have a new girl working at the kid's club, and she is making eyes at Franco at the dive shop. Is that the kind of gossip you wanted to know, or are you looking for something specific?"

Megan cringed inside. Beth was just too smart for her own good.

"You know it's not. Tell me about the people I met last night, Vicki for starters. What's her last name by the way?"

"Ah, so now we're getting somewhere. Brenten is her last name. She's been here for at least six months, maybe even a little longer. She's renting a little house in South Akumal. She doesn't do anything other than shop and flirt with men that I know of. She socializes with everyone, but doesn't seem to have any really close friends."

"What about Mrs. Cowen? Last evening I heard her and Vicki making plans to go see some Mayan dig."

"I guess she might be the closest thing to a friend Vicki has, but I don't think Ruth likes her flirting with Vince. I've seen them having lunch together a few times, and they have mentioned going shopping in Cancun together. I don't think they particularly like each other, though. Don't ask me why, it's just a feeling I get when I'm around them."

"How about Rex Higgins? What is he doing here and has he been here very long?"

"I'd hate to be his wife. I know he'll go after anything with boobs. He's been here about four weeks this time, but he's been here before. He talked to me and several others about investing in a satellite communications company that he tells us will replace what we already have. He keeps trying to convince us that he could provide more services than what we get now and that if we invest in it, we could make a huge profit. It was his assurance that we would make tons of money that turned off most of the people he talked to. He's just too sleazy for any of us to trust him."

"Let's see, who else was there last night? How about Josh Brown?"

"He seems like a real nice guy, always polite and pays his bill on time. I just get the feeling he isn't exactly what he seems. Stuart was there, too. He is such a fun man. Everyone likes him, and he can talk you into anything. If he were the one trying to sell the satellite company he would probably have several investors already. Actually, he said that he's just here to have a break from his former job. I take it he worked in the computer business and that he made a lot of money at it. He got burned out, though, and needed a break."

Megan had to smile to herself. Stuart could even fool Beth, and she could read most people like a book.

"Anyone else you want to know about?"

"As of right now, I can't think of anyone. Are there any other new and interesting people you want to tell me about? Or is there anything new or different happening here?"

"I can't think of anyone else new since you were here last. We do get some of the people from the Mayan archeological dig in town on Saturday nights, and they usually stay here overnight. They seem like a nice group. They're all either students or professors from different colleges. I know some of the tourists and even some of the locals have gone out to the dig to see what's going on. They'll take you on a short tour if you go out, but they're very careful and don't let anybody just wander around. I guess they're afraid someone might walk off with a valuable artifact."

Megan was afraid she could be treading in dangerous water, but she also knew that if anybody from the U.S. locals had heard anything about the drug ring it would be Beth, so she asked, "Has there been any increase in crime lately?"

Beth looked a little taken aback by the question.

"What are you getting yourself into? I don't know if I like where I think these questions are going." Then taking a deep breath and frowning at Megan she said, "Petty theft and occasional brawls still happen, just like always. Some of the people use recreational drugs, too, but I wouldn't classify any of them as real addicts. I'm sure you are aware that some drugs come in along the coast and make their way inland, but that isn't anything new. I've heard it whispered that the influx of drugs has increased and are more controlled than they used to be. I have no idea who's involved though, if that is what you're asking. And if it is, why are you asking?"

"No reason. I had just heard the same thing and hated the idea of this little town having such a thing start here," Megan said and shrugged her shoulders as if to dismiss it.

Beth wasn't comfortable with her answer but decided to let it drop. She knew Kaleb and Katie would be really upset if they thought Megan was involving herself somehow with drugs, even if it were an attempt to stop them. She would have to keep an eye on her to make sure she didn't get hurt.

Megan promised to stop by some other time and left. So, the word was getting out. She would bet that the native population knew a lot more about it than Beth did. She would see what her other friends had to say by the end of the week.

Wednesday night Megan went to dinner and dancing with Josh. They had a nice time. She likened it to going out with a brother, though. She played up her part of being a spoiled rich girl, and he remained the rich beach bum. She was sure she thought more kindly of him than he did of her. Of course, she knew he wasn't really what he pretended to be, while he thought she was exactly what she acted like. Good thing she didn't have a crush on him.

Josh didn't ask her out again, so she figured he had dismissed her as a suspect in the drug cartel.

On Thursday, she stopped by Olivia's and met her two little boys. They were two and four and very fun to be around. After giving the boys a lot of attention and asking about her husband, Megan brought up the subject of drugs.

Olivia seemed a little nervous, but then leaned near Megan and whispered, "Not good. Not good at all. No one will say anything because they are afraid. Some of the men used to pick up packages and deliver them to other men that came down from Mexico City, but now they either don't do it anymore or they have to give them to just one person. Nobody knows who he is, but they are told where to deliver. They are threatened with their lives if they take it anywhere but where they are told. A couple of men tried to give it to the people they used to give it to and now they have disappeared. We think they were killed. It's bad business. I'm so glad my family is not involved."

"I won't say anything. I had just heard rumors and wondered what was happening. I worry about my friends and don't want to see anyone get hurt."

Megan changed the subject and asked Olivia about all the new building going on and asked if wages were any better than they used to be. Olivia relaxed with the new topic and they had a nice visit before Megan left.

Megan went to Cancun Thursday afternoon and checked in with the Mexican Drug Enforcement Agency. She was shown into the director's office and briefed on the little bit of information they had accumulated.

They were convinced that the head of the operation was an American, from what the informants had said. They always referred to the person in charge as the Boss. The informants only spoke Spanish but still referred to the person in English and called him the Boss, as if that was his name.

They knew that the drugs came in mostly by boat and were dropped off along the coastline. They couldn't figure out how the drugs were getting to Mexico City or to the U.S. Prior to the takeover of the new cartel several shipments would be intercepted on their way through the jungle, but for the past several months not one was intercepted by its normal route. Agents in Mexico City knew that shipments had arrived, however; in fact, more than usual.

"We are missing an important link somewhere. We hope you can find out where it is. I will give you my personal telephone number so you can call me if you learn anything."

"Have the other American agents checked in with you?" Megan asked.

"Yes, but I have not told them of your arrival as was requested by your director. He is suspicious of one of them, yes?"

"I'm afraid so. I sure hope he is wrong about that. They all have good records and I would hate to see one of my co-workers turn bad."

"I understand. I would feel the same about my own people. Be careful. You are very young to be involved in such a dangerous business."

"I'll be careful, and my youth gives me the edge."

She smiled and then took her leave.

Lunch on Friday was spent with Raul and Maria. Maria was an excellent cook and the meal was delicious. They asked Megan about her family and especially about Katie. They had known Katie since she was twenty years old.

After lunch, Megan again brought up the subject of drugs coming in along the coast. Maria gave Raul a warning look, but he pretended he hadn't seen it.

He gave Megan a searching look and then said, "I wondered what you were really doing here. The water plant is coming along fine, and I know your dad trusts both me as the foreman and Keith, the director of the site. You showing up to look over our shoulders didn't seem right. I don't know what you have gotten yourself into and I won't ask, but I will try to help. Word has it that someone has taken over the business of drugs and anyone who tries to defy him winds up dead. I'm sure it has something to do with the new Americans in town, but I haven't figured out whom. Maybe some of them are working together. If I learn anything specific, I will let you know. You come by the site though, so no one wonders what you are doing here."

"Thanks, Raul. Please don't say anything about me to anyone else or you could put my life in danger. Not even to Keith. If he is upset with my being here, he will just have to live with it. I can't afford to have anyone suspect me of being anything but a spoiled rich girl checking up for her daddy."

"Okay honey, but you be cautious."

Maria and Raul each gave her a warm hug goodbye when she left. She really did love the people who lived here.

When she got home she checked her computer again. She had put Victoria's name into the computer to try to get some background on her, but had come up empty-handed. She then contacted her boss and asked him to see if he could find anything. She was still waiting for an answer. No reply yet.

Megan spent the weekend trying to organize what little she knew. Whoever was in charge liked to be called the Boss. He was most likely an American and he was deadly. He had the native Mexicans afraid of him and he had figured out a way to get the drugs out of the area without sending them through the jungle.

What came and went from this area? Planes, of course, but they were under heavy security and were checked both here and again when they landed in the U.S. Ships came and went, but why bother to bring them into the country in the first place if you were going to send it by ship, unless it was going in special cargo. But ships didn't go to Mexico City, and some of the drugs were making their way there.

She played all this over and over in her head. No answers came.

Chapter 31

Megan spent the next two weeks between the water plant and hanging around on the beaches, eating at the local restaurants and hitting the nightspots. Tourists came and went, but the people she had met the first night remained.

Rex and Vicki appeared to be having a fling. On one occasion, when Vicki was not around, Rex tried to pick up on Megan. She played along for a while and then suggested that maybe they could get a little cocaine and have a party. He backed off after she had made the suggestion.

Stuart didn't pay much attention to her. Megan figured Stuart and Josh were working together and Josh had already checked her out and decided she wasn't of interest to them. They did seem to spend a lot of time with the others though, so they must have had some leads that kept them focused in their direction.

Megan watched the Cowens closely whenever she was around them. They usually ate dinner out, but otherwise they weren't seen in town often. One evening Megan mentioned that she was thinking of going out to the Mayan excavation site just to see what was going on. Mr. Cowen said that he had been out there once and that he found it rather interesting. Ruth Cowen didn't say anything. That seemed funny, since she knew that she had gone with Vicki. Maybe they hadn't made it out there after all.

After being around Vicki more, Megan decided she was definitely closer to forty than she was to thirty. She also had gotten word back from her boss that Victoria Brenten was either a miracle worker or had risen from the dead. They had only found six Victoria Brentens in their complete search; one was sixty-five, another was five, one had died six months ago at the age of eighty, one lived on a farm in Iowa with her husband and five kids, and the other two reported every day to their jobs in Chicago, Illinois, and Norfolk, Nebraska.

Why was she using an alias? Maybe she was running from the law or maybe an irate husband. She wondered if she had forged documents to enter the country or if she had used her real identity and just used a different name once she got into Mexico. Since the borders between Mexico and the U.S. had been opened two years ago, anyone could enter or leave the country as long as they had proper identification. A visitor's visa was no longer needed.

She wanted to get a picture of Vicki to send to headquarters. She would bring a camera with her from now on and would try to get a group picture sometime in the near future. If that didn't work, she would have to think about breaking into her house to see if she could locate a passport or a driver's license.

Richard Trent hadn't been able to find out anything of value either. He seemed to be putting in a lot of time on his fake job. Maybe he was enjoying using his college degree for something other than fighting crime. For some reason his lack of interest kept her from telling him anything she learned, too.

By the time the third week had passed, Megan was getting frustrated. She decided to have a look around Vicki's house. She had learned which house she rented and had watched from a side street until she saw Vicki leave. This was one part of her job she didn't like. It always made her a bit nervous to break and enter. Usually she had someone else with her, too. That way one could keep an eye out for anyone returning. Well, she didn't have anyone there to help, so she would have to do it on her own. It should be a quick in and out job since she was just looking for a driver's license or anything with Vicki's picture on it that she could copy on her little copy machine. Modern gadgets were a godsend in her line of work.

She made her way to the front door of the house and looked over the entrance. She needed to be sure there were no security devices that would sound an alarm. She had just reached for the door handle when she glanced up again and saw a blinking red light at the very top of the doorframe. She recognized it for what it was. It was a well-hidden surveillance camera. She was quick on her feet and immediately reached out and rang the doorbell. When no one answered she knocked and called out, "Is anyone home?"

Acting as though she was distressed she muttered to herself, "Just my luck. No one here when I need help."

Turning, she headed across the street to the next house. She didn't know how far the camera viewed so she rang the doorbell at the next house and when someone answered she asked to use their telephone. They let her in and she called Maria.

"I'm having some trouble with my car. Could you have Raul come and see if he can fix it or give me a ride? I'm over in South Akumal on Quanta Street."

After she hung up she thanked the woman and walked back to her car. Waiting for Raul to come, she had time to think. She was shaking a little and had to take several deep breaths to calm her nerves. That had been very close. Once she was calm she began to wonder why Vicki would have such a high-tech camera at a rented house. Something was definitely not right with Miss Victoria Brenten.

Raul showed up a few minutes later and Megan got of the car and lifted the hood.

"Do something in there to make it look like you're fixing my car," she told him.

He gave her a worried look but nodded and bent over the engine. He pulled one of the wires loose from her battery and told her to try to start the car. When she did, of course it wouldn't start.

"Wait just a minute and let me try cleaning this cable. There, now try it."

The car started right up. Megan sat behind the steering wheel as Raul walked over to the window.

"Okay, young lady, what was that all about?"

"I can't tell you, but thanks for coming to my rescue. No questions please."

Raul shook his head and said, "I told you to be careful. I'll just tell anyone who asked that you had a loose battery cable and that it was corroded. Okay?"

Megan smiled and said, "That is exactly what the problem was. Thanks again, Raul."

They both pulled away. No picture, but she now wanted to get into that house more than ever. She had a little camera that she could probably conceal well enough that no one would know if she took their photo. She would try it first on one of her friends to see if they noticed her snapping a picture.

The following afternoon turned out to be her lucky moment. She had just walked out of Beth's office and had taken a picture of Beth without her noticing. The camera was in her hand and she had her beach towel folded over it. She looked out the door to see Vicki and Mrs. Cowen walking towards her. They both greeted her and asked how she was.

"I'm good today. Now, if I had seen you yesterday, I would have said not so well. I was over in South Akumal and had pulled over because my Coke fell and was spilling all over the car. The car died and I couldn't get it started again. I had to walk to someone's house and get Raul, my dad's foreman from the construction site, to come and fix the car. There wasn't anybody home at the first house I went to, so I had to walk to another house. I'm thinking of complaining to the rental agency for the inconvenience it caused me. What do you think? Shouldn't they be sure their cars are in good shape before they rent them?"

She added a little whine to her voice and acted really upset.

Mrs. Cowen rolled her eyes at Vicki as if to say, "What a spoiled brat."

Vicki smiled and said, "You poor dear. Where in South Akumal did it happen?"

"I was on the corner off of Quanta Street. Do you know where that is?"

"Why, I live on Quanta Street. I wonder if you might have come to my house. I wasn't home most of the day."

"I wouldn't know. I had an appointment for a facial at Thesa's and when I left there I grabbed a Coke and had it on the floor. I had heard that there was a new villa going up somewhere in the area and thought I would have a look. I hear it's supposed to be something. I guess I got turned around. There's so much new construction since the last time I was in that part of Akumal. I decided I was going the wrong way and when I turned, the stupid can fell over, and you know the rest. You would think that when you rent a car they would put drink holders in them, too. I miss the BMW I have at home."

"We're sorry you had such a bad day. Do be careful and don't set any more cans on the floor of your car. Your face looks lovely by the way. We're on our way to do some shopping, so we'll catch you later."

"Okay. Maybe I'll see you at dinner tonight."

As they walked away, Megan was relieved and excited. She had snapped a picture just as she walked up to them, so now she had to get it sent off to headquarters. She would drive into Cancun and have it developed at one of those one-hour photo places. She was also glad that she really had a facial at Thesa's before going to Vicki's house. She had the feeling that Vicki would check out her story.

It was on the way home from Cancun that she suddenly began to wonder about the Mayan excavation site. It seemed to come up in conversations, and Vicki was leading the pack of suspects as far as she was concerned. It was from Vicki's mouth that she had first heard of the excavation. Maybe she should go have a look for herself.

When she got home she sent a copy of the picture she had taken of Vicki and Ruth off to headquarters. For some reason she didn't destroy the picture right away. She decided to see if she could find someone to trust at the site and find out if either woman had ever been there.

The following morning, Thursday, she made plans to visit the site. She knew that they only did tours on Tuesdays and Saturdays, but she preferred to have a personal tour with no one else with her. She would take her chances and see if she could convince them to let her have a look around today.

She put on a pair of slacks and long-sleeved blouse that she tucked in. Socks and tennis shoes went on next. She was dressing for the jungle and knew enough about it to stay away from shorts and sleeveless tops. She gave herself a quick once-over in the mirror and decided to put her hair up. Once that was done she took a wide-brimmed straw hat from her closet and went to her car.

She had been to the Mayan ruins in the area several times, so she knew the way. The road would be bumpy, but the car was in good shape and up to the trip. She wondered if she would find anything of interest once she got there.

Chapter 32

Max stared intently into the mesh wiring as he swished it back and forth. He thought he glimpsed something shining in the dirt. A female voice interrupted his thoughts.

"Hi! Something interesting in that dirt?"

Looking up he saw a young woman standing several feet in front of him.

"How did you get in here? This isn't one of the days that we give tours."

"So I just found out. I bribed the guard to let me in," Megan said with a smile.

Giving her a calculated look, Max frowned. He knew that Pedro didn't let people bribe their way into the dig, so how had she gotten in?

"I don't think Pedro is open to bribes, so a better explanation is needed."

"You're right about that. He is an honest man. Actually, I have known Pedro since I was a little girl and I used to play with his children. I didn't realize until he told me that you only conducted tours on Tuesdays and Saturdays. I begged him to let me at least talk to you and see if you could make an exception this time. It was a bumpy road and I would hate to have to come back again. Please."

"Are you from around here? I don't recall seeing you the few times I've been in town."

"I'm down here to check on my dad's construction project, but my family owns a villa in Akumal. When I was a child we would spend at least three months a year here. This is the first time I've been here in the past couple of years. My name is Megan Dalton, by the way, and Pedro told me that you are Max Parker and the one in charge. It's nice to meet you."

"Since Pedro knows you and let you in, I can hardly turn you away. I'll get someone to show you around."

Max immediately thought of Kevin. He hadn't left the dig site since he got here a month ago. He needed to lighten up a bit, and this young lady looked like a good start. One of the workers had just arrived with a load of dirt. Max spoke to him.

"Would you go to hole number four and tell the Professor that I need him up here?"

Megan's heart gave a little lurch when she heard his words. *Was Richard Trent out here working at the site, and why?* she thought. She just stood smiling and decided she would just have to play dumb when he got there.

A few minutes later she saw a young man walking towards them. This wasn't Mr. Trent. She felt a wave of relief. As the man came nearer and she could see his features, she was sure she had met him before. She just couldn't place where or when.

Max called out, "Hey, Professor, I have a special job for you. I want you to give this young lady a tour of the area. She's a friend of Pedro's, so we're making an exception."

Kevin wasn't pleased when he heard what his special job was. Why couldn't she wait and take the tour when it was offered? He couldn't see her clearly as he approached since the sun was in his eyes, but at least she was dressed for the jungle.

When he reached them, Max made the introductions. Looking at Megan he said, "This is Kevin Mackenzie." Then turning to Kevin, he continued, "And this is Megan Dalton."

Both of them recognized the name of the other from that long-ago cold evening in Boston. Megan recovered from her surprise first and spoke without thinking.

"What are you doing here? Oh, that's right; you told me you were an archeology professor. I just never dreamed I would meet you again in the jungles of Mexico."

Kevin could see her face clearly now and his heart gave a little jump. He had wondered about her for some time after that unconventional meeting.

"I got lucky and landed a position working on this dig. What are you doing here?"

Max felt like a fifth wheel.

"I didn't realize that the two of you knew each other."

Megan laughed and said, "We've met, but we really don't know each other. Kevin stopped and kept me company one night when my car broke down in freezing weather in Boston. He kept me from getting frostbite."

Max grinned and said, "I'll bet he enjoyed that."

A blush rose on Megan's face but she stood her ground and explained that he had allowed her to wait in his car until the tow truck arrived. Kevin just stood there smiling. He had remembered thinking that she was very attractive and he had been sorry that she had never looked him up at the college.

Second chance, he thought.

"I still don't know what you're doing here? I never dreamt I would meet you again in Mexico."

"My dad is constructing a water purification plant in Akumal and he sent me down to do some checking on it. I work for his company. Plus, my parents own a villa here, and it's a semi-vacation for me."

So, she is Kaleb Dalton's daughter, he thought.

"I guess, since Max here gave his okay, we can begin the tour."

He explained what Max was doing first and then took her around the campsite. Next he walked with her down to the actual dig. She asked several questions and commented on the small tools used by the workers. He explained that they had to do everything slowly and gently so that they wouldn't damage anything that was buried in the earth.

As they walked back up to the campsite she asked, "What do you do with the things you find?"

"We catalog them and then box them up and ship them either to Mexico City or to the States. The actual study of the artifacts takes place after they leave here."

"How do they keep them straight as to where you found them, if you put them in boxes and send them away?"

"Each item goes in its own box and has any information we have attached to that item. We keep the boxes over in this tent and every evening we package up anything we found that day. At the end of the week we take them to Cancun and ship them by special cargo to their destination."

He showed her into the tent where the packaging took place. There were several boxes sitting on a table, and several more tables set up about the tent.

"We catalog the items and write out a description of each one in here."

"How do you decide where to send each item?"

"All bones and anything with what appears to be writing or pictures that might tell a story go to the United States. Everything else, like things made out of metals or pottery or wood, goes to Mexico City. Each of the two institutes that study these items has their own specialties. Eventually, everything is returned to Mexico."

"I bet you have to package everything very carefully."

"We handle the artifacts as if they were newborn babies. The boxes are special and protect the items. As far as I know we have never harmed anything in the shipping process. The group that is funding the study sends us new boxes every couple of weeks; that way the boxes don't get damaged from the moisture here. They have special linings that keep everything safe. I'm not a chemist, so I don't know what the lining is made of, but it works."

"This has been so interesting. I'm glad I came. A couple of my friends told me that they had come on a tour and I just had to come myself."

She reached into her purse and pulled out the photo of Vicki and Ruth.

"These are my friends. Did you take them on the tour?" she asked.

Kevin glanced down at the picture. He thought it a little strange that she would ask him about her friends, but then who knew how some people's minds worked. He gave the picture a second look and knew he had seen one of the ladies before.

"I think I might have seen the one on the left, but I haven't done many tours and I usually don't pay any attention to the tourists when they come."

Megan just shrugged her shoulders and returned the picture to her purse. He had pointed out Vicki. She was easier to remember because of her flirtatious manners, and she just bet she had noticed Kevin.

As they walked back to her car, Kevin decided not to let her get away this time without making an effort to see her again.

"Some of the people go into town on Saturday night. I was wondering; would you like to have dinner with me this weekend if I come to town?"

Megan was pleased with the request.

"I think I would enjoy that. I could meet you somewhere. Where do you like to eat?"

"I have no idea. I've never been in Akumal. Why don't you name a place and I'll find it? I think they usually arrive around six."

"Okay, we can meet at Quz Onda. It's a little Italian restaurant that has great food and is quiet so we can talk. I'll see you there at six."

Kevin smiled as she walked away. He still didn't know what her hair was like, since she had on a big straw hat with her hair pulled up under it. He was looking forward to Saturday. As he turned to go back to work, Max motioned him over.

"If that smile is any indication, I would say you just made some plans for Saturday night."

"That I did. See you later, Max."

Chapter 33

As Megan drove away, she thought over all she had learned. Kevin had almost seemed embarrassed when he said that he thought he had seen Vicki at the site. She would bet that Vicki had made a play for him. The site and the work itself had been interesting, and she could understand how people interested in archeology would enjoy being there.

It was the shipping of the artifacts that interested Megan. They sent their items to the two places that the drugs went. She hadn't asked exactly where in the U.S. the items went because she was afraid to ask any more questions, but if she developed a relationship with Kevin she would get a chance to find out more.

Any items coming into the United States were searched both by x-ray and dogs. If they couldn't be searched by x-ray they were physically searched. Had someone in the customs department gotten sloppy with the boxes coming from the site, or was there some other means of concealing the drugs in the boxes that was going undetected? Her gut feeling told her that the drugs were getting shipped with the artifacts.

Kevin said they got new boxes every two weeks, so that would work perfectly for the drug runs. Where the boxes were made and who purchased them were the next things to find out.

She hadn't heard from headquarters yet, either. She wondered if they had found out who Vicki really was. She planned on checking her computer when she got back, and then she really should find some time to meet with Richard and fill him in on what she suspected.

When she arrived at the villa she had a message on her computer from headquarters. They wrote that the picture she had sent was black and out of focus. It was a good thing she hadn't destroyed the picture yet, as was the proper procedure, or she would be back to square one in that area. She re-sent the picture.

Deciding to wait until she heard back from headquarters before she talked with Richard, her mind turned to Kevin. He was a nice man and very good-looking. She was glad that they had met again and was looking forward to dinner on Saturday. Her life after college hadn't left much time for socializing, and sometimes she wondered if she would ever meet the man of her dreams.

On Friday she went to the restaurant that seemed to be the meeting place for all her suspects. All were there, including Josh, Stuart and Beth. They asked if she would like to join them for dinner.

During the meal, Mr. Cowen announced that he was going back to the States the next day. Everyone was surprised and asked why he was going. He began to answer saying, "I miss my..." and that was as far as he got when his wife interrupted him.

"He has so many friends there and he gets lonely for his old golf partners. I love it here though, so I'm staying. He is only going home for a month."

Mr. Cowen gave his wife a frown but said no more. Rex spoke up then and said that he planned to leave a week from Sunday.

"I have to get back to work. I still wish some of you would invest in the company. I know you would make a lot of money. Megan, sometime when you talk to your dad, why don't you ask him if he would be interested? I can leave you all kinds of information about the venture."

"That would be fine. I'll keep the information and the next time I see him, I'll pass it on. You can drop it off at the villa tomorrow."

It just appeared easier to go along with him than to tell him that her dad wouldn't ever consider such an investment. The rest of the evening passed pleasantly enough without any more surprises.

Megan hadn't received any messages from her director on Saturday. She supposed they were unable to do much work since it was the weekend. Maybe Monday she would get the information she had requested.

As evening approached, Megan found herself getting excited about her date. She looked through her closet several times to try to find just the right outfit. She settled for a sundress in a dark shade of blue. It set off the blue of her eyes. She slipped on a pair of sandals and let her hair down. Her hair reached the middle of her back and had a little natural wave. She didn't like to wear jewelry, but did so to play up the part of being a rich girl. She decided a bracelet that had several sapphires on it would be enough for tonight.

Taking one last look in the full-length mirror, and dabbing some perfume behind her ears, she picked up her purse and set out for the restaurant. She had decided to walk, as she lived close to the main part of Akumal. When she arrived, Kevin was already there.

"We got here a little early. You sure look great. This is the first time I've seen your hair. It's gorgeous."

"Thank you. You look different, too. You have on regular clothes without dirt all over them. Let's go in and find a table. The food here is really special. I hope you like Italian."

"My mother's Italian and does the cooking for the restaurant my folks own. I definitely like Italian food."

Megan laughed. "I would never have guessed that you were Italian with the last name of Mackenzie. You must have gotten your coloring from your dad. You're tanned from being in the sun, but seem quite fair, and with blonde hair I would never have suspected that your mother was Italian."

"Well, she is, but actually I was adopted as a baby, so I don't know what nationality my birth parents were."

"I understand. After my mom died my dad remarried and my step-mom is fair with blonde hair. I got my dark complexion and hair from my mother. Whenever I introduce my parents, people study us to see who I look like, but they can't seem to pick up much resemblance."

They found a little table for two in the back and ordered a glass of wine to start with. Megan noticed a little silver pin on the lapel of Kevin's shirt collar. Other than that, the only other jewelry he had on was a wristwatch.

Kevin noticed where her eyes had settled and he reached up and fingered the little pin.

"I consider this my good luck charm. I don't wear it too often, but I wanted to have luck on my side tonight," he said with a grin.

Megan felt a little blush creep up her face. Changing the subject she asked him how long he would be working at the site.

"I'm going to be here until the middle of December. Then I'll go to Santa Barbara for the holidays before I return to Boston for the spring semester. How about you?"

"I'm not sure how long I'll stay. I'm doing some work for my dad. It could take a while; a few more weeks at least. By the way, I was in California in March and I made it a point to go to Santa Barbara. You were right; it is a very nice place."

"Did you have business there?"

"No, I was actually at a construction site in Santa Monica, but I made a special trip to Santa Barbara just because you had told me how much you liked it."

"You went there on the word of a stranger."

"Yes, but then you were a very nice stranger. Thank you again for stopping that night."

"I think that was my lucky night. If we hadn't met then, you probably wouldn't have agreed to have dinner with me."

"If we hadn't met then, you wouldn't have asked me."

"Don't be too sure about that. You're very pretty, and I told my family before I left that I was going to find me a jungle girl."

Laughing, Megan said, "I don't know that I qualify as a jungle girl. I am from Boston."

"Ah, but it was in the jungle that I got the chance to ask you out."

"That's true. How do you like Mexico?"

"I haven't seen much of it. I'm spending the night here and tomorrow I'm going to see how the beach compares to California's. You want to go to the beach with me tomorrow?"

"That sounds like a good plan. You'll be surprised at how warm the water is. How did you wind up in Boston anyway?"

"My dad graduated from Boston College and pushed me to go there. I like it except for the winters. Do you have any brothers or sisters?"

"I have twin brothers and a sister. They're several years younger than me. The boys are in high school and my sister is an eighth grader this year. How about you?"

"I'm an only child. I have tons of cousins and other family, though. Even though I don't have brothers or sisters, I feel like I grew up in a large family. I suppose we should order."

They studied the menu and made their selections. The food was as good as Megan had promised. Conversation remained comfortable and they both enjoyed themselves. After eating, Kevin suggested that they go somewhere to dance.

As they entered the nightclub Megan saw Rex, Vicki, Josh and Stuart sitting together at a table. They all saw them enter and waved them over. Kevin was introduced and Vicki smiled at him, saying, "You probably don't remember me, but I remember you from the dig site. How did you ever get him to come to town, Megan?"

Kevin spoke up, "I met Megan months ago in Boston. When we found out we were both here, we decided to renew our old acquaintance. We came in here to dance, so if you'll excuse us."

He guided Megan onto the dance floor.

"You really don't like her, do you?"

Kevin didn't have to ask to whom she was referring.

"Not particularly. She is much too pushy and tries to act several years younger than she is. You asked me the other day if I had seen her. I'll tell you now that she's been to the site a couple of times and tries to pick up any guy that will give her the time of day."

Kevin was an excellent dancer and it felt good to be held in his arms. The music switched to a faster beat and they agreed to sit this one out. When they returned to the table Rex and Vicki were gone. Josh and Stuart visited a short while longer and then made their way to the bar.

"Thank God they all decided to leave. I want to have you all to myself," Kevin said.

Megan felt the same. Plus, she really didn't want to try to play the spoiled-rich-girl role in front of Kevin. The evening passed quickly and soon it was time to say goodnight. Kevin insisted on walking Megan home and they shared a goodnight kiss on her doorstep.

When Megan entered her house she was floating on cloud nine. It had been a long time since she had spent such a nice evening with a man. In fact, it was the best time she could ever remember having. He was wonderful.

Kevin almost skipped back to the hotel. She sure was terrific. He was going to come back to the villa at nine the next morning. She said she would fix him breakfast and then they could go to the beach. This beat the heck out of reading books all weekend long.

Megan didn't even check her computer but went straight to bed. When the alarm woke her in the morning, she showered and dressed in a swimsuit and then put a cover-up over it. Making her way to the kitchen she started to prepare waffles and clean strawberries to put over them.

The ringing of the doorbell told her that Kevin had arrived. He had on his swim trunks and a T-shirt. They ate the waffles on the patio. When they finished, he helped her clean the kitchen, saying that he was a pro at clean-up from his years of working for his folks at the restaurant.

Megan grabbed some beach towels and they headed to the beach. Kevin stood with his mouth gaping when Megan took off her cover-up and walked into the water. She had on a bikini that showed her figure at its best. Kevin pulled his T-shirt off and followed her into the water.

"You're right, the water is warm, or maybe it's just me. You raised my temperature by several degrees when you took off that thing you had on."

Megan splashed some water at him and replied, "I think you like to see me blush. Come on. I'll race you to that rock out there."

She pointed to a rock that stood in the water several yards away. Kevin dived into the water and the race was on. He beat her, but just barely. They were both laughing when they surfaced.

"You're good but you can't beat a native California beach bum," Kevin remarked.

Megan decided it was payback time. She looked him over and said, "I could have, but the scenery was just too good from behind."

He pulled her into his arms and said, "I think you're getting just a little bit too mouthy," and with that he pulled her under the water and tight up against him. He found her mouth and melded their lips. They came to the surface in a full embrace with their lips sealed together. When they both had to take in some air, they broke the contact.

"I think I'm the one that's got a fever now," Megan said.

Kevin grinned and flipped onto his back to let the water carry him back to shore. The water was still, so he had to aid his progress. Megan swam easily beside him until they were back on land.

"So what do you think of the sea shore as compared to California?"

"I think I fell in love the moment we set foot in the water."

He hadn't really answered her question, and she had the feeling he wasn't talking about the beach. She didn't know what to say, so she began to lay the towels out for them to sit on. They relaxed in the sun. The water was beautiful and clear and the sand was snow white. It really was the perfect place to fall in love. Time for Kevin to return to camp came much too soon.

"I'll be back next Saturday."

"Okay; I think I'm going to miss you and I hardly know you."

"The same for me."

He gave her a hug and got into the van. They waved to each other as he pulled away.

The following week, both Megan and Kevin were kept occupied with their own work, but on Saturday night they again spent the evening together. Megan fixed dinner at the villa and they spent the time getting to know each other better. Later in the evening they went dancing.

On Sunday they rented snorkeling equipment and went snorkeling in the lagoon. Kevin was impressed with the coral and sea life. It was a pleasant afternoon and they strolled on the beach until it was time for Kevin to once again leave for the dig site.

"If you get lonely and want another tour, you come by any time. I'm not in the army or prison, you know," Kevin said as he kissed her goodbye.

"I'll see how the week goes, but I'll try to get there in a few days."

Chapter 34

Returning to the villa, Megan changed out of her swimsuit and went straight to her computer; nothing there. She would have to talk to Richard tomorrow. She had to see if he knew anything that might help her find out about Vicki. She wasn't any closer to figuring out who might be betraying the agency either.

The ring of the doorbell startled her. She didn't expect any company tonight. She looked through her peephole and was surprised to see Stuart standing on her step. She knew she had been a little careless the past few days, so she went to the table and took out a small handgun from her purse. She slipped it into her pocket and pulled her top over it to conceal it from view. When she got the gun out, the picture she had taken of Vicki and Ruth fell onto the table. Deciding it wasn't good to leave it lying around and not having time to destroy it, she stuck it in her other pocket.

Opening the door, she was about to speak when Stuart placed his fingers over her mouth and shook his head. Then he motioned her to follow him out. She did.

He walked to the end of her drive and started towards the beach. She followed behind, wondering what was going on. She felt a sliver of fear but continued down the path with him in the lead.

A short distance away from her home he stopped, turned toward her, and then smiled.

"So you're the Gypsy," he said.

That was the last thing she expected to hear. He had caught her off guard and she didn't know how to respond. She gave him a puzzled look as though she didn't know what he was talking about. She slipped her hand into her pocket and waited.

"Sorry. I didn't mean to frighten you, and don't pull that gun out of your pocket yet. I know that you know who I am. I went to Cancun today and contacted headquarters. They told me about you and said I would have a hard time convincing you that I'm supposed to deliver this message, but they had no choice. Someone has been intercepting our e-mails to headquarters. I got suspicious when half of the information I requested didn't come. They either didn't receive my requests or I never got their answers. I asked you to come out here because I have a feeling that our homes or rooms are bugged. I found a tracking device and receiver in my car, too. I've been trying to think of a way to convince you that I'm not the one that is double-crossing the agency. I think the only way to do that is for us to go to Cancun, and you can call headquarters from any phone you choose. That way you can talk to the director yourself and also know that the phone call isn't being monitored on this end. I went to Cancun on the bus so as not to let whoever was tracking me know that I had found the devices. You didn't put them there did you?"

When Megan gave him a blank look he said, "I didn't think so. I know you were supposed to check me out, but wire tapes and tracking devices aren't your style."

He was so easy to believe, but how could she trust him. She didn't know what to do. She didn't want to go off somewhere with him by herself, but she had to find out what was going on or she could walk into a real trap. If Kevin was still in town she would ask him to go with her, but he wasn't. If she suggested that either Josh or Richard come along she could be inviting the very person they were trying to catch to observe their every move.

One of her best qualities had always been her gut instinct, and it was telling her to trust this man. Could she go with her instinct when her life might depend on it? He seemed to be willing to wait for her to make up her mind and didn't push.

"Don't you think a pay phone from Akumal would be safe?"

"It might, but there are only four that I know of, so they could easily be wired. Cancun is a different matter, lots of phones there."

He had a point. It wasn't as if she would be in a car alone with him, and he already knew who she was, so if he meant to do her harm he would find a way.

"Okay, let's go. I take it you have some money on you so I don't have to go back to the house."

"That's my girl, already thinking ahead. Let's go, the bus leaves in five minutes."

They walked to the bus stop. Megan was happy to see several others waiting to get on. She didn't know any of the people though. That was probably good, since she didn't want whoever was behind this to see her leave or hear that she had been seen leaving on the bus. They might get suspicious since she had her own car and rich people didn't ride the bus.

An hour and fifteen minutes later they were in Cancun. It was already seven in the evening and the last bus going back left at eight-thirty. They left the bus and walked several blocks before Megan found a phone. She had memorized the special number the director had given her to use in case of an emergency. She asked Stuart to wait a half a block away and then stepped into the phone booth.

Picking up the phone, she dialed the number. She recognized her boss's voice when he answered.

"Hi, this is Megan."

"So the Preacher still has his touch. I was afraid he wouldn't be able to convince you to call me. Where are you calling from?"

"I'm at a pay phone in Cancun."

"Good. That should be safe. Is Stuart there with you?"

"Yes and no. He rode here on the bus with me, but he's about half a block away from the phone booth. What have you found out that makes you trust Stuart?"

"We kept getting what seemed like partial requests or requests for information that we had already sent from you and Stuart and Josh. It didn't make any sense, so we tried a new gadget that one of our men was working on. We've had it up and running for the past week. It's a device that can track e-mails and tell where they're received and if they're intercepted. We can then trace the interruption to wherever it goes, kind of like tracing a phone call. We have known for some time that e-mails could be intercepted if one of the computers that is sending or receiving the message is wired with a special device, but we didn't know how to trace the interruption before now. All of your computers have had that device installed in them by someone."

"Have you been able to find out who is interrupting the messages?"

"The messages are going to a house on Quanta Street in South

Akumal."

"Vicki. Did you ever get the picture I sent of her?"

"I'm afraid not. You can be sure that she knows who you are though. I'm thinking that maybe I should pull all of you off the case. I don't see how you can be effective with the bad guys knowing who you are."

"Before you do that, do you have a fax machine where you are?"

"Yes, of course. Why?"

"Give me your fax number and I'll send you a picture of Vicki. I'll send it and then call you back in an hour. I want to see if you can find out who she is. Maybe if we know the answer to that we can figure this out."

"All right, but after I get the picture if I decide you need to come back I'll make it an order. Understood?"

"Okay. I'll talk to you in an hour."

Megan broke the connection and walked back to where Stuart stood waiting.

"We need to find a fax machine."

He didn't question her but looked about for a likely place to find a machine.

"I would bet that a hotel would have one. The Hilton is just a couple of blocks from here."

"Let's go."

After Megan faxed the picture, she and Stuart found a table in the little coffee shop and ordered coffee. She started to go over everything in her mind and said out loud, "I just wish I knew who Vicki Brenten was. I think that is the key."

She repeated Vicki Brenten several more times in her mind and then the last time she repeated it, her mind seemed to tangle and she heard Vicki Trenten. A light seemed to go on in her head.

"Oh, my God! Do you know anything about Richard Trent's personal life?" she asked Stuart.

"Not really. I think he was married once. I worked with him a few years ago and it seems like he mentioned her in passing. That was a long time ago."

"It could be important. Do you know her name?"

Stuart sat frowning, "It seems like it was an unusual name, like Michala or Michlea. I think he just called her Micki."

"That's got to be it. Come on. I need to call headquarters."

"I thought you were supposed to give them an hour."

"I would, but they won't be looking in the right place."

Megan found a pay phone in the lobby of the hotel and dialed the emergency number again. When it was answered she said, "I think I know who she is."

"That would be good, since so far she isn't matching up to any of the women in our criminal files."

"Do you keep files on our families?"

There was a brief pause and then he answered, "I'm afraid so. Why?"

"How about pictures of our families?"

Another pause and then, "Yes."

"Good. Check Richard Trent's file and see what his wife or ex-wife looks like."

Megan could hear the phone being set down and several long minutes later her boss came back on the line.

"I don't know how you figured it out, but you hit it right on the head."

"I'm almost sorry I did. I just remembered in one of my criminal law classes that most aliases were close to the person's real name. I kept repeating her name in my head until I said Trenten instead of Brenten. Stuart remembered that Richard had referred to his wife as Micki; Micki Trent and Vicki Brenten, one and the same."

"I guess now that we know who our rotten agent is; you three can take care of each other until we can prove everything. You can stay on the job. I would suggest that you leave all the wiretapping equipment in place and meet at safe locations. You have to continue to report to Richard. Just give him enough information to let him know you're working on the case and then let him hang himself. You all be careful and tell Stuart and Josh I'm sorry I suspected them, but I have a feeling Richard planted enough evidence against them to make it look like a possibility. Keep me informed of anything else you find out, but use a pay phone like you did this time."

"Okay, and while I have you on the phone I need you to check something else for me. Can you see who is financing the archeological dig that is going on at the Mayan site outside of Akumal? I'll check back with you as soon as I can. We have to catch a bus now. Bye."

Stuart and Megan ran to make the departure. They both spoke little, as there were several others on the bus and they were both leery of whom to trust.

When they arrived back in Akumal, Megan made her way to a small café and ordered a sandwich. A few minutes later she saw Stuart enter the usual restaurant and nightclub. She finished her sandwich and then walked to the club. Vicki was sitting at a table with Josh, and Stuart was at the bar having a drink with one of the local men.

Megan went to the table and greeted the two. "Pretty quiet tonight. Did Rex get off on his flight?"

Vicki sighed and said, "He left this morning. I don't think he was too thrilled with the idea of going home to his wife and kids, and now I don't have anyone to dance with. I wish that hunk you were with the last couple of weekends were here. I'd like to get my claws into him."

Megan was red with jealousy just at the idea of Vicki coming anywhere near Kevin, but she smiled and said, "I wish he was here, too. He is quite a hunk, isn't he?"

"Where have you been all evening? I thought the van from the dig left hours ago."

"It did. I went home and changed and then one of the women I know dropped by and we went for a walk and talked about things. Her husband was home with her kids and she just wanted to get out of the house for a while. But married women with kids have to go home early, so here I am."

Vicki said, "Well, married or not, I think it's time for me to go home. I'll probably see you guys tomorrow." She picked up her purse and left.

Megan smiled at Josh and then said, "What do you have on?"

Josh frowned at her and said, "What do you mean what do I have on?"

"Humor me. Stand up and let me see what you're wearing."

Josh shrugged his shoulders and stood. He had on a pair of swim trunks and a short-sleeved shirt. She could see his chest through the open vee of the shirt, nothing on under the shirt and no pockets. He wasn't wearing a watch, so he must have come straight from swimming.

Megan stood and said, "Let's go for a walk. I want to talk to you."

"Sure, why not?"

She caught Stuart's eye as they left. He followed a ways behind and then turned down a side path that led to the beach.

Megan noticed Vicki's car that had been parked in front of the club was gone, so she felt comfortable about walking with Josh.

"I want to go down on the beach. Okay?"

"Fine with me. Is there something special you wanted to talk about?"

They were just on the edge of the sand when Megan answered him.

"Yes. I think it's time for the Preacher, the Bum and the Gypsy to have a little meeting."

Josh looked surprised.

"You're the Gypsy? I should have guessed."

Stuart joined them a few moments later. They told Josh all they knew about the wiretaps and the tracking devices. She also informed them that the e-mails were being intercepted and about the new device the agency had used to track it.

Josh was surprised to learn he had been a suspect, but then understood when Megan told him what the director had said about planted material. He hadn't figured out who Vicki was, but he had decided she was definitely involved.

After talking for some time, they tried to speculate on who else they thought might be involved. Richard, of course, but did Rex Higgins or the Cowens have any connection? It was still an open question. Megan did tell them she thought the drugs were being smuggled in the boxes from the dig site, but she didn't know how.

"Do you think someone who is actually working there is involved?"

"I suppose someone could be, but I don't think there is any reason for them to have to be there. I would bet the drugs are already in the boxes before they arrive. Having someone in the camp would just be a waste of their time."

"What are you going to tell Richard? And what should we be e-mailing? It would seem pretty strange if we don't communicate at all with headquarters," Stuart said.

"I guess I'll have to tell him I suspect one of you as the traitor. Who wants the privilege?"

"I think it should be me," Josh said. "Vicki knew you and I were left alone and she may have even found a place to watch to see if we left together. I'll be waiting to see if they try to plant some kind of evidence on me after you tell Richard what you think. You might even e-mail your suspicions to headquarters. I'll try to act the same in my room and in my car, but it will be hard."

"Now, that I find hard to believe. You are the consummate actor, according to the file I read on you. You better walk me back to my house so if anyone is watching they'll think we just took a walk. Take care, Stuart. Thanks."

Josh saw Megan to her door and left. Megan was nervous about her place being wired, but she decided she could handle it. After taking a shower she fixed herself a glass of ice tea and then lay down in her bed and switched the television on.

She figured she would be unable to sleep, but soon she was dozing off. She caught herself nodding and switched the TV off. As she fell to sleep she was thinking about Kevin. She missed him and wished he could be there to keep her safe.

Kevin was lying in his cot thinking about Megan. He couldn't believe how beautiful she was, and so nice. Maybe his family was right. He should be looking for a nice girl to settle down with. She was perfect. She was well-educated and understood family commitment, since she worked in the family business. She was fun, and he bet her family had kept her innocent of all the ugly things in the world, and he would like to protect and keep her that way.

Chapter 35

Megan made plans to meet with Richard on Tuesday afternoon. She went to the plant and asked to see him in the construction site's office. She told Keith, the director of the operation, that she would need his office for a private meeting with Mr. Trent. She indicated there were some recommendations he had made upon which she wanted clarification and she would like to handle it herself. Keith appeared to be a little upset by her request, but she was the boss's daughter, so he had no choice. At noon, Richard came in and closed the door.

"I take it this is not about my recommendations. Have you learned anything?"

"I've narrowed my suspects down to Vicki—the woman I told you about—and Rex Higgins. Rex left on Sunday, supposedly to go home. I e-mailed headquarters to see if they can confirm that is where he really is. He has a criminal record, so that moves him way up on my list. I haven't figured out how the drugs are moved out of the area. It's a real puzzle. What about you? Have you learned anything?"

"I have to agree with you on Rex Higgins. I'm not sure why you think Vicki is involved though. Has she said or done something to make you suspicious?"

"No, she hasn't done anything, but headquarters can't seem to find a trace of her. I just have a feeling about her. I guess that's what has me looking her way. Have you learned anything about her?"

"Not really. Maybe I can just do some checking of my own and see if I can find anyone by that name who might fit her description. I still have some ties with some people at the old agency I used to work at, maybe they can find a DMV record or something. You have to have more than feelings to base your conclusions on."

Megan shrugged her shoulders and just made a face.

"Oh, I think our traitor is most likely going to turn out to be Josh. I saw him the other night talking with some pretty scuzzy-looking people down by one of the bars. It looked like money was being exchanged. I tried to play up to him the next night and thought maybe I'd see if I could get him to show a little interest. I don't think he finds me very appealing though."

Megan said the last with a bit of a pathetic whine.

"Maybe I should tell him that Daddy is threatening to cut off my money supply and see if he offers me a way to make a little extra cash."

Richard almost seemed disgusted with her, like she was somehow beneath him and he didn't think she was worth his time. Their previous contact had been very brief, so he didn't really know what she was like.

"I guess that might be a workable plan. I hate to think Josh would betray us."

"I know. It makes me kind of sick to my stomach. You better tell me something you've recommended to Keith before I leave, something he has already decided to do."

"Okay, let's see. I told them to use a particular kind of filter for the uptake system. It really is the best there is on the market and I know what a stickler your dad is about using the best. I think they've already ordered them. By the way, I saw you with some man last Saturday night. Is he involved in this?"

"You must mean Kevin. No, he's someone I knew back in Boston. In fact, he's a professor from Boston College just down here to take part in the archeological dig that's going on outside of Akumal. He's personal, if you know what I mean."

"You take care and let me know if anything else turns up. I'll fill you in if I find out anything about Vicki."

They left the office and Megan found Keith.

"I think his recommendation on the kind of filters we should use sounds good. Do you agree?"

Keith frowned and said, "I already ordered them. Is there anything else you want done?"

"No, that's all. I'll see you later in the week."

As Megan left the site she could almost feel Richard's eyes on her.

She hoped she had convinced him she wasn't smart enough to be a real threat.

Megan and the other two agents met at the dive shop on Wednesday morning. She told them what she had told Richard. She also told them she planned to go to visit Kevin that afternoon and, if she had to, she was going to tell him what she did and see if he could help her get one of the boxes so they could study it. They wanted to be sure he could be trusted, and she told them about how they had met and that he was trustworthy. They decided she should go with her instincts and do whatever she thought necessary.

Stuart planned to take the bus into Cancun again and would check with headquarters to see who was financing the dig. Josh said he better stay in town and act like he was wasting time. They all laughed and went their separate ways.

When Megan pulled up to the site, she noticed Pedro was again on duty at the entrance. She told him Kevin had extended an open invitation for her to visit.

"He's working at sifting dirt today, so he should be the first one you see. Go on up."

As she drew near to the tent she could see Kevin busy at work shaking the dirt through the meshing.

"Hi, good-looking. You finding any lost treasures in there?"

Kevin lowered the sieve and smiled up at her "The only treasure I've seen today is standing in front of me. I'm so glad you found time to stop by. I've been thinking about you ever since I waved goodbye on Sunday." He turned towards the back of the tent and called out, "Hey Max, I'm taking a break. Okay?"

Max spotted Megan and hollered back, "Take your time, there's nothing here that hasn't been here for a few hundred years already."

"Let's walk up behind the ruins. There are some pretty places up there."

"Okay. How's it going? Are you finding lots of important things?"

"Some days we find a lot of stuff and other days, like today, nothing."

They had walked up behind the camp and were now making their way to some stones that sat a few feet from the Mayan statues. Kevin was holding her hand, and when they reached the stones he helped her to sit on top of a smooth rock. He was leaning towards her to give her a welcoming kiss but she put her hand up to stop him.

"Before you kiss me, I have something to say. The first day I came out here, I had no idea that you were here. Our dates have been strictly pleasure and because I like you but, so things don't get mixed up, I have to tell you today I'm here on business."

"Business? What could I possibly have to do with a water treatment plant?" Kevin asked in confusion.

"Not a thing, but that's not the business I'm here for. What I am about to tell you must never go any further or you could be putting my life in danger. Promise you won't tell anyone what I am about to say."

A look of total bafflement crossed Kevin's face. "What could you possibly tell me that could put you in any kind of danger?"

"I'm not really in Mexico to work at my dad's construction site. That's just a cover. I'm an agent with the United States Drug Enforcement Agency, an undercover agent. In the past year this region of the Yucatan Peninsula has been organized into one of the most successful drug smuggling operations around. I was sent here to try to find out who was in charge and also to uncover a traitor within the agency. I need your help."

Kevin couldn't have been any more shocked by what she said than if she had told him she was a mermaid and she had to go back to the sea.

"You're not joking about this, are you?"

"I'm not joking. I think the smuggling ring is using this operation to ship the drugs to Mexico City and to the U.S."

Kevin plopped down on the rock beside her. She was serious.

My God, he thought, *I was going to protect her from the world, and she knows more about the ugly part of society than I could begin to imagine.*

"How did you ever get mixed up in something like this?"

"Remember I told you I had gotten my degree in criminal justice from Boston College. The agency recruited me before I even graduated. I've been working for them for the past four years. I don't usually tell anyone what I really do. Other than the people who work in the agency, my dad is the only one who knows, and now you. The fewer people who know, the safer I am. I'm sorry I told you because it could put you in danger too, but I just couldn't use you as a means to an end and have you thinking that is the only reason I went out with you. Does this make you feel differently about me?"

"It scares the hell out of me. You're just a fragile little thing and shouldn't be messing around in this kind of business."

"I'm not fragile. I told you I had a black belt and that wasn't a lie. I'm also a crack shot and can handle a knife with some expertise. I'm usually far away before the bust actually goes down though. I have to remain unknown if I'm to be of any value to the agency. I dig for the evidence and then let someone else do the clean-up. We both dig in dirt, mine's just a different kind."

Kevin sat shaking his head. He still couldn't believe it.

"What are you hoping I can help you with? I don't know anything about a drug ring."

"One of the biggest problems we're having is trying to figure out how the drugs are getting from the coast to their destinations. I think they're going with your artifacts every time you ship."

"I've helped package those things many times, and I can assure you no one is putting anything illegal in them."

"I agree. Tell me this, when they go through the airport security systems are they x-rayed?"

"No, that could damage some of the articles and cause the dating of them to be off. But they are opened and inspected by at least two people working together. It's customs' way of making sure everything remains on the right side of the law. I know they have trained dogs there, too. If there were drugs, the dogs would sniff them out."

"That's what I thought at first, but you told me the boxes are specially made and delivered every two weeks. I think the drugs are already stored in the boxes before they get here. I hoped you could sneak one out for me so I can study it. There has to be a way for them to be using the boxes. It's the only thing that fits. The Mexican government is the one who first realized the movement of drugs through this area had changed. They still intercept drugs coming in on boats along the coast. That means they're probably stopping about ten to twenty percent of everything coming this way. But suddenly, last winter, they didn't intercept any moving through the jungle. Mexico City has had an increase in drugs, so how are they getting there?"

"I can't believe I'm sitting here having a conversation with you about the movement of illegal drugs through Mexico. This picture seems totally wrong. You're supposed to talk about friends and family and maybe a little about your father's business, like what new construction projects he's starting and how much they cost, maybe even some concerns over their environmental impact, but not the sleazy world of drugs."

"Can you get me a box? And does this mean you don't want to get to know me any better? I was really looking forward to another night on the town with you and maybe some snorkeling on Sunday."

"I'm finding it hard to even think right now. The new shipment of boxes came yesterday. They won't be bringing any more for two weeks. I can probably sneak one out when I come on Saturday night, but I'll have to bring it back with me on Sunday. I'll bring the smallest one I can find and put it in my camera case. Should I bring it to your house?"

"Yes, but I'm afraid my house and car are bugged. Someone is trying to keep track of everything I do. Don't look so horrified. It's okay now that I know. I'm really careful to only say the things I want them to know. Why don't you come to my house and we can talk about anything but drugs and boxes? That way, whoever is listening will know we are just friends. We can walk to the beach from my house and drop the box off with two other agents before we go out to dinner. They can check it out. Once the box is out of our hands then business is done for the night and we can just have our date like we planned. Is that all right with you?"

"You may be able to just forget about your business, but I have a feeling it won't be as easy for me. I'll do my best though. I know I have to act normal or I might endanger you. That will be my biggest incentive." He leaned toward her and said, "I think we should start practicing going from one mode to another right now. No more business talk. Now it's pleasure."

He started to nibble his way from her ear down her cheekbone and finally kissed her lips. She reached up and put her hands on the nape of his neck and kissed him back. His hands began to wander up and

236

down her back and came to rest under her breasts. He smoothed his thumbs on the undersides of them and he heard her quick intake of air. His heart was pounding at an accelerated rate. They broke off the kiss and sat gazing at each other.

"I like pleasure much more than business," he said with a grin.

She was still trying to gather her wits. "Mmm, so do I."

"I hate to break this up, but I do need to get back to work. Be very cautious. You got that."

"Anything for you," Megan replied.

Chapter 36

The midnight moon was glowing long before Megan, Josh and Stuart were able to meet on the beach. Vicki seemed to want to stay at the bar, and even Mrs. Cowen was there and appeared reluctant to call it a night. Richard had shown up for the first time at the restaurant. Megan made the introductions, introducing Richard as a consultant at her father's business.

Megan had easily slipped into the rich pampered ditzy role she had been playing. She almost felt like Richard believed her act to be real. He treated her in an almost condescending manner. She was sure that was a good thing.

Once everyone made their excuses and left the nightclub, Megan walked to her villa and went inside. She knew her activities were being monitored in some fashion. She changed into a comfortable lounging suit and then got herself a glass of juice and went out on the patio. There was a garden down from the patio, so she walked into the garden and then made her way down the path leading to the beach. Stuart and Josh were already there.

"It's about time you got here. We were getting worried," Josh said.

"I wanted to take my time so it wouldn't appear as though I rushed home to leave again," Megan replied.

Stuart spoke up, "Makes sense. I have some interesting information to share. It seems the funding for the archeological dig is coming straight out of the Cowen bank account. I also found out their son is mentally and physically handicapped and has been in a private institution since he was five years old. Private institutions and archeological projects don't come cheap. Considering what Mr. Cowen has done for a living for the past twenty years, I would guess the real money was gotten by Mrs. Cowen. I had their finances checked and there hasn't been any new money coming in, only withdrawals. At the rate they're spending they'll go through their savings in a few years."

"Do you think they may have hidden accounts somewhere else?" Megan asked.

"I suppose it's a possibility, but I would bet on some kind of blackmail," Stuart replied.

"Beth told me the first day I was here that Mrs. Cowen didn't really like Vicki, and I would bet she is right. I wonder if the probe that was started into Senator Cowen's finances would have turned up some shady deals and now they're paying for it. Vicki probably has proof of some kind of illegal activity and is using Mrs. Cowen for her fall person along with using her money," Megan said.

"That makes sense. Most white-collar criminals don't like getting mixed up with the underground running of illegal drugs. It's much too dirty for them," Josh commented.

"We still have to figure out if they're really shipping the drugs in the boxes with the Mayan artifacts. If we can get proof of that, it will probably be time to find out where the boxes come from and then have a little chat with Mrs. Cowen. If we're right, we can probably get her some kind of deal in exchange for her testimony. I want to nail Richard and Vicki on this more than anyone else. They've got to be the brains behind the whole operation," Stuart said.

Josh readily agreed, "I hate traitors, and especially ones who try to set me up. I'm going to expect them to try to plant some kind of evidence on me for you to find, Megan."

"I guess we'll just have to see what develops. I told Kevin the broad picture and he's going to bring us a box on Saturday. I told him we would drop it off somewhere for you two to find. I didn't tell him who you were, of course, just said that two other agents would study it and get it back to us by Sunday before he leaves. We could bring it down from my place and store it under the big fern at the end of the path. You'll have to figure out when and where to take it to check it out. Have it back at the same place by four on Sunday. Okay?"

Josh and Stuart agreed and decided they would just have to wait for Saturday to come.

An observer would have thought the next two days were a peaceful interlude for all those involved. Sunbathing on the beach with a novel in hand, eating at the local restaurants, and visiting while sipping exotic local specialties gave the appearance of tranquility. Megan was filled with tension and anxiety. She could hardly wait for Saturday to arrive. She wanted to get this whole business over with and at the same time she was giddy with the idea of spending time with Kevin.

Friday night Josh and Megan went dancing and saw Vicki latched to the arm of a tourist who had been in town for only two days.

"She works fast," Josh commented.

"So it seems. The way he is looking at her, you would think she was a piece of chocolate ready to be tasted. Sometimes I can't figure out men. If she and Richard are still married, and from what I was told they are, how can he stand to have her carrying on right in front of him?"

"Don't ask me. If I ever get married, fidelity will be a must."

"For me, too."

The ringing of the phone brought Megan rushing in from the patio. She seldom received phone calls. Since it was Saturday afternoon she thought it must be her parents calling.

"Hi, I'm so glad you called."

The voice on the other end replied, "You are? Why might that be?"

"Oh. I thought you were my family. What's up, Richard?"

"I wanted to let you know I ran into Vicki this morning and while we were talking I found out why the agency couldn't find anything out about her. I asked her what nationality Brenten was and she laughed and told me Brenten wasn't her full name. She said her name was really Henrietta Victoria VanBrenten. She indicated she had always hated her name, so she told everyone when she got here it was Victoria Brenten. I'm sure if you have the agency check her out under her full name, you'll be able to get some information on her. Let me know what you find."

"Wow. Now I know why they call you the Professor. I would never have thought to ask her about her name. I'll e-mail the agency right away. I'll let you know what they report as soon as I get it. By the way, Josh said something about being out of town tonight. Do you think we should try to follow him to see where he goes?"

"You can if you want, but if he's meeting someone involved in the drug ring, I would think he would be extra careful and you'll probably have trouble trailing him."

"I wasn't thinking I should follow him. I have a date tonight. I figured you could do it."

"Pleasure first for you, huh? I doubt if following him would do us any good, but maybe I can check out his room while he's gone. Did he say when he was leaving?"

"I'm afraid not. I'd love to come with you, but..."

"Yeah, I know. You've got a date. Call me when you hear back from the agency. See you around."

Richard hung up the phone, shaking his head.

Her daddy must have bought her the position with the agency, he thought. His mind continued, *I can outsmart anyone, but it really isn't any fun when she is so stupid and pathetic. At least not everyone in the agency is so dumb. Vicki is always impressed with my schemes and she is ten times smarter than Megan.*

After hanging up the phone, Megan e-mailed the request to check out Vicki with the name Richard had supplied. She bet they would find a very benign history for Henrietta VanBrenten. Then she thought about Josh. She better let him know she had suggested Richard follow him tonight. She didn't think he would, but it was never wise to leave things to chance. If she was a gambler she would wager Josh was going to have something found in his room tonight that would incriminate him in the drug ring. Whether Richard would find it, or someone else would be set up to discover it, remained to be seen.

If the boxes turned out to be the means for transport, they still were left with finding a way to prove Richard and Vicki's involvement. That was going to be the hard part.

Kevin was nervous. He had never done anything like this before. He knew no one counted the boxes and wouldn't realize one of them was missing, but taking something that didn't belong to him made him edgy. *It's for a good purpose,* he kept reminding himself as he rode along in the van with the other workers. If anyone noticed he was quieter than usual, they didn't say anything.

As soon as the van stopped, he headed straight to Megan's house. He would be glad to get rid of the damn thing.

How could she stand to be involved in these kinds of things all the time? he wondered.

The only mystery he liked was that of the past, not of the present. The past, that he loved, didn't hurt you. It could teach you and help you, but the present could get you in real trouble.

He stood fidgeting at the door, waiting for Megan to answer. The door swung open and he forgot momentarily that he was there on a mission. She looked great in her sundress with her hair down. He was always stunned when he saw her hair. It was so beautiful.

"Hi there, handsome. I didn't think tonight would ever get here. How have you been?"

"I'm great now that I'm finally here. You look wonderful."

They stood drinking in the sight of each other.

"Are you going to invite me in or just let me stand on your step all night?" Kevin finally asked.

Megan laughed and said, "I'm sorry. Come on in. I think my brain just kind of shuts down when you're around."

"It's the same for me. If we should wind up together for any period of time, everyone will think we're both brain dead. I didn't even take time to drop off my overnight bag at the hotel. We'll have to go there before we go out to eat. I brought my camera, too. I want to take some pictures of the scenery and of you."

"You can just put your bag on the table. I'll get us a drink and we can go out on the patio for a little while before we head to dinner. Why don't you bring your camera, and after we have a drink we can walk down to the beach from the verandah and take some pictures. The sights are great from down there."

"That sounds great. Do you have any scotch? A scotch and soda sounds good to me."

"Coming right up. How is the dig coming? Did you find anything of interest this week?"

"Just a few items which appear to be housewares and one stone square that has some kind of writing on it. Everything progressing okay at the water plant site?"

"So far so good. No real problems, but then my dad has good people working for him. Here's your drink."

Once they were on the patio they sat down and talked about what news they had from home and about their plans for the evening. When they finished their drinks they took the camera case and walked toward the beach. When they were some distance from the house, Megan whispered, "Did you get it?"

Kevin just nodded his head and pointed at the case slung over his shoulder. When they reached the large fern, Megan stopped and opened the camera case, removing a small box from inside. She shoved it under the bush and then continued down the path. As soon as they were on the beach, she turned to Kevin and smiled.

"Personal time now."

Then she leaned towards him and brushed his lips lightly. Kevin didn't hesitate, but pulled her into his arms for a more satisfactory kiss.

"I've been waiting forever to do that," he said.

"If I remember right, it has only been a couple of days."

"Two days to a starving man is forever."

Laughing, she said, "I thought we came down here to take some pictures. You do have film in the camera, don't you?"

"I have film. Why don't you stand over there so I can get part of the ocean and the jungle as a background? I want a picture of you I can send to my family."

"If you get to have one of me, I get to take one of you. I'll have to go back to the house and get my camera."

"Just use mine. I'll give you the picture when I get it developed."

"If you use up the whole roll while you're here I can take it to Cancun and get it developed this week. They have a place where I can get the pictures in an hour."

"That sounds great. Since we're so far from home, I can't take you to meet my parents and family, but I can at least send them a picture."

"If we were nearer to them, would you really take me home to meet them?"

"Yes, I would. I know we just met, but it seems like we've known each other for a long time. You're already special to me."

A smile spread across Megan's face. "I feel the same about you. I have never believed in love at first sight, but I definitely know I'm a whole lot in like with you."

"Well, you may not believe in love at first sight, but I do. I guess I'll just have to change your mind, because I already know you're the one for me."

Megan couldn't seem to find an appropriate response. All she could think about was the fact that he had implied he was in love with her. Could that be possible? She knew her dad and Katie had fallen in love very fast and it worked. So maybe!

"You really do know how to muddle my brain," she finally said.

Kevin grinned and said, "Let's get these pictures taken and go get me a room so we can go to dinner. This man is getting hungry."

After they used the whole role of film, they returned to the villa.

"I think you should have some really good pictures of the area. I'll probably be able to get to Cancun the first part of the week, so I'll bring them out to you as soon as I can. That is, if you don't mind me coming to the site again."

"Now, what do you think? You better come out or I'll be a wreck before next weekend gets here."

They walked to the hotel and checked Kevin in. From there they went to La Buena Vita for dinner. They had a beautiful view of the ocean from the upstairs dining area. The food was wonderful and they were relaxed and comfortable with each other's company. After their meal was completed they decided to go downstairs to the bar and dance area. The band was just warming up.

As they were looking for a table they saw Vicki and her newest male companion enter. Stuart was at the bar getting drinks for himself and Mrs. Cowen. There was no sign of Richard.

"Hi, Megan."

Megan had been so intent in observing the other Americans she hadn't noticed Raul and Maria at a table near them.

"Oh, I'm sorry. I didn't see you. How are the two of you?"

"We're fine. I see the band is about to start playing. That's usually our cue to go home."

"Before you leave, I would like you to meet my friend, Kevin. He is a professor from Boston College, down here to take part in the Mayan dig. We met once before in Boston. Kevin, these are friends of my family. Raul is the foreman at the construction site and Maria is the best cook you'll ever meet."

Kevin shook hands with Raul and then bent over Maria's hand and kissed it in a courtly fashion.

Maria blushed and said to Megan in Spanish, "He is very handsome and very polite. You look at each other with stars in your eyes. He is special to you, yes?"

Megan replied, "Yes, he is."

"I am glad to hear it. It is time for you to settle down and make babies."

It was Megan's turn to blush. She was glad they were speaking in Spanish. She didn't think Kevin understood everything that was being said.

Raul and Maria said their goodbyes and left.

"Let's get a table so when the band starts we can dance," Kevin said.

"Hey you two, aren't you going to say hello?" Vicki had spoken and was standing behind them with her male friend.

Megan and Kevin both turned and said hello. After introductions were made, Vicki looked at Megan and in a sugary sweet voice said, "My, don't you look lovely tonight. I think I like this dress better than the one you were wearing last night when you were out dancing with Josh."

There was almost a malicious look in Vicki's eyes and Megan noted a slight stiffness in Kevin.

Now what is she up to? Megan wondered.

"Thank you. I think this is my favorite dress. I wear it for special occasions," Megan responded smoothly.

Vicki then turned her attention to Kevin. She reached up and smoothed her hand down the front of his shirt.

"Come dance with me. Fred here isn't very good, and I so love to dance."

Fred turned red and said, "Go on and dance with her. She's right; I'm not any good at dancing. I'll wait here at the table with Megan."

Kevin had never felt jealousy before, but he knew that was what he was feeling now.

Who is Josh? he wondered.

With his thoughts on Josh, he had missed the rest of the conversation. Before he realized what was happening, Vicki was grabbing his hand and trying to pull him toward the dance floor. He looked down at her hand on his and then seemed to snap out of his daze.

"I'm sorry Vicki, but the first dance and all my others belong to Megan."

He then shook off Vicki's grasp and reached for Megan's hand. Megan smiled at Kevin and walked with him onto the dance floor.

"Josh is just a friend. Nothing more," she reassured him.

Kevin visibly relaxed.

"I'm glad. I don't think I would like competition."

"I think you just made an enemy out of Vicki though. She likes to get her man and she definitely wants you."

"Well, she can't have me. She gives me the creeps. I don't know what men see in someone like that."

"I would say they see a quick tumble with no strings attached. Besides, she really is quite pretty, and to have her attention makes them feel sexy."

"You're probably right, but I only want your attention."

When they returned to the table, Vicki seemed to be pouting. She tried one more time to get Kevin to dance and when he turned her down, she and Fred left.

"I'm glad that's over. Do you think she finally got the message that I'm not interested?" Kevin asked.

"She got the message, but she's not happy about it."

"That's her problem, not ours. Let's dance again. I like the nice slow ones so I have an excuse to hold you."

They danced to several more songs and then decided to go for a walk on the beach. As they left the restaurant, they ran into Richard. He stopped and greeted them.

"Hi Megan, and you must be the professor from Boston College. I'm Richard Trent. I'm working as a consultant for the water treatment plant Megan's dad is building. It's a nice evening, isn't it?"

"Very pleasant. I'm Kevin. It was nice to meet you, but we were just heading to the beach to enjoy some of this great atmosphere, so if you'll excuse us," Kevin said.

"No problem. Have a nice evening."

They parted company and Kevin and Megan made their way to the beach. Kevin took off his shoes and socks and rolled his pant legs up while Megan kicked off her sandals.

They walked hand in hand along the shore, occasionally walking into the warm, still water of the lagoon. The moon cast a romantic glow upon the water and the snow-white sand. It was a perfect night for lovers.

Eventually, Kevin stopped and pulled Megan into his arms. He began to kiss his way from her lips to the side of her neck and down to the edge of her sundress that began just above the swell of her breast.

"You taste so good. I want to taste all of you," he whispered.

Megan had twined her fingers in Kevin's hair and was just trying to remain standing. Her heart was beating rapidly and her legs felt like Jell-O. The vision of him kissing her all over was a heady thought. In time, Kevin lifted his head and kissed her soundly on the lips.

"I want the first time for us to be perfect and somehow making love in the sand without a blanket doesn't seem right. Besides, I think we need a little more time to get to know each other. I want you so bad, but I want this to be forever, so I think I better slow things down a bit."

Megan was just starting to come back to reality and in a faraway voice said, "Okay. If you insist."

He laughed and hugged her to him.

"I promise we won't wait too long."

Chapter 37

Kevin and Megan ate breakfast together and then packed a picnic lunch. They spent the day snorkeling and swimming. Several of Megan's friends and their families were on the beach, and Megan introduced them to Kevin. Beth was there but didn't need an introduction since she already knew him from his staying at her hotel. She did tell Megan she needed to see her this evening alone and to come by the office after Kevin left.

A little after four, they made their way to Megan's house and retrieved the box from the site. They put it back in Kevin's camera case. At that point, Kevin seemed to retreat a little.

Back to business, Megan thought.

When Kevin had left, Megan made her way to Beth's hotel and knocked on her office door. Beth was sitting behind her desk going over some account books. As Megan walked in, she motioned her to the chair sitting in front of her desk. Then, taking off her reading glasses, she regarded Megan for a brief time.

"I'm not sure if I should be showing you this or not, but I have the feeling it is just the kind of thing you wanted me to keep my eyes open for."

She reached in her desk drawer and pulled out a little plastic bag that appeared to have some kind of white powder in it.

"One of my trusted maids told me she found this in Josh's room along with a note. She didn't know what the note said, since she doesn't read English. After she reported it, I went to his room and read the note left with the bag."

Beth handed the note to Megan.

It said, "Here is the sample you wanted to check. I assure you it is the best quality. Whoever told you we had started to send a bad grade was wrong."

"You were right. Thank you for showing this to me. Where exactly did the maid find it?

"It was stuck under some folded towels on the bathroom counter. She moved the towels to wipe off the top. She lost a cousin in Mexico City to drugs and is very upset from finding this. Any of my other maids would probably have ignored it. I really hate this. Josh seems like such a nice man."

"I know. Maybe it is just a plant. That was a pretty obvious place to leave something like this, don't you think?"

"Maybe to you, but he's been here a long time and knows most of my maids are not so thorough. What do you want me to do with it?"

"I think you should just put it back. I have a friend that I'll call and let know about this. Did you see anyone unusual hanging around who might have put this in his room?"

"No one I can remember. I still don't understand your connection to all of this." When Megan didn't reply, Beth continued, "You be careful. This isn't a game."

"I know. Thanks for telling me. I'd better go now. I'll talk to you later."

Megan made her way back to the house. She checked her e-mail and found a complete report on Henrietta Van Brenten. It indicated that her father had died two years ago and she had inherited a large sum of money, plus she had been the beneficiary to a life insurance policy for one million dollars. She supposedly quit her job at an electronics firm after that and had been living off of her inheritance. Last known address was a house in Middletown, Rhode Island. No criminal record, no marriages and no children.

Megan felt certain the report had come from headquarters. Richard was very clever and extremely smart, she decided. He had somehow created a cover that even headquarters found, and if they didn't already know Vicki's true identity, they would have believed this was accurate. How were they ever going to prove his and Vicki's involvement? Even if Mrs. Cowen turned state's evidence, her word against that of an agent without any criminal record would be useless.

Megan decided to take a long bath in her tub and then make her way back to the beach around ten o'clock to meet Josh and Stuart.

As she descended the path to the beach she could hear voices speaking in low murmurs. They were waiting for her, but trained conditioning made her slow her pace and look the area over before she ran headlong onto the beach. She saw two figures standing a few feet away and almost called out to them. Then she realized it wasn't Josh and Stuart. She pulled back to the protection of the jungle vegetation and waited.

The voices grew louder at times and she realized it was a man and a woman arguing. A strange sound came from the other side of the beach and both people turned. The moon hit their faces and Megan could make out their features. It was Richard and Vicki. With the change in their position she could hear them more easily.

Vicki said, "I'm not leaving. With the cover story you gave me, I shouldn't be a suspect anymore and I have some unfinished personal business."

"I guess you're probably right about the cover story. What kind of personal business do you have?"

"You know I always get what I want, one way or another, and there is a certain man that is playing hard to get. I won't leave until I have him."

"It's the professor who's been seeing Megan, isn't it?"

"Yes. I don't understand what he sees in that scatter-brained little twit. I am so much more of a woman than she is."

"There's just no accounting for taste," Richard replied in a sardonic tone.

"Don't get smart with me."

Then Vicki seemed to change right before her eyes.

"Don't be mean to me. You know you're the only one who has ever understood my needs, and I always help you play your little games just to prove how clever you are, don't I? You are so shrewd," she added in a bolstering tone.

He stood looking at her and then peals of laughter could be heard and he hugged her close.

"You and I are quite a pair. Neither of us is any good without the other. Come on, I'll walk you back to your car. Things will go according to our plans. No one will ever figure out that the linings in the boxes are made with a new plastic only laser can pierce. It was rather clever of me to think of putting metal containers inside the plastic coating. The drugs go in the metal tubes and then you can just smear on the plastic. Ten minutes in a freezer and the plastic is so hard no one can get in. Some day I'll have to sell it to a plastics company and find a new invention to try out. I get to use my brain and you get all the money you need to live the lifestyle you like."

Megan stayed hidden for at least fifteen minutes after they left. She stepped from her hiding place and was about to return to her house when she heard movement just a few feet from her. Her heart began to pound, but then Josh and Stuart stepped out from a tree just a few feet away.

"Oh my, you just about gave me a heart attack."

"We thought you were going to walk right into that one. Thank God you're cautious. I guess we all heard the same thing. We were going to report that we hadn't found out anything about the boxes, but now I guess we know why. We tried everything we could think of to break the lining but nothing worked," Stuart said.

"Did you get the feeling this was just some kind of game to them? Like they're trying to see how much they can get away with before they get caught," Megan asked.

"I think it is definitely a game for Richard. I think Vicki just likes men and money and she'll do anything to have them. I don't know what she'll do if Kevin doesn't play her game. She seemed pretty upset with him for not falling all over her. Did something happen while he was here to make her mad?" Josh replied.

"We happened to run into her and her latest fling when we were out dancing last night. She insinuated that I was seeing you and Kevin at the same time. She then tried to get Kevin to dance with her, but he said he planned to share all his dances with me. She got upset and left. I knew she wasn't happy. Kevin won't need to have any more to do with this though, so hopefully he can stay out of her way. By the way, Josh, you have a bag of what I'm sure is cocaine in your room, along with a note. One of the maids found it and reported it to Beth. She then let me know about it. I'll have to tell Richard tomorrow. I also got a call from Richard yesterday morning, and he told me Vicki's real name was Henrietta Victoria VanBrenten. I got a complete report back on her from headquarters. It seems Richard is indeed very clever. If I'd talked to him first about her, I would have gotten the report and dismissed her as a suspect."

"I guess I'll have to get rid of the note and the cocaine. Too bad I can't just stick it in Richard's place and then have the local cops come and bust him. Of course, that would be a minor charge and Vicki would still be in the clear. We need to think up a plan to either get them to confess or catch them actually working with the drugs. Anyone have an idea?" Josh asked.

No one had a ready answer so they decided to wait a couple of days and see if Megan's report to Richard would stir anything up. She told them she was going to Cancun on Tuesday to get Kevin's film developed, and she would report to headquarters what they had found out. They were going to meet at the dive shop on Wednesday and decide what to do from there.

"We'll have to see if any of us can come up with a plan by then," Stuart said.

On Monday, Megan again asked to use the office at the construction site to talk with Richard. She filled him in on the report about Vicki and indicated she no longer considered her a suspect. She also informed him of her visit with Beth. She told him she had talked with Beth when she first arrived and had asked her to let her know if there were any unusual happenings at the hotel. He seemed satisfied with her explanations.

He agreed Josh had probably gotten rid of the evidence by now and agreed she should let headquarters know what she had seen and been told. He acted upset with her.

"Next time, don't wait so long before you report something like that to me. We could have nailed him and he might have given away his contacts to save his own hide," Richard scolded.

"He just seems so nice and is so good-looking—I wanted to make sure," Megan said in a pouty voice.

Richard was thinking, *Lord, save me from idiots.*

Megan hummed along with the music on the radio as she drove to Cancun. She parked her car and set out for the department store to have the film developed. After dropping it off, she made her way to the Hilton Hotel and had a sandwich and a Coke. She watched the people come and go, and when she felt certain she hadn't been followed she went to the payphone outside the ladies' room.

She dialed headquarters and asked to talk to the director. She told him about the boxes from the Mayan dig site and about what they had overheard on the beach.

"That scum," was his reply. "I want him real bad. Do you have any ideas on how to nab him?"

"I wonder if you can trace the boxes from the delivery site and see who picks them up. I would guess they don't send the boxes back since they have to laser the plastic. They might send the metal tubes back though. If they do, I want to know where they're sent. I haven't informed the Mexican agency. Do you want me to?"

"I think you should do that now. You may need their help soon."

"What about talking to Mrs. Cowen? I'm sure she is their fall guy, and she might be able to shed some light on a way to catch the others. Are you willing to grant her some kind of immunity if she talks?"

"I think it's a real possibility, since you think she's being blackmailed. Whatever they are using to trap her may be something illegal. She could get in trouble for that, depending on what it is, and it won't be up to me."

"Okay, I'll see what we can do here and I'll go to the Mexican agency before I leave Cancun. I'll keep in touch."

Megan went to the agency and talked to the man in charge of this particular case. They were pleased that she had discovered how the drugs were leaving the area and planned to watch the delivery of the artifacts to Mexico City to see who picked up the boxes and where they went after they left the university. As far as the people involved, she said she was still working on that.

The pictures were ready when she returned to the store. She went through them and found several she liked of Kevin. She wouldn't be back in time to take them to him that day, but she would go to the site tomorrow after she met with Stuart and Josh.

It was another sunny day and the temperature was in the nineties. It was normal weather for this time of year in Akumal. Megan wished it were a little cooler. She walked about the dive shop trying to decide if she should make arrangements for her and Kevin to go scuba diving on Sunday. She decided to wait and see if Kevin had ever been diving.

Josh walked in and said Stuart couldn't make it. Vicki had cornered him at lunch and he wasn't able to get away.

"Why don't we meet tonight on the beach? Make it a little further down from your house. I hate predictability; too chancy."

"All right, I'll see you around ten on the beach."

Leaving the dive shop, Megan drove to the dig site. Kevin was happy to see her and liked the pictures, especially the ones of her. He picked out one to send to his parents.

"I guess this will have to go Fed-Ex or we'll be married with two kids before they get it. The regular mail is very slow."

Megan was again struck by his belief in their relationship. In the few male alliances she'd had before, the men were always skittish about long-term commitments, and now Kevin was acting as though it was a forgone conclusion. It was a very heady thought and made her feel warm all over.

"Let's take a walk," he said.

As they made their way to the spot behind the Mayan statues, Kevin took hold of her hand and walked beside her in companionable silence. As they got further away from the main campsite, Megan spoke.

"Thank you again for getting the box for us. Hopefully this whole thing will be solved soon."

"As much as I hate this business that you are involved with, I have to ask, were you right?"

"I'm afraid so. We couldn't figure it out, but then Sunday night I overheard a conversation that explained how the boxes are used. We know who's doing it, but we haven't been able to prove a thing yet."

"What are you going to do?"

"I don't know yet. Try to set up some kind of trap, I guess."

"You don't have anything in mind yet?"

"Not really. It's like this vague kind of image in my head, but I haven't pinned it down yet. Don't worry; I'll leave you out of anything else to do with this business."

"I don't know if I want you to do that. If the plan involves any kind of danger to you, I want to be there."

She smiled then and asked, "Why? Do you want to protect me?"

"If I can," he said in complete seriousness. "I would never forgive myself if something happened to you."

"That isn't your responsibility."

"Of course it is. You're the woman I love, and I should take care of you. You can take care of me, too. This is a partnership."

Megan was overcome with emotion. He had said he loved her.

"You love me?" she asked.

Kevin frowned and said, "Of course. What do you think I said the other night when we talked about this? I was serious then and I'm serious now."

"Just hold me for a minute. I have never had a man tell me he loves me, so this is a very special moment."

"Well, aren't you going to tell me you love me, too?"

"I don't know if I do. I hadn't thought about it."

"What's to think about? It isn't a thought; it's just the way you feel. If you're not ready to tell me, that's okay, because I know you do love me."

Kevin then swept her up in his arms and sat down on one of the stones. Holding her on his lap he began to kiss her. She lost all sense of time and place. He unbuttoned the front of her blouse and his hands were roving over her breasts and nipples. She could hardly breathe.

"You feel so good. It seems I always get us in these predicaments at the most inopportune times and places. Next time we will have to try for a better spot."

He rebuttoned her blouse and then glanced at her face. She had a kind of glazed look.

Oh yes, you love me, he thought. *You're just afraid to admit it.*

He set her back on her feet, took her hand and started back to her car.

"I want you to know Vicki came with the tour again yesterday and hounded my every step. She tried to talk me into meeting her when I come to town on Saturday. I'm telling you this so if she says anything, you'll know I turned her down. She's a very devious person and I don't want her to come between us."

"I'll remember. I'll miss you between now and Saturday. By the way, do you scuba dive?"

"It's been a while, but I'm fully certified. Why?"

"I just wondered if you want to go on Sunday."

"Let's wait until Sunday and see. That's not too late to make arrangements is it?"

"This isn't high season, so it should be fine. I'll see you at the house on Saturday then. Bye."

Megan would have gotten in the car, but Kevin spun her around and into his arms for one more kiss goodbye. Megan wasn't sure how she got into her car, as her head was still spinning with emotion even as she was driving back to Akumal.

He had said he loved her and acted as though they were going to get married and have a family. How did she really feel? She tried to categorize her feelings and then she had to admit whatever she felt, she had never felt it before.

She gave a sigh and giving in, she said out loud to no one, "I guess he's right. I do love him."

Then her face turned to an almost giddy expression and she said out loud again, "I love him and he loves me. This is really quite wonderful. I need to call my family as soon as I get home."

Then she remembered her phone was tapped and she didn't want to share this personal information with those creeps who had her place bugged. She would just have to wait.

By the time she reached home she changed her mind again and decided to send her family a scanned picture of Kevin. She wrote on the bottom of the page, picture of someone special to me. They would probably all pass the picture around and try to speculate on what she meant by special. She would explain when this mess was all cleaned up.

Chapter 38

Thousands of stars twinkled above and a half-moon smiled down on the land. The water of the lagoon shimmered beneath the night sky. Megan meandered along the shore lost in thoughts of Kevin. He was handsome and had a great body. She loved his smile and the way his eyes twinkled when he laughed. Obviously he was intelligent and had a promising future. He loved his family and spoke of them often. His kisses were to die for and he wanted to protect her.

She smiled to herself when she thought about how he was afraid for her and wanted to be there to keep her safe. That was probably a little old-fashioned, but she decided she liked old-fashioned. It felt good to think he was so concerned for her well-being.

She was lost in her thoughts and didn't hear the approach of the man until he was taking a hold of her arm. She turned sharply and almost threw him to the ground before she realized it was Josh.

"Wow, I didn't mean to startle you, but I called your name a couple of times and you didn't answer. Lost in a dream world somewhere, I think."

"Sorry about that. I guess I was daydreaming a bit. Is Stuart here?"

"He should be along any minute. Any news from headquarters?"

Stuart came strolling down the beach about that time so Megan waited until he arrived and then said, "I told them what we had overheard, and they will try to trace the boxes after they leave the institute in New York. I also talked to the Mexican drug agency, and they will do the same in Mexico City. I'm wondering if there is any way to follow the truck when it delivers the boxes to the site. They have to be putting the boxes together somewhere in this area before they are sent to the site. We know the drugs come in along the coast, so it has to be somewhere near here."

"I've been thinking about that myself. I would almost bet either Vicki or Richard helps put them together since it's his invention they're using. Maybe we need to start staking them out," Josh said.

"They know us, so it won't be easy. Do you have any idea as to when they are expected to deliver another load of boxes to the dig?" Stuart asked.

"Kevin said they bring new boxes about every two weeks. He was told they only bring a few at a time so the moisture in the jungle won't damage the boxes before shipping. It all seems pretty innocuous. They got boxes last week, so next week should be delivery time," Megan answered.

Stuart thought for a moment and then said, "I think you should find out how much time Richard really spends at the construction site. It seems to me we hardly see him. If he's not at the water treatment plant, where is he? As for Vicki, maybe Josh and I can split up the duty and see where she spends her days and nights. She's pretty visible in the evenings."

"If we can get some clue as to where they're filling the boxes, it might be time to talk to Ruth Cowen. We can offer her immunity as far as the drugs go, if she'll cooperate, but if she's prosecuted for some other shady deal, we can't help her there. Her husband is due back in another week or so. Let's hope we know something and can talk to her before he comes," Megan said.

"I think it's time to pull the tracking devices out of our vehicles, and any other gadgets they may have on them. You better leave yours alone though, Megan. Richard will get suspicious if you pull yours at the same time as Stuart and I do. I'll clear my room and telephone, but I'll leave the computer alone. What do you think, Stuart?"

Stuart nodded in agreement. "I'm sorry you have to stay under surveillance, Megan, but I think it's important they not guess we're all working together. Besides, you're not supposed to be bright enough to find it on your own. I think we better break up this little meeting before someone sees us. Night all, and stay in touch."

Josh left shortly after Stuart, and Megan continued her slow progress along the shore. She wasn't ready to return to her villa yet, so she walked further down the beach. She had her handgun in her pocket, so she felt safe.

The shoreline was uneven and wove in and out, with the jungle coming close to the water in places. As she reached a curve she thought she heard someone dive into the water on the other side of the outcropping of land and jungle. She slipped into the undergrowth and made her way silently to the other side. Staying concealed, she watched as a man came swimming back to shore with a pouch pulled over his shoulder.

She could see the outline of a yacht on the horizon. There was probably a small dinghy on its way back to the boat, but with only the moon to light the area she couldn't see it. The man came ashore and then looked about as though to make sure no one was near. He headed into the jungle just a short distance from where Megan stood. She held her breath as he passed by.

She wanted to follow him but she wasn't dressed for a hike through the jungle and she knew the dangers that lay within its smoldering existence. Maybe she could go just a little ways and see if he met anyone. She had only gone a few feet when she saw a car waiting on a narrow road.

The man approached the car and then in Spanish said to the driver, "I have it. Do you want to deliver it tonight or should we wait until tomorrow?"

"We better deliver it tonight or the Boss will be upset, and we don't want to make her mad."

"Okay, let's go then."

They started the car and pulled away. They were headed in the direction of a little town a few miles east of Akumal. Whether they were actually going to the town or somewhere along the way Megan couldn't be sure. At least she now knew what direction to look.

She made her way back to the beach and eventually to her home. She had managed to avoid being observed. Tomorrow she would find out where Richard spent most of his time.

Hammering, drilling and all the assorted sounds that accompany a construction site greeted Megan as she made her way from her car to the temporary office at the water treatment site. Raul and Keith were both working at a desk situated at the rear of the small building. They looked up at her entrance.

Keith said, "Hi, Megan. I didn't know you planned on coming over today. Do you need the office again?"

"No, I just stopped by to see how things were going. Have you been in contact with my dad lately?"

Raul answered, "I talked to him just yesterday. He asked about you and said to tell you hello when I saw you. He is pleased at the way things are going."

Megan asked about the plans they were studying on the desk and then asked if Mr. Trent was around. She was informed he usually didn't come in until later in the day and he tended to take Thursdays off. Keith wanted to know if there was a special problem she wanted to talk to him about and she assured him there wasn't. Keith seemed to relax some after that.

After spending a little more time looking over some of the accounting figures and inspecting some of the actual work, Megan left.

So Thursday was the day to follow Richard, she thought, *too late today.*

That evening she spent her time at home catching up on household chores. On Friday she went to dinner at the usual place and ran into Vicki and Mrs. Cowen. She greeted them and asked Mrs. Cowen when her husband was due back. She said she was picking him up at the airport in Cancun next Friday morning.

Vicki listened to their conversation and then said to Megan, "Oh, by the way, I saw Kevin the other day and he said he would be coming to the dance club on Saturday. Are you planning on being here?"

Megan smiled and replied, "I'm not sure what my plans are. I guess that will be up to Kevin."

"Oh my, I didn't mean to insinuate Kevin would come without you, but I did make him promise I got at least one dance. He is so good-looking, don't you think?" Vicki almost purred.

"Yes, he is. I was just on my way home, so I'll probably see you tomorrow night. Bye."

Megan walked away. She was glad Kevin had warned her about seeing Vicki. She really was something else.

When Megan got home she noticed she had a message on her answering machine. It was from her family wanting to know who Kevin was and what did she mean by special. This was the second call she had missed from them since she sent the picture. It was too late to call now. She would try to call them from a payphone tomorrow.

Kevin was a little later than usual and Megan was getting upset. She had watched the clock all day waiting for six o'clock to get here, and now it was twenty minutes after. Where was he?

The doorbell rang and Megan went dashing to the door. She flung the door wide to see Kevin standing on her step with a bottle of wine and a basket of cheese and fruit and what appeared to be fresh bread from the Italian restaurant.

"Sorry I'm late, but I had to do a little shopping before I got here. You cooked for me last week, and since I couldn't cook I thought I'd do the next best thing and bring you an Italian picnic."

Laughing, Megan said, "It looks great. Come on in. We can have a picnic out on the patio."

Kevin followed her out onto the verandah and set everything down on the table. He picked her up and kissed her soundly.

"I really missed you. You taste so sweet," he whispered in her ear.

"I missed you, too. I'll go get some wineglasses and a corkscrew. Do we need a knife to cut the bread and cheese?"

"I'll help. We'll need to cut the cheese and the apples, but you don't cut the bread, you just rip it apart. That's the real Italian way of doing things."

They settled on the swing on the patio and placed the food and wine on the little table sitting in front of it. Soon they were feeding each other bites of bread and sipping wine. They interspersed kisses between the food they nibbled on.

Megan was giddy with wine and Kevin's presence. Kevin refilled her glass and she asked if he was trying to get her tipsy so he could have his way with her. He answered, "Yes."

"Oh! I guess I should tell you I decided I do love you," she said and then giggled.

He reached across and took her wine glass from her.

"I really don't want you drunk, just relaxed."

"That's only my second glass of wine. I think I'm just giddy from having you here."

Kevin pulled her into his arms and started a gentle seduction. He kissed her thoroughly and ran his hands up and down her body. She moved closer to him as though she wanted to become part of him. They were lost in each other and were startled back to reality when the doorbell rang.

Kevin almost growled with frustration, "That better be something really important."

Megan managed to pull herself together and went to the door.

"Daddy, what are you doing here?"

"Don't just stand there. Give your old dad a hug."

Megan threw her arms around him and gave him a big kiss.

"Now, why haven't you called and what do you mean by just sending a picture of some guy none of us know and writing 'someone special' on it? You have the whole family up in arms wondering what's going on."

"You came down here just because I sent the picture?"

"Actually, it was just an excuse. I missed you and decided to check on you and the construction. I also have instructions to find out everything about this young man," Kaleb said as he noticed Kevin walking in from the patio.

Megan turned towards Kevin and put out her hand to him.

"Come here and meet my father. Dad, this is Kevin Mackenzie. Kevin, this is my dad, Kaleb Dalton."

The men shook hands.

"I met you once before when you were the guest speaker at graduation exercises at Boston College," Kevin said. "I'm sure you don't remember, there were so many of us."

"I do remember giving the address, but you're right, I don't remember you. Are you a professor there?"

"Yes; I'm down here taking part in a Mayan dig. I have a leave from my teaching job until next January."

"How long are you staying, and how is everyone else? I really miss them," Megan said.

"I'm just here for a few days. I have to be back in Boston by Wednesday. It's a short trip."

"Are you hungry? We were just having some cheese and bread and fruit out on the patio. I'll get you a glass for some wine."

They made their way out to the patio and sat visiting until quite late into the night. Megan told her father she had something to show him down in the garden, and when they were some distance from the house she told him the house was bugged. She also told him Kevin knew she worked for the DEA and she was in love with him. Kaleb was happy for her and said, so far, he liked what he had seen of Kevin.

"You can tell the rest of the family he is really wonderful and he loves me," Megan said, as they made their way back to the patio.

Kaleb laughed and said, "No one will ever be good enough for you in my eyes, but as long as you love him and he makes you happy I will give you my blessing."

"Thanks, Daddy. I love you," Megan said as she leaned up and kissed her father on the cheek.

The three of them spent most of Sunday together until it was time for Kevin to return to camp. He was sorry to leave and made Megan promise to come see him during the week. He told Kaleb he loved his daughter and would do what he could to keep her safe.

Kaleb was pleased with Kevin and liked his honesty concerning his feelings for Megan.

Megan spent most of the next few days with her father. They visited the construction site and also spent time visiting some of Kaleb's old friends from the area. It was time for Kaleb to return home much too soon for both of them.

Chapter 39

Having waved goodbye to her father as he exited through the loading gate, Megan turned and started to retrace her steps out of the airport. As she came into the main lobby she saw Josh and Stuart enter. They acknowledged her with a look and then went into the coffee shop. She followed them in and sat down in the booth they had secured.

"Okay, what's up?" she questioned.

"We decided this was probably the safest place to meet. We've been following Vicki for several days now and haven't learned a thing," Stuart said.

"I found out Richard often takes Thursdays off. I think tomorrow will be the day to follow him. I also ran across one of the people bringing in drugs the other night after we had talked on the beach. I followed him a short way and he met someone in a car. They headed east out of Akumal. I'm thinking we should borrow a car from one of my friends and just stake out that road starting tonight and see if we find our quarry materializing. It's almost time for the dig site to get a new shipment of boxes. What do you guys think?" Megan asked.

Josh nodded his agreement and said, "It's as good a plan as any. What about Mrs. Cowen? We still haven't approached her. Her husband gets into town some time on Friday. I'm wondering if she comes here to the airport to pick him up if one of us should be here to question her. Her car and house are probably wired. I'm sure we could get one of the rooms security uses here at the airport for our little interrogation."

Megan and Josh looked at Stuart as though he was the most likely candidate for the job.

"She'll tell you anything," they both said at the same time.

"I can try," was Stuart's only reply.

"Josh and I can stake out the road tonight and tomorrow and see what we can learn. Does that sound all right with everyone?" Megan asked.

Josh replied, "Do you think you can get a car? Richard and Vicki know ours and if they should glimpse them it would be over."

"I'll borrow one from my friends. They're very generous. I'll just tell them there's something wrong with mine and I need to go to Cancun tonight and I'll get it back to them sometime tomorrow. Where do you want to meet, Josh?"

"I'll come by your place around ten. I'll just wait out by the end of the drive. Has anyone heard anything from headquarters?"

They all shook their heads no and decided they would contact headquarters after they saw what materialized in the next two days.

The road saw little traffic in the daylight hours but at night it was practically deserted. Only one car had passed in the last three hours. Megan was trying to sleep while Josh remained vigilant. They were sitting in an older model Ford pickup. One of Megan's friends used it just to haul things and had been happy to let her borrow it.

They were on a little dirt path just off of the main road leading from Akumal to a small village called Tulare. The village was inland and about twenty miles from Akumal.

Megan couldn't find a comfortable position and was about to tell Josh she would stay awake and he could get some sleep when they saw headlights coming down the road. They both watched closely as the car passed. They couldn't see who was in it but they both recognized it as Mrs. Cowen's car.

"Now where do you think she is going at two in the morning?" Josh asked.

"I think we should find out. Do you think we can drive on the road with only the moon for light? With no other traffic they would see our headlights right away."

As Josh started the pickup he said, "We'll give it a try. I'm sure we'll hit every rut there is, so hold on tight."

They could see the car ahead of them and remained quite a

distance back. After about ten minutes, the car turned off the road. Josh slowed and then pulled off on the shoulder.

"Is there something up ahead or did they just spot us?"

"There are little houses interspersed all along this road. I bet they stopped at one. We can get out and walk. If we stay near the jungle we can always hide if someone comes back this way."

"Let's go then."

They walked about a mile and then came to a dirt road that led off of the main road. They stayed on the edge of the jungle as they made their way toward a small house sitting several yards off of the road. Mrs. Cowen's car and a van were parked outside the house.

Josh and Megan made their way to one side of the structure. There was an open window and they could hear voices coming from inside. What little conversation they could hear was in Spanish. Megan overheard one man say to the other, "The Boss seems anxious tonight, pacing back and forth."

His cohort responded, "It's better when she doesn't come. The other two get things done fast, even if they do make me nervous with their masks on. I don't like this whole business. It was better before they came."

Megan and Josh decided they had heard and seen enough. They made their way back to the pickup and then drove back to Akumal. The other two people they heard talked about could only be Richard and Vicki. If they could get Mrs. Cowen to cooperate they would try to catch them all in the act of putting the drugs into the boxes.

They decided they were going to go to the airport with Stuart on Friday and would wait to see what Mrs. Cowen said.

"I don't know what you are talking about," Ruth Cowen said as she sat in a chair in the security office at the airport.

"I wouldn't be too quick to deny anything, if I were you. I know a lot about the operation and everything points straight to you. The drugs come and go in the boxes from the Mayan dig site, which you are paying for. Your car has been seen driving to the site where the boxes are prepared, and if I'm not mistaken you are known as the Boss. It doesn't sound real good for you," Stuart said.

Ruth just sat staring straight ahead and said nothing. Her mind was in a tangle. What was she going to do? She had never wanted anything to do with this in the first place, but she had to protect herself and her family. She began to wring her hands and a fine sweat broke out on her forehead. Noting her body language, Stuart started his gentle push.

"I know this couldn't have been your idea. It just doesn't sound like something you would do, so I figure someone else is responsible. They must have offered you a lot of money to get you to cooperate."

Ruth gave a little hysterical laugh, "Give me money? You have got to be joking. They're bankrupting me."

"Then why would you help them?" Stuart said.

Ruth looked at him and said, "I think I better wait and get a lawyer before I say anything."

Stuart shrugged his shoulders and said, "If you want. I can offer you immunity for anything involving the drugs if you cooperate now. As far as anything illegal that you've done outside of the present situation, I have no control. Your husband should be arriving soon. Do you want to wait and talk to him?"

She shook her head no.

"He won't understand. He has never understood that money doesn't go as far as he thinks it should, and the things I've done have been so he can be comfortable and so we can keep our son in the institution. He always thought I should have our son at home and take care of him myself. I just couldn't do it." Taking a deep breath, she continued, "What do you want to know?"

"I want you to tell me who is behind the drug ring and anything you know about it. I'll be tape-recording everything you say."

"Okay, but they said if I told anyone I would be the only one prosecuted. I pay for all the shipping of the drugs and I'm the only one any of the locals have actually seen. There is no proof about the others and it's just my word against theirs. They supposedly have spotless records, where mine wouldn't be so good if someone looked into my finances more closely."

"Let us worry about the proof and you just tell us what you know."

"You're sure I can get immunity?"

"Yes."

"All right. Vicki Brenten approached me almost a year ago. First she just acted like she wanted a friend, but then one day she invited me to her home and told me she had proof of some wrongdoing concerning my campaign finances and also my dealings with the real estate group I lobbied for. She told me she wanted me to do some small things for her in exchange for keeping quiet. She had papers to back up her threats. She told me I was to finance an archeological dig in Mexico. She told me who to contact and what needed to be done to set it all up. After that was done, she again contacted me and said they had decided my husband and I should buy a house in Akumal as a retirement home and it would be best if we spent most of our time here. I had to do a lot of talking to get Vince to agree to buy a house here. Since we've been here, she has made me go with her and a man, sometimes late at night, to a little house outside of Akumal. They put drugs into metal tubes and then dunk them into some kind of mixture. After that they stick the tubes in a freezer for a few minutes. When they take them out the outside is hard. The tubes then latch into grooves on the sides of the boxes with a layer of foam over them. The boxes then go to the dig site to be used for the transport of any artifacts they discover. I don't know what happens once the boxes leave the dig site. When they make me go with them, I drive my car and go as I am. Vicki and whoever the man is who comes along always wear some kind of disguise and masks on their faces. I am the only one the other people, all of Mexican descent, have ever seen. I don't speak Spanish, but I think Vicki has told them I am the boss. I hear them say things in Spanish and then say 'the boss' as they are looking at me. That's all I can tell you."

"Do they always go to the house on the same day?"

"No, but of late it seems like it has been on Thursdays. They change it around sometimes though."

"I need you to return to Akumal and continue as you have been. I might warn you that your car and house are probably bugged, so don't say anything to your husband about this. I need some kind of signal to let me know when you are going to the house again. Do you get any warning?"

"Usually Vicki will just say she's coming over later, so stay up so she doesn't have to wake me. When Vince was here she would tell him she was afraid to spend the night alone and just needed someone to keep her company. Vince didn't seem to mind if I left with her."

"I guess there is no way for you to signal me, but since you just went it will probably be a couple of weeks. I'll just keep a stakeout posted. Remember, as long as you continue to cooperate, you will get immunity, but if you double-cross me you will be prosecuted. I might add we feel they have committed more crimes than you are aware of, so don't try to play their game."

"I want out of this more than you could possibly know. I'll do whatever I can to help you."

"Your husband is probably about through customs, so you better go meet him. I'll be in touch."

Stuart ushered her out the door and then let one of the airport security personnel take her back to the lobby to await her husband.

Megan and Josh came into the room and said, "Well?"

"It's as we suspected. They are blackmailing her. She doesn't even know Richard is the man involved. The only person she can identify is Vicki. We're going to have to let the local Mexican Drug Enforcement Agency know where the house is that they use to make the boxes and have them keep it under surveillance. The only way to catch both Vicki and Richard is when they are there. Megan, maybe you better go talk to the agency since you are the one who is supposed to be figuring out which one of us is on the take."

"Okay. Why don't you two let headquarters know our plan? I guess we will just have to hope both of them go next time. I guess until then we all just sit tight. I'll probably talk to Richard and ask if he's found out anything about Rex Higgins. That should make him think he's safe. I rode in with Josh, but I'm going to take the bus back so we don't take any chances on being seen together."

"We better stay here a while longer so we're sure the Cowens have left. I just don't understand why Richard would do something like this," Stuart said.

"From what we heard that night on the beach it seems like it's a game to him. It's like he wants to see if he can outsmart everyone else. I wonder if he did anything like this when he was with the New York police force. Have you ever heard why he left them and came to us?" Megan asked.

"I think it was something to do with his partner and that he had killed himself. Supposedly, Richard was too upset to remain with the force. Now I wonder what really happened. I think you're right though, it's all just a game to him."

Chapter 40

The moon was full and its light cast a silvery glow over the stone in the patio. Kevin held Megan's hand as they let the swing carry them back and forth.

"It's such a beautiful night. I wish we could just stay here forever. I'm going to miss you so much when I go back to Boston," Megan said.

"I wanted to come on this dig so badly, and now all I want to do is go back to Boston with you."

"Since the Cowens won't be footing the bill for the dig anymore, I wonder how long it will be able to keep going. Do you think they'll be able to get funding from somewhere else?"

"I'm sure they will eventually, but how soon I don't know. I still can't believe Richard and Vicki got away. I wonder where they are right now."

"They've probably made their way to Central or South America. They must have had an escape route planned ever since they started this operation. Mrs. Cowen said it was as though one minute they were there and the next minute the two of them were gone. I'm sure the Mexican patrol is still looking for them, but I would bet they're long gone."

"At least the agency won't have him working for them anymore. It's too bad his old partner from the police force probably got framed by him and who knows, probably even killed. His family, at least, is grateful that a new probe is going to be made into the whole incident."

"Have you disconnected all the wiretaps and tracking devices? I always felt like I was on display when I came here."

"You bet. I couldn't believe all the electronic devices they had at

Vicki's house. It looked like a military control center."

"Enough talk about them. I'm just so glad you are safe and here with me. When are we going to get married?"

"Are you proposing?"

"I guess I am. I can't make it official with a diamond and everything since I'm stuck out in the jungle, but when I get back to Boston I promise to buy you a ring. So what do you say? Will you marry me and spend the rest of your life with me?"

"I can't think of anything I would like better."

They just sat smiling at each other and then finally, Kevin pulled her into his arms for a passionate kiss.

"Mmm, you always taste so good."

"It must be the mouthwash I use," Megan said with a laugh. "Will your parents like me, do you think?"

"My parents will adore you. I may be adopted, but we have similar taste and if I love you, they will love you."

"I'm glad. Do you ever wonder about your birth parents?"

"I suppose all adopted kids wonder about their birth parents at times, but I don't think I'll ever want to look for mine. I love my parents and I don't need another mom. I have this feeling that my birth mother gave me to them for a good reason and not because she didn't love me. I think that is really the reason most adopted kids look for their birth parents. They want to know that it wasn't really them, but that it was circumstances."

"This day and age a lot of unwanted pregnancies end in abortion. I would think if a woman carried a child to full term and then gave the baby up for adoption it would be because she thought it was best for the child."

"Enough on that subject, back to a date for our wedding. Do you want a big wedding?"

"You bet. I only plan on getting married once and I want the whole church thing with flowers and music and you in a tux."

"That's good, because my family would have a fit if that wasn't the case. They are into weddings. I suppose it will take a few months to plan. It's August now. How about sometime in February? I know it will still be cold but I don't want to wait any longer."

"That sounds good to me. That way if the dig gets financing, you'll still be back a couple of months before the wedding to help with some of the plans."

"We'll talk more of the plans later. Right now I just want to hold you and kiss you into sweet surrender."

"Why don't we go in? This swing isn't the least bit comfortable when it comes to more intimate engagements."

"I'm right behind you. You lead the way."

Megan walked into the first-floor bedroom that she had been using since her arrival.

"Does this look more comfortable?" she asked.

Kevin grabbed her around the waist and tumbled her onto the bed. He followed her down and landed half on top of her. They began to kiss and soon were shedding pieces of clothing. As Kevin rearranged one of the pillows he noted a wicked-looking knife under it.

"What is this?" he questioned.

"I kept that there while the investigation was going on. It gave me a sense of security. I just left it there out of habit."

Kevin was already kissing her neck and seemed not to care about her answer. Soon they were lost in passion's embrace.

"Isn't this just the sweetest thing you ever saw? They haven't even finished getting undressed," a voice drawled.

Kevin and Megan jerked apart, with Megan grabbing the sheet to cover her naked top. Vicki and Richard had walked into the bedroom. Richard was holding a pistol and had it pointed at the two on the bed.

"Now you didn't really expect us to just walk away, did you?" Richard said. "I really hate to lose. I don't know for sure who figured it all out, but I'm betting Stuart and Josh played a major role. Sorry, little Megan, but I just don't think you are smart enough. I wanted to go find Josh and Stuart right off, but Vicki figured Kevin would be here with you since it is Saturday night and she just can't stand to have someone turn her away, can you Vicki? Or should I say Micki?"

"I kind of like Vicki. It has a certain ring to it," Vicki said as she reached to the floor, picked up Megan's blouse and threw it at her. "Here. Put it on and get off the bed."

Megan did as she was instructed. Kevin lay on his side and watched the two for any sign that he could overpower them. Then he remembered the knife under the pillow. He would bide his time and wait for the best time to attack.

Megan walked toward Richard and in a whimper said, "What are you going to do with us?"

Richard just shook his head at her.

"Vicki wants to show Kevin what a real woman is like, and then we're all going to take a little drive. After we pick up our other two guests, we'll take you for a nice walk in the jungle. No one thwarts my plans and gets away with it."

Vicki was beginning to strip.

Megan looked at Richard and said, "I don't understand you. How can you let your wife go to bed with someone else, especially while you're just standing here?"

Richard roared with laughter, "That has been our best joke yet. You see, when I was in college, I didn't have any money and married guys got all the help they needed. So Vicki and I decided we would get married. We had to change her birth certificate a little, but no one ever checked on it, so no problem. Vicki is my sister. We had the same mother but different fathers. Vicki liked being married, too. You see, she has this little personality quirk that makes her want lots of men, and most men feel more comfortable making it with a married woman. They feel sure there will be no strings attached. I get to play my games and show how brilliant I am, and Vicki gets what she wants; all very simple."

Both Megan and Kevin were thinking that these were two very sick people. Megan was gradually getting closer to Richard as he talked. It was like he thought she was totally inconsequential.

As Vicki lowered herself to the bed she said, "Now you do just what I tell you and your little Megan won't get hurt."

Richard stood watching the scene on the bed. Megan had moved within a short distance in front and to the side of Richard. She gave Kevin a quick look that seemed to say, "Now!" Then she reached for Richard's arm that held the gun and jerked him over her shoulder and onto the floor.

As Megan made her move, Kevin grabbed the knife from under the pillow and placed it at Vicki's neck. He got up gradually and just as he stood, he saw Richard reach for the gun that had fallen on the floor. He pushed Vicki down on the bed and threw the knife. It hit Richard in the shoulder and had him yelling with pain. Megan quickly grabbed the gun and moved back from Richard.

"Good throw. I didn't know you could handle a knife."

Kevin just said, "Boy Scouts."

He pulled Vicki's shirt and shorts back on her and after tying her hands behind her back with a sheet he placed her back on the bed. Next he picked up the phone and called the police. He told them to notify the Mexican Drug Enforcement Agency that they had two people they were searching for and they would wait for their arrival. Next, he rang the hotel and asked for Josh's room.

"I have a present for you and Stuart here at Megan's house. Could the two of you come right over?"

After he hung up, Megan said, "I guess you know who the other two agents are now. I'm sure you won't give their secret away."

A few minutes later Josh and Stuart arrived. They were stunned and pleased to see what the present was. After the police came and took Vicki and Richard away they all breathed a sigh of relief.

"We should have known they wouldn't just walk away. You are both lucky to be alive," Stuart said.

"You were on their list, too. If we hadn't stopped them, you would have gotten your chance. They are really sick people," Kevin informed them.

"By the way, Kevin and I are getting married and I would like both of you to come to our wedding," Megan said.

"I have every intention of getting this lady wed and pregnant as soon as possible so she'll have to resign from her present job. I hope this is the last time you get to work with her," Kevin added.

They all laughed and said considering the dangers of the job they thought it was a good idea. Megan even conceded she wouldn't mind giving up this line of work so she could pursue a career as wife and mother.

Flowers decorated the altar and ribbons and bows were attached to the pews. Sunlight streaming through the stained glass windows had shards of colors dancing on the floor. Guests were arriving and were being ushered to their seats on the arms of dashing young men.

Megan was having the finishing touches made to her hair and the veil was being placed on her head. Katie had tears in her eyes as she gave her a big hug and kiss and wished her all the happiness in the world.

It was then someone noticed the boutonnieres for the men were in a box in the bride's dressing area.

"I'll take them to the men," Jessica offered.

Jessica made her way to the basement of the church where the men were getting ready for their appearance. She knocked on the door and then entered the room.

"I brought your flowers. Do you need help pinning them on?"

It almost sounded like a chorus when they all answered yes. She pinned on the groomsmen's first and then turned to Kevin to fasten it to his lapel. As she was pinning the flower in place she caught sight of a little silver pin fastened to his tie. Her hands began to shake and she had to stop what she was doing. She had turned pale and Kevin became concerned.

"What's the matter? Are you sick?" he asked.

Jessica took a couple of deep breaths and then seemed to pull herself together.

"I guess it's just all the excitement. Just give me a minute and I'll be fine."

After she was again composed, she returned to the task at hand.

"I couldn't help but notice that little pin on your tie. It is rather unusual. May I ask where you got it?"

Kevin reached to his tie and gave the little pin a fond touch. He said, "This is my lucky pin. I wear it for all special occasions."

Jessica stood looking at him with what seemed to be almost a pleading kind of expression that said, "Tell me more." He didn't usually go into any more detail than that, but for some reason he couldn't ignore her unvoiced plea.

"I'm sure Megan has probably mentioned that I was adopted as a baby. My parents always told me I was a special gift to them. When I was somewhere around ten, I asked my mother why I was their special gift. She told me my birth mother had given me to them because she loved me and couldn't take care of me herself. Then she went into her bedroom and brought me back this little pin. She told me this was a special gift my birth mother had given to me and it was her way of letting me know how much she loved me and I should always take care of it. I have worn it on all the special occasions in my life since then. It was on my tie at every graduation and at confirmation. I wore it to my prom and I wore it on the first date I had with Megan. Today is the most special day of all, and it will be here with me."

When he finished speaking, Jessica had tears in her eyes.

"Thank you for sharing that with me. I better go now or you'll keep your bride waiting."

Jessica barely made it out of the door before she had to hold onto the wall to stand up. She stood there for several minutes and then she heard John call her name.

"I wondered where you went. Are you all right? You look like you just saw a ghost."

Jessica laughed, "In a way I did. Come on and walk me outside. I need to talk to you."

When they were outside they found a little bench on the side of the church. They sat down and Jessica told John what Kevin had shared.

"Oh, my God, Jessie, Kevin is your son. How do you feel about this?"

"It's a shock, but a nice shock. From what he said, and from what Megan has said in the past, I don't think he will ever try to find me, so this has to stay just between the two of us. I feel like God has truly blessed me. Now I know my son has had a good life and has turned into a wonderful man. I even get to be at his wedding. I can't imagine anything better."

John just held her for a few minutes and then said, "You are wonderful, and I'm so happy for you. I know you have always wondered about him. If we don't get in the church now, however, we'll miss the wedding."

The church was packed. On one side of the aisle was all of Kevin's family—mother and father, grandparents, uncles and aunts, and cousins too numerous to count. Behind them were his friends and colleagues from Boston College.

On the other side of the church were Megan's family and grandparents, Jessica and her family, Katie's parents and her brother and sisters and their families. Behind all these relatives were Megan's friends and a couple of lone men known as the Bum and the Preacher.

Kevin and his groomsmen were standing at the front of the church as the bridesmaids walked down the aisle. When they reached the altar, the music changed and Kevin could see Megan at the back of the church with her hand tucked under her father's arm. She was radiant and he knew that his love for her would last a lifetime.

Epilogue

"You better hurry; we don't want to be late to Cousin Jessica's birthday party."

"I'll be right down," Megan called out to Kevin. As she came down the stairs she added, "I'm so glad were here to celebrate her seventy-fifth birthday. We've missed so many of the family's special occasions because of our traveling. It's nice to be settled here in Boston."

"We've had a good life traveling to various sites all over the world, but you're right, Boston does feel like home. Between your parents and Jessica, we always stayed informed of the latest happenings in your family. I have to admit there are times when I envy you your brothers and sister."

"They're your brothers and sister too."

"I know, but sometimes I wonder if I have a brother or a sister out there somewhere. I don't think I gave it much thought until after my parents died. I miss them a lot, and I wouldn't wish my life any different then it was, but maybe that's why I question whether my birth parents are still alive and if they ever think of me. Even at fifty-nine, I suppose we still wish we had our parents. Besides, I have spent my whole adult life searching out the past of humanity and I know nothing of my own."

"I see you are wearing your pin today, in fact you have been wearing it a lot more recently. Does this mean you are thinking of looking for them?"

"Maybe, I don't know. I might."

"We can talk about this some more when we get back, but right now we best be going."

Karen, one of Jessica's daughters, answered the door. "Oh, Kevin and Megan, we're so glad you could come. Mom will be so happy you made it. Everyone is gathered in the dining room. You know Mom; she is in seventh heaven having all of her family together."

"Knowing her, she is probably rushing around trying to make sure everything is perfect and that no one is left stewing by themselves," Megan said.

"She would be, but Christine and I made our brothers take her and Dad for a drive while we prepared some food and got her birthday cake ready," Karen replied as she led the way down the hall.

"Hey, everyone, look who I found."

Greetings were exchanged, conversation never ended, and lunch was served. Finally, it was time for the birthday cake. As soon as the candles were lit, the group sang a loud rendition of "Happy Birthday."

"Now make a wish before you blow out your candles," John whispered in Jessica's ear.

Jessica closed her eyes to make her wish and then she blew as hard as she could. Every flame flickered and died. The crowd clapped and cheered.

"Are you going to tell us what you wished for?" one of Jessica's grandchildren asked.

"If I tell you, my wish won't come true. Before we cut the cake though, I want to thank all of you for coming. John and I love it when the family all gathers. I am especially happy to have all my children here with me."

At her words, Kevin smiled at Karen, who stood next to him. It was at that moment he noticed a small pin on Karen's blouse. He couldn't take his eyes off of it. It had a small opal dangling from a small replica of a teacup. Across the top were the words, "I will only put good things in here."

His startled gaze quickly sought out Jessica's other five children. Each one had a small pin on their collar or lapel. All the pins were slightly different, but they all had a teacup somewhere in the pin.

He must have seen them at some other family gathering. Had he just realized what it meant now that he was seriously thinking of searching for his family? He once again studied Jessica's six children and he realized his eyes were the same shape and color of some of them. He had Karen's nose, and if he were about twenty years younger he could be mistaken for Robbie, Jessica's youngest son.

His heartbeat had spiraled but now it began to slow. He had no need to search, for he knew he had already found his family.

Each person gave Jessica a happy birthday hug and when it was his turn, he held her a little longer than the others and then whispered, "Happy Birthday, Mother."

Jessica gasped and then as she looked into Kevin's eyes tears blurred her vision and clogged her throat. "I've always loved you," she managed to say.

With a gentle smile and a fingertip touching the little pin on his collar, Kevin replied, "I know."

Love can heal
Love can mend
A bracelet can be a symbol of love

Love is shared by two
Love is what makes a family
A ring can be a symbol of love

Love never ends
Love brings peace to the heart
A teacup can be a symbol of love